Gate to Gate Trilogy

Gate to Gate Trilogy

Stories from the Seatback Pocket

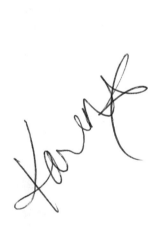

Betty Gossell and Karen Pickens

Library of Congress Control Number: 2020916600

HARDBACK: 978-1-952155-92-5
PAPERBACK: 978-1-952155-91-8
EBOOK: 978-1-952155-93-2

Ordering Information:

For orders and inquiries, please contact:
1-888-404-1388
www.goldtouchpress.com
book.orders@goldtouchpress.com

Printed in the United States of America

THE BOARDING PASS

BETTY GOSSELL AND

KAREN PICKENS

Praise for

The Boarding Pass

"I absolutely loved this book. I felt like I was there. Passed it on to my daughter." Roberta C.

"An easy-to-read look into the lives of passengers on a plane. I want to know more." Rosemary F.

"I loved this book! I TOTALLY am not a reader, but I couldn't put it down!!! Every chapter left me wanting more!!!" Karen H.

"It is an intriguing book. Didn't put it down till I finished it." Susan H.

"The book is a Fine Restaurant decadent dessert with a beautiful coffee! I want to take it slow and absorb - not dash through it! What a great concept. It's like a book you wish to read a page, then pause...not wishing it over." Tara S.

"Since reading this wonderful book, I now find myself gazing each time at many passengers on my flights and wondering where they are going and what their story might be. LOVED it!" Marlene F.

"Hard to put down! Only downside is that I found myself hooked on each person's story, and it left me wanting to read more about each of them. Guess that leaves room for the follow-up book(s)." Christie K.

"Great story line! It would make a great movie!!" Mark L.

"Really enjoyed the book. It was well written." Carolyn R.

"I found it to be very interesting! It left me hoping for more!" Wanda G.

"An interesting look into the lives of eight people as they all go about their day, linked only by a shared airplane seat. Despite the brevity of our glimpse into their lives, you become invested almost instantly, and quickly find yourself wondering what happened to them after they got off the plane." Jackie D.

"It was a good read – You guys have the talent! Awesome!" Mary Sue R.

"A brilliantly written book about everyday people, but with a twist." Linda H.

Dedication

To my family and friends, who were always supportive of my dreams and encouraged me to never settle for less than my best;

To my co-workers and fellow road warriors, who know all too well the trials and tribulations of the crazy life that we lead;

But most of all to my fabulous daughter Karen. You have been the light of my life and my inspiration since before you were born. I never could have done this without you! I love you more!

Betty Gossell

To the Gossell and Pickens clans, for loving me as I am, for giving me more happy memories than anyone has a right to wish for, and for never being more than a phone call away;

To my friends, past and present, who shaped me and fueled me and made me better. Thank you for being beautiful and talented and forgiving;

To my wonderful husband Chris. I don't have enough words, and for me, that's saying something! You're the closest thing to perfect, and my life is immeasurably better with you by my side;

To my gorgeous daughter Lilah Joy. You are a dream come true, so bright and funny and challenging. You make me a better person every day. I'm so grateful that you're mine;

And of course, to my mother. You gave me life and you gave me so much of yourself that we're practically the same person sometimes. I love you more than you will ever know. I couldn't ask for a better mom or friend.

Karen Pickens

Foreword

The world and how we perceive it has changed drastically, even in my relatively short lifespan. The planet has gotten smaller and simpler to traverse. Stereotypes have been discarded and new ones erected. Definitions of success, family, happiness - all have undergone massive renovations, but there are a few truths that hold.

We still glorify the "special" moments in life, those with measurable quantities of interest. And we shun and almost dread the "ordinary." It seems that we must be reminded that even in the most exemplary life, a snapshot may reveal that which is static and mundane.

So how would it be possible to find a true cross-section of life amongst ordinary people? That would probably depend upon your definition of ordinary. Maybe it's running to the grocery store to pick up food for your family for the week. Maybe it's standing in line at the bank to deposit a paycheck. Maybe ordinary is pushing a lawnmower or a swing. Maybe it's sitting in a classroom, a traffic jam, or an airplane seat.

Though our actions and even our words cannot always be revolutionary, even the most cynical among us cannot deny that chance encounters and other so-called ordinary events have the potential to change our little piece of the world. These unsuspecting snapshots may not start or end a war. They may not crumble an empire or spark a new dream. But that they exist is cause for research into to the human condition, those warring desires for stability and change. Only a little dissection will show that everyone has a story – a past, a future. Every person has a place of origin and a destination, as well as somewhere in between. And somewhere on this journey, for every blessed one of us, there are moments - more frequently than you would expect - when we are the direct opposite of ordinary.

--Karen Pickens

Contents

Prologue - Jean

What a lousy way to spend her 50th birthday. Instead of celebrating a successful job interview in Dallas, Jean found herself jammed into the window seat on an overly-crowed and delayed flight back to St. Louis, sweltering in the 105 degree Texas heat.

She hated sitting next to the window, often feeling trapped into the small space by strangers who may or may not let her get up to stretch her legs. Ironically, this was much the same way she felt trapped by her life after years of questionable career decisions. She looked into the seat back pocket in front of her for anything she could use as a fan, and noticed something sticking out of the in-flight magazine. The crumpled piece of paper was a boarding pass for a woman named Lisa Davis, who flew from Des Moines to Chicago earlier that morning. Also folded neatly in the bottom of the pocket was today's *Des Moines Register*, open to the sports section.

Glancing at the boarding pass, she began to wonder about Lisa's life. Who was she? Where was she going so early in the morning? Was Lisa's life any more fulfilling than her own? Did she have a family or anyone to care if she made the trip, or care if she came back home? Jean turned the small piece of paper over and over in her hands, almost willing it to tell Lisa's story.

Davis, Lisa

DSM - ORD

Global Air

SEAT NUMBER

19F

JUNE 09, 2017 06:00 AM

Chapter One

Chapter One

DSM to ORD (Lisa)

The only light in the room was the soft red glow from the alarm clock. 1:57 AM. With a resolute sigh, Lisa slipped quietly from the warm bed she had shared with her husband Kevin for the past 27 years and walked silently across the room. The alarm was set to ring in a few minutes, but she turned it off so Kevin could sleep undisturbed. After a quick hot shower, she dressed in the clothes she had laid out the night before. Pulling her long blond hair into a pony tail, she applied a little bit of makeup and picked up her small red suitcase and matching carry-on bag. She paused at her bedroom door to blow a silent kiss in Kevin's direction. He was so handsome while he slept, and had to resist brushing her fingers through his tussled dark hair. She loved him so much, and leaving without saying goodbye was so difficult.

She walked quietly down the hall and glanced into the dark bedroom of their teenage son Shane. His long gangly frame was sprawled across his bed, and he was buried under a mound of covers. She tiptoed past Shane's door, trying to avoid tripping over the dog sleeping in the hallway. The Irish Setter was 15 years old now, and almost completely deaf. They had gotten him when Shane was little, and the two were inseparable. After making her way downstairs, she took one quick look around her recently remodeled kitchen to assure herself that all was in order. Shane had done a great job putting things away after his party last night. She looked in the fridge one last time and saw that it was well stocked with Kevin's favorites and Shane's necessities. Taking her cardigan from the hall closet, she turned off the lights and walked out the back door into the cool Iowa night. She had about an hour's drive to Des Moines before her 6 AM flight to Chicago. Even though it was early June, the air had a chill that made her wish for a warmer sweater.

The gravel in the driveway crunched under her tires as she backed her old Honda out of the garage. She paused to admire the large house that she and Kevin had worked so hard to restore after they first got married. As young teachers in the local school system, money was always tight. But they had found a run-down farmhouse on the edge of Winterset and worked nights and weekends for over a year to make it their own. Their first child, Miranda, was born just weeks after they moved in. Their son Tyler came three years later, and then Shane made his appearance just as Tyler was going to Kindergarten. Even in the dark she could see the outline of the basketball hoop on the driveway and the old swing set in the back yard. Her garden was growing well, and they had enjoyed their first vegetable pickings just last week. She inhaled the fresh country air, and knew this was the life she had always wanted. At the end of the driveway, she stopped and checked the box for the *Des Moines Register* and found that the delivery person had already been there. Tucking the paper in her carry-on bag, she turned from the driveway out onto the highway. She loved driving in the early morning, and left her window down just a bit to inhale the cool air, noticing the familiar and intoxicating scent of freshly mowed grass.

When she met Kevin all those years ago, they were both education students at the University of Iowa in Iowa City. Introduced by mutual friends, Lisa had fallen for Kevin's dark good looks and hazel eyes almost immediately. He was a star on the track team, and Lisa had been his biggest supporter in the stands. He graduated while Lisa was just a sophomore, and moved to Winterset to teach Jr. High math and coach the track team. Lisa was miserable being a few hours away from him, and they were married the weekend after her own college graduation two years later. Wearing her mother's ivory wedding gown, she proudly stood with Kevin to say their vows in front of a very small group of family and friends.

"I, Lisa, take you, Kevin, as my lawfully wedded husband, to have and to hold from this day forward." Lisa had said those words bravely but with a slight quiver in her voice. Looking into Kevin's eyes with love and trust, she had pledged her life and soul to him that day. Her sisters were beside her in their pale yellow bridesmaid dresses, and she held a bouquet of roses and daisies. Her mother wiped a silent tear from her eye, and her father gave her a wink of encouragement. But all she could really see was the amazing man she loved more than life itself.

"I, Kevin, take you Lisa." She heard his voice break and knew he was nervous about saying the vows just right. But no matter the words, she believed they were knit together with a bond that would last forever. As much as she had loved him then, it paled in comparison to her feelings for him today, so many years later. She glanced down at the ring he had put on her finger that day and knew that being Mrs. Kevin Davis was who she was meant to be.

She was fortunate to get a job teaching 4th grade at one of Winterset's two elementary schools, and she moved into Kevin's tiny apartment on the edge of town. They saved every spare penny for a full year before finding their "dream home" on a small piece of land just west of town. Their parents helped with the down payment and Kevin's dad (who owned a construction company) spent many weekends assisting with the major renovations. When they discovered that Lisa was pregnant with Miranda, Lisa was thrilled to spend her weekends fixing up the tiny nursery, decorating with Winnie the Pooh and Tigger. Kevin was nervous at the thought of being a father, but soon it was obvious that he was a great dad. He loved his children, and had built the swing set and a playhouse that they had all used for years. Now Miranda was a court reporter in Des Moines, and Tyler had just finished his junior year at Drake University; following in his dad's footsteps and staring on the track and baseball teams. Lisa was a bit disappointed that he did not move home this summer, opting instead to stay in Des Moines and work in the university's athletic department as an intern. But she understood his need to "spread his wings" a bit, and knew she would see him often in the coming year.

Shane, on the other hand, loved living at home. He was 17 now, and appeared to be in no hurry to leave. Like his dad and brother, he excelled in sports, especially baseball and wrestling. He hit a homerun in last night's game and drove in the winning runs. Lisa was glad she was able to see the game – this trip to Chicago had been planned for quite some time, but his game had been rescheduled because of rain the previous week. She stood in the stands and cheered as he rounded the bases and then listened to him retell the story later after he had gotten home. Several of his team-mates had come to the house after the game and were up late talking and laughing in the back yard. Lisa had gone to bed early, since she had this early morning flight, but Kevin had stayed up to supervise things. Shane had just started looking at colleges, but his heart had never really been on his studies. He loved fixing cars, and spent most of his free time rebuilding an old Chevy in his friend Tommy's garage.

The drive to Des Moines went quickly, and Lisa pulled into the almost deserted airport parking lot. After taking her bags from the car, she walked quickly into the terminal. There were few people awake at this time of the morning, so she did not have to wait in line to check in. The ticket agent was friendly and efficient.

"Where to, this early morning?" the young woman asked. "Chicago, on the 6 AM flight," Lisa answered.

"I need to see your ID. How many bags are you checking?"

Lisa pulled her driver's license from her wallet, and handed it across the counter. "Just one bag." The agent quickly printed her boarding pass and tagged her suitcase. She handed her license and boarding pass back to Lisa, and set the suitcase on the conveyor belt behind her.

"You are all set, Ms. Davis – everything is on time, and you will be boarding in about an hour. Go down this hall and to your right. There is an escalator that will take you upstairs to security."

"Thanks so much, have a good day," Lisa answered. Picking up her purse and small carry-on, she moved away from the counter and slowly down the hall. They had remodeled this part of the airport since the last time she had been there, and she admired the changes. After riding up the escalator, she took her place in the short security line. Off came her shoes and sweater, and she put them in the gray tub for scanning, along with her purse and carry-on bag. After walking through the x-ray machine, she picked up her belongings and headed toward her gate. This was the first time she had flown in almost a year – actually, the last time was when she rushed to Chicago last fall when her mother Nancy had been critically injured in an auto accident. She had lived just a few days after Lisa got to the hospital; the drunk driver who hit her had walked away without a scratch. That flight was one of fear and worry; this one was supposed to be one of fun and friendship. So why was she dreading it so?

She sat alone in the boarding area and pulled a granola bar from her bag. Several colorful "Visit Chicago" flyers were tucked in the pocket of the bag, but she could not bring herself to open them. She hated being forced into uncomfortable situations, and feared that the next few days with her sisters would be extremely unpleasant. How she wished she could have found an excuse not to go today.

This trip had been the brainchild of her younger sister Susan. As the baby of the family, and the favorite of their parents, Susan seemed to do everything right. She married her childhood sweetheart 19 years ago, and was a stay-at-home mom for their twin preteen daughters. She lived in a cute little house just a few miles from where their parents had lived. She also had been the primary caregiver for their father during the final stages of his battle with Alzheimer's before he passed away just a month after their mother's accident. Lisa and Susan had always gotten along ok, but Lisa often felt alienated since she had moved so far away from everyone. Her busy school schedule, plus keeping track of a large house, garden, and three children, did not leave her much time for visits, and Susan commented more than once that she needed a break from the daily stress of caring for their aging parents. Lisa felt very guilty that she had not found a way to be more helpful during those stressful weeks, and months, and years.

Their older sister Rebecca was another story altogether. She and her husband Lawrence were partners in one of Chicago's largest and most prestigious law firms, and lived in an upscale condo on the waterfront. Too busy for children or pets, their hectic work and social schedules left little time for family or close friends. They chose not to have children, a concept foreign to Lisa who had trouble imaging a life without her children. They were the joys of her life, and she loved being a mom. Rebecca *did* handle the probate on both of their parents' wills, but had been too busy to spend much time with either of them in their final days. There was a certain level of friction between the sisters because of Rebecca's busy schedule and Lisa's inability to be of much help because of caring for her own family. Harsh words had been said at their father's funeral; words that left the sting of anger and frustration with all three sisters. Susan, in an effort to assume the role of peacemaker, had thought that the sisters should get together for some fun and to explore Chicago together. Hopefully this would be a start to mending their fractured relationships. Even though they had grown up in the Chicago area, they had never gone as sisters to do many of the "touristy" things that visitors from out of town usually did, and Susan was hoping the three girls could bond as sisters again.

"I think it will be so good for the three of us to spend some quality time together," Susan had said a few months ago, when they first started planning the trip. "We have not seen each other since the funerals, and I don't know about you, but I could use a little sister time about now."

Rebecca had been noncommittal, of course, saying she would have to see what her trial schedule was like, but would do her best to squeeze in some time for them. Lisa didn't have the heart to disappoint her little sister, and had reluctantly agreed. Susan was excited, and had planned four days of sightseeing and shopping. They even had tickets to an off-Broadway show for tomorrow night.

About 45 minutes before her flight, the gate agents arrived and took their place behind the small counter. Lisa double checked with them and found the flight was still on time. The gate area began to fill with other sleepy travelers, and before long, Lisa boarded the plane and settled into seat 19F. She enjoyed sitting by the window, and was hoping to catch a quick nap before landing in Chicago in a little over an hour. She knew that Susan would be at the airport to pick her up, but Rebecca had not returned her latest phone calls, so Lisa was not sure when they would meet up with her, if at all.

The flight attendants seemed overly perky for such an early hour of the day. Lisa admired the fact that they looked so ‘pulled together’ and glanced down at her own slightly frumpy travel outfit. She was just a few weeks short of her 50th birthday and was starting to look her age. Perhaps she should have spent a little more time on her own appearance today. Her khaki pants were rather rumpled, and her tan and green plaid tunic was comfortable but did little to camouflage her sagging curves. Her loafers were scuffed and well worn, and she could not remember how old they were. She tried to smooth the wrinkles from her slacks, but was sure that Rebecca would not have been caught dead in an outfit like this. For some reason, Lisa was always comparing herself to Rebecca, and usually felt that she came up short.

The plane was filling up now, mostly businessmen heading into Chicago for meetings, but also a few families dragging sleepy children along. A professional-looking Asian woman in an expensive and well- tailored business suit sat down in the aisle seat and slid her briefcase under the seat in front of her. Barely acknowledging Lisa's presence, she pulled a Wall Street Journal from her bag while talking on her Blackberry. Obviously there was important business to conduct, even at 5:30 in the morning. Lisa was relieved to be on summer vacation from school, and was looking forward to leisurely months with her husband and kids, and working in her garden. "Lisa's Secret Garden" as her kids loved to call it, had become a real joy to her, much to everyone's surprise. After growing up in the city with nothing but a few house plants, Kevin had been skeptical about her ambitions to grow her own vegetables. But after a few years of practice and some trial and error, her garden was now quite prolific. With Miranda and Tyler both living just an hour away in Des Moines, she knew she would see them often over the summer months. She and Kevin were even hoping to take a mini-vacation of their own without the kids this year; the first time since their 20th anniversary. They were not planning anything too fancy or expensive, maybe just a long weekend in Kansas

City or Memphis. She was sure that Shane could spend the weekend with Tommy and she and Kevin would not have to worry about him. Kevin had the summer off from school, too, but had taken a part-time job at the local Home Depot to make a little extra money. They still had another year of tuition to help Tyler with, and Shane's senior year was coming up. There were always so many expenses involved with that.

Lisa sat up with a jolt when the reality of Shane's graduation next year sank in. One year from now, she would have no children at home, and she and Kevin would be starting a new phase of their life together. After all these years, they would be alone again. The big farmhouse was already starting to feel a bit empty, but Shane was a lively and funny kid who had helped to fill the voids left by Miranda and Tyler. The house certainly would be quiet after he left, IF he left, that is. He just might decide to stay around a little longer, and Lisa admitted that she would not mind. She really did enjoy being a mom.

The plane was in the air now, and the flight attendants passed out coffee and juice. Not even a muffin – things sure had changed in the past few years. Lisa remembered when you actually got a meal on a plane, but not anymore. She was glad she had that granola bar earlier. Once the announcement was made that it was safe to use electronic devices, the businesswoman near her started typing enthusiastically on her laptop. She sure was focused on her job! Lisa was glad to be on summer break and could let her brain rest for a while.

She pulled the *Register* from her bag and turned to the sports section. There was a nice write-up about Shane's homerun from last night, and Lisa could not help but feel pride for her younger son. There was even a picture of him rounding third base, one arm raised above his head and a fist pumping toward the sky. Lisa smiled as her fingers traced his outline in the paper. Oh, how she loved her children, all of them. Rebecca had no idea how much she was missing.

Lisa turned to the special section about the upcoming State Fair. She had been involved in 4H for most of her adult life, ever since moving to Iowa. This year she had been selected to serve as a judge for the bakery entries. Her specialty was in the pastry area, and she was excited to be named as one of the lead judges. Her kids used to tease her about being able to just "whip up a pie" when many of the other mothers at school could not even make a tolerable pie crust. It was just something that came easy to her, and she loved to experiment with different fillings and techniques. The crust recipe was a secret from her mother, however, and she refused to share it with anyone outside the family.

After finishing the paper, she folded it neatly and slipped most of it into the seat pocket in front of her, putting the Fair section into her bag for future reference. She could no longer ignore the fact that she was about to spend four potentially friction-filled days with her sisters. The unresolved tension between them had become even more obvious as time went on. Why Susan thought that forcing the three of them to spend "quality time" with each other would solve anything was beyond her. They were three very different people who had chosen three very different paths for their lives. Why could they not just leave things alone? She stared out the window and tried to quell the sense of dread she felt.

Lisa noticed the in-flight magazine in the seat pocket, and decided to read instead of thinking more about her dysfunctional family. She flipped through the pages without finding much of interest, stopping finally on the airport maps in the back. She never did like flying into Chicago O'Hare airport, and found the terminals a bit confusing. She was supposed to meet Susan at the baggage claim area, but Lisa was hoping to stop first at a coffee shop to grab something more substantial than her granola bar to eat. Her stomach had started to grumble, and she had no idea how long it would be before they had lunch. She loved fixing big breakfasts for her family, and wondered what Kevin and Shane would do without her today. She had left plenty of things in the fridge for while she was gone to Chicago, and Kevin had promised Shane at least one cookout on the grill with some of his school friends. There would be plenty of burgers and dogs, and probably a touch football game in the back yard. In fact, they were looking forward to a little time with just the guys, although there would probably be a few girls there, too. Shane was a really likable kid, and quite popular at school. She knew she had no reason to worry about them. But she missed them already.

The flight attendants collected the cups and napkins, and told everyone to put their laptops and IPods away. The businesswoman sitting on the aisle seemed annoyed that her work would have to wait a few more minutes. One again, Lisa felt a sense of pity for her, and was glad her life was not so stressed or high-pressured.

The pilot announced that they were making their descent into Chicago, and Lisa put the magazine away, not realizing that she had left her boarding pass tucked inside the back cover. Looking out the window, she scanned the familiar

Chicago skyline and identified the Sears Tower and other landmarks. Once on the ground, she took her cell phone from her purse and called Kevin to let him know she had arrived safely. The businesswoman sitting next to her was back on her Blackberry again, checking for messages and emails. Kevin answered on the second ring, sounding sleepy and sexy. Even after all these years, she melted when she heard his voice, and couldn't wait to get home to see him again.

"Hi, honey. Did I wake you?"

"Mmmmm," he mumbled. "Where are you?"

"We just landed and I am waiting my turn to get off the plane. Go back to sleep – I just wanted to let you know that I got here OK."

"I'm glad everything was on time. Susan is picking you up, right?"

"Yes, she's gonna meet me at baggage claim. Have a good day, honey. I'll call you later – I love you."

"Love you more…" he said sleepily.

Lisa put the phone back into her purse, made her way up the aisle and out onto the jet bridge. The "Blackberry Lady" was chatting away, rushing ahead of her. There were quite a number of people waiting in the gate area as she picked her way through the crowd and into the main terminal. After grabbing a biscuit at McDonald's and then stopping at the restroom to freshen up a bit, Lisa found the escalator that carried her down to the baggage claim area. It took her a few minutes to find the correct carousel, and then she saw Susan. They always did look so much alike, and bore a striking resemblance to their mother, who was fairly short but with lots of curves. Rebecca, on the other hand, looked much more like their father – tall and with striking, angular features. Too bad she did not have his caring and sensitive personality.

Susan was scanning the crowd, looking for Lisa, and then a big smile broke out onto both of their faces when they made eye contact. Lisa put aside her dread of the upcoming days to give her little sister a big hug. While waiting for Lisa's bag to arrive, Susan was bubbly and talked excitedly about the plans for the upcoming days. Lisa told Susan about Shane's game last night, and Susan filled her in about the twins' latest summer camp adventures. She then told Lisa that Rebecca was too busy to be there to meet her, but had promised to join them for lunch at a trendy restaurant in the Loop. She was in the middle of a big trial and was not sure how much time she would have for them over the next few days. Typical Rebecca.

Lisa's bag finally arrived, and after making their way through the crowd near the baggage claim area, the sisters walked toward the exit and out into the early morning Chicago sunshine.

Back at the gate area, Gerald MacNamara was boarding a flight to New York and wondering how he was going to survive the day.

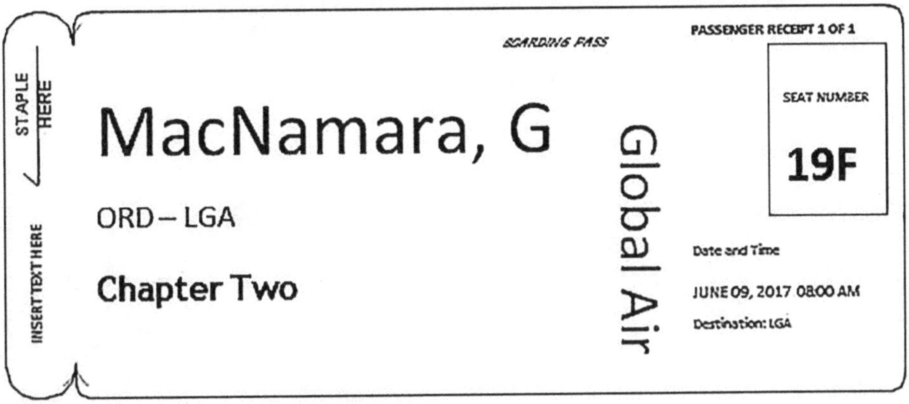
BOARDING PASS
PASSENGER RECEIPT 1 OF 1
STAPLE HERE
INSERT TEXT HERE
MacNamara, G
ORD – LGA
Chapter Two
Global Air
SEAT NUMBER
19F
Date and Time
JUNE 09, 2017 08:00 AM
Destination: LGA

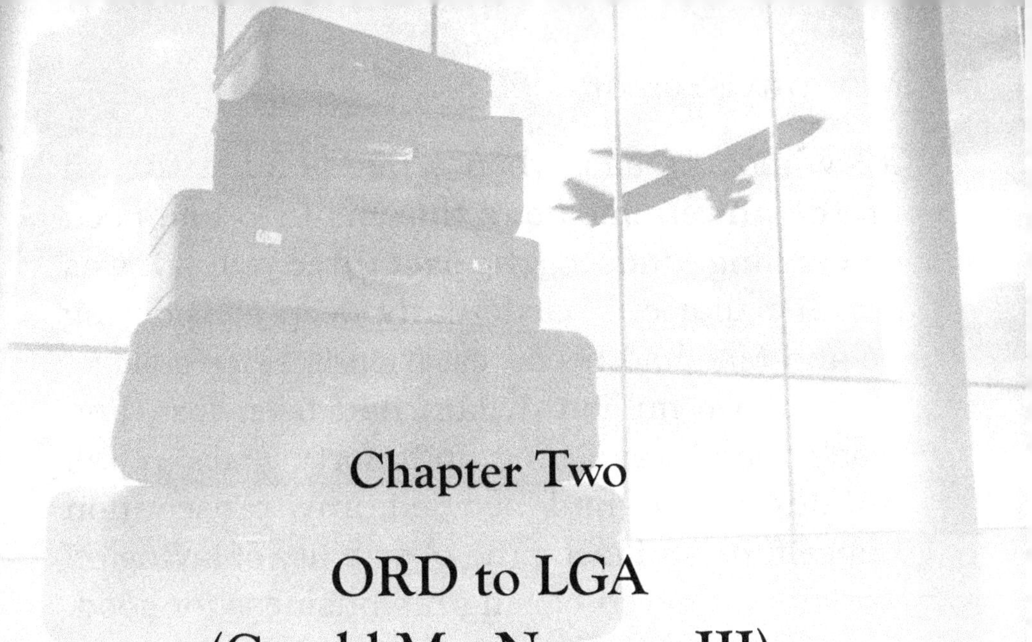

Chapter Two

ORD to LGA
(Gerald MacNamara III)

Oh, how the mighty have fallen. He might as well have that imprinted on his business card. For Gerald MacNamara III (Mac to his friends), those six words summed up his entire life—professional, personal, financial, and spiritual.

It was 6:00 AM and Mac was sitting dejectedly in the crowded boarding area at Chicago O'Hare airport, waiting to board his flight to New York City. This was his last chance, his only hope of saving his floundering architectural firm, which he'd not so modestly named Mac III. The recent housing bust had crushed his business and depleted his savings. But the final blow came a few months ago, when a messy audit turned up the unwelcome news that his CFO had been embezzling funds for the past three years. It was a crime that cut particularly deep considering he and Mac had been best friends since college.

Over five million dollars had been lost, and Mac's friend was facing up to forty years in jail. Although Mac had avoided any prosecution himself, he still faced the possibility of laying off workers and even closing his business for good. He had this one last chance to save his firm and his reputation. Quite literally, everything was resting on the presentation he was to make this afternoon to a group of investors who were interested in constructing a spectacular office building near the former World Trade Center site. Mac had the floor plans and elevation drawings in a crush-proof plastic tube, and his briefcase was filled with financial projections and testimonials from previous clients. He refused to take his hands off either of these, knowing how important they were. It was too bad that the sun hadn't even risen—Mac really needed a drink to steady his nerves.

He glanced subconsciously at his left hand and rubbed the place where his wedding ring used to be. His finger looked so different without the gold band that had been there for over twenty years, but the failing business and Mac's fondness for afternoon cocktails drove away the only person he had ever truly loved: his beautiful wife Misty.

Mac and Misty used to be the toast of the town, invited to all the exclusive parties and red carpet events. They thrived in a world of fast cars, expensive jewels, and the lavish lifestyle that came with being the CEO of one of Chicago's most prestigious businesses. Misty was ten years his junior and he had loved spoiling her with all the trappings of a trophy wife. They had just over two adventurous decades together, wild years of success and opulence, but when the market started to fail, Mac had to cut back on some of those luxuries, and Misty didn't take it well. She might have been more gracious about what she had to give up if he had given up his afternoon drinks in his home office. He never missed a Scotch and soda though, which later became mostly Scotch with very little soda, and then Scotch straight up. Mac became more and more withdrawn, and eventually Misty moved out of their bedroom into a spare room on the opposite side of their high-rise condo. And then she moved out altogether.

Within a week of her leaving, Mac was served divorce papers. His lawyer was appalled to find out that they'd never signed a prenuptial agreement, and that without working a day in her life, Misty would get half of everything. But even though she'd broken his heart, and even though half of everything wasn't all that much anymore, Mac would have gladly given her even more.

The architect and the socialite had met over twenty years ago at a Fourth of July party hosted by an up-and-coming real estate mogul. Mac was a rising star and Misty was the type of girl that always seemed to appear when rising stars congregated. She was a stunner, tall and blonde and curvaceous. He was average looking at best, but Misty seemed to genuinely like Mac. He fell hard for her, and would go on to tell anyone who asked that he was now a believer in love at first sight. He refused to consider that his money was the only thing keeping someone so young and beautiful at his side, but that didn't stop him from lavishing all he could upon her. Within months of their first meeting, he proposed with a massive diamond ring. They were married in a candlelight service on Christmas Eve in front of hundreds of guests. Their honeymoon was a cruise in the Mediterranean and a week in the south of France.

Mac's business really began to take off, and Misty was excited to play the gracious hostess. He could count on her to throw posh parties and invite all the A-list celebrities she could find. Every few years they moved to a larger and more luxurious home, filling it with clothes and trinkets purchased on their many international vacations. But the busier Mac got at work, the more he worried that Misty would be lonely at home. Due to a surgery she'd had after a boating accident when she was a teenager, Misty was unable to have children. Mac suggested that they adopt a child, but Misty swore that she was fine on her own and refused even the company of a dog or cat. She claimed that she didn't feel cut out to be a mom and Mac had grieved this decision in his own way, but now, he supposed it was the right call. He couldn't imagine navigating this tumultuous phase of his life with a child or two in the mix.

He supposed it was possible that being a father might have held him together when the stock market crashed and he was trading lavish vacations for long hours trying to salvage his company. But more than likely, any child of his would have been just as neglected and frustrated as Misty was when their lifestyle suffered. And just like Misty, this fantasy child would fail to see the severity of their situation, and would hold him accountable for things far out of his control.

Without children, Mac had made his business his true legacy, and had nurtured it over the years. To see it hanging on by a thread now was agonizing. If the men and women he met with today didn't see potential in his designs, if they didn't hire him, it was all over. His mouth went dry at the thought.

Mac glanced at his watch. He'd been concerned about delays when he learned that he wouldn't be on the first flight of the morning, but was pleased to see his plane arriving right on time from wherever it had been in the pre-dawn hours. He pulled his boarding pass from his suit pocket and his mood sunk even further. Seat 19F. Coach. Back of the plane. His ticket felt like a badge of dishonor for a man used to flying in private jets, or First Class if he was forced to fly commercial. Now he was just like the average people around him, only from the occasional bursts of laughter and the hum of excited chatter, they did not have the feeling of impending doom that he had.

After a crowd of sleepy passengers piled off the plane and the flight attendants took a moment to tidy up and restock refreshments, the gate agent announced that they were ready for First Class boarding. Mac instinctively stood and then self-consciously dropped back into his uncomfortable chair. With gritted teeth, he waited his turn and filed along with the fidgeting babies, sleepy teenagers and over-caffeinated businessmen. Slowly they marched through the drafty jet bridge and into the metal fuselage of the plane.

As Mac shuffled past the First Class passengers, already comfortably seated and with drinks in hand, he looked down at the floor, trying not to make eye contact. The last thing he needed was for one of these elite flyers to recognize him. There had been enough rumors and gossip about him and Misty in the local tabloids. Wouldn't they just *love* to know he was now flying Coach?

Further and further toward the back of the plane he went. It felt like a different planet back here. He gently put his document tube in the overhead bin and slid his briefcase under the seat in front of him. Crawling into his window seat, he noticed the lack of leg room. At just shy of six feet, he wasn't overly tall, but still felt like his knees were up under his chin and wondered how he would survive this two hour flight to New York.

Mac leaned his head against the cool window and closed his eyes. Air travel didn't really frighten him, but anxiety about his meeting had heightened his discomfort. The whining of the engines and the stale taste of the recycled air had him wishing that all of his senses could be dulled for a few hours. Maybe then he could get the rest he needed on this flight.

He might have actually dozed for a few moments when he felt someone moving beside him, heard the buckling of a seatbelt. Sitting up slightly, he glanced to his left and almost cried out. The young woman beside him reminded him forcefully of Misty as she had looked so many years ago. She had long, slim legs and a tumble of golden hair and a movie star smile when she made eye contact with him.

"Sorry, I didn't mean to wake you," she said in a hushed voice. "You didn't, don't worry," he managed to say. He knew it would be impolite to keep staring at her, but she just kept smiling. The more he looked, the less she really looked like Misty except for the hair. This girl's eyes were a greenish-hazel, not blue, and she was wearing a t-shirt and distressed jeans and sturdy boots, which Misty never would have done.

"Was that your big plastic tube thing in the overhead compartment?" she asked boldly, kind of out of nowhere.

Mac gave a little laugh. "Yes, it's mine. Was it in the way or something?"

"Oh, not at all," the young woman assured him. "I was just wondering what was in there. Are they super-secret government documents or maybe blueprints for a building you're going to rob?"

Mac couldn't help but chuckle loudly. "I think you've read a few too many novels. It's nothing as glamorous as that. I'm an architect and those are my design plans."

He expected her to be underwhelmed, but she seemed plenty impressed. "That's very cool. I thought about being an architect when I was younger. But someone told me they are the most boring students on a college campus because all they do is draw non-stop."

Mac grinned. "Your friend is right about that. No time for beer parties or extracurricular things in design school. It's worth it though, when you see your first building on the skyline."

The girl's pretty hazel eyes got a bit sparkly at his words. "I'd love that, to leave a legacy somehow. I've been accepted to UIC in the fall, which I suppose is a good start."

Mac's eyebrows rose a bit. The University of Illinois at Chicago was no joke. "Congratulations. What do you plan to study?"

"Bioengineering," she replied in a matter-of-fact tone. Then she smiled warmly at Mac's perplexed expression. "It's what you pick to major in when you can't decide between biology, chemistry, or computer science."

Mac let out a grunt. "You've just named every subject I would choose to never take again in school."

She giggled. "You sound like my dad."

Mac winced. He'd forgotten for a moment how much older than this girl he was. She was probably just eighteen. He could easily be her father; in fact, if he and Misty had been able to have a biological daughter, she would probably look just like this young woman. "Well, I'm sure your father is very proud of you."

"He is," she said softly, looking past him then out the window. Without Mac really being aware of it, the plane had taxied away from the terminal and was now racing down the runway. A moment later, after a second of weightlessness followed by a little swoop as gravity kicked back in, they were airborne, climbing up into the early morning sky.

To his surprise, the girl began to giggle quietly, trying to stifle it with her hands over her mouth. "What's so funny?" Mac asked.

"I just can't believe I'm actually doing this!" she gushed. "I've never left the country before!"

Mac frowned. "You know this plane is only going to New York, right?"

She rolled her eyes at him. "Yes, but I'm catching a connecting flight.

I'm going to Spain! I can't believe it!"

Catching on, Mac nodded at her. "I love Spain. My wife and I went many times."

"Oh, that's lucky! How long have you been married?"

"Um, we were married for about twenty-three years. And we've been divorced for about eighteen months now, I guess."

The girl's eyes went wide and she looked so devastated at his words, like she'd never heard of something so sad in her life. "That's awful. We don't have to talk about her if you don't want to. We don't have to talk at all, I guess. I'm just feeling excited and chatty. I'll just read or something."

"You're not bothering me," Mac said gently. "Misty and I were great together, but she had expensive tastes and I've had a run of bad luck lately. Hopefully I can turn that around today."

"And then you'll try and win her back?" the girl pressed, staring openly at him.

Mac felt his brow furrow and he turned away from her. "I can't say that I've thought about that. I don't think she'd take me back."

"Well, I don't think it's very fair of her to only love you if you're rich, but if you became rich again, doesn't that mean that she would love you again?"

Mac grinned sadly. "What's your name?"

"I'm Tess," she said sweetly and reached over the armrest to shake his hand.

"Hi Tess, I'm Mac. And it's sweet of you to think that getting back with my wife would be that easy, but it's a lot more complicated than me making some money."

"Oh, I'm sure," Tess said. "When I was little, my parents had money troubles and it really brings out the worst in people. When you're tired from working or looking for work, and you're hungry and stressed, it just takes all of your flaws and puts them under a magnifying glass."

It was easy to brush away Tess's words, to minimize them because of her age and inexperience, but honestly, Mac found her story to be very accurate. Mac had always been a drinker, and under the microscope of financial instability, that particular vice had become his most prominent character trait. His kindness and generosity, his creativity and his drive, all of that had fallen aside in favor of his addiction.

So no, it had never been difficult to see why Misty left, how he had driven her away. But it shocked him how until this very moment, he'd never considered trying to win her back. When the divorce papers had showed up at his office, he'd seen that as the end of the line. He'd given her everything she'd asked for and hadn't put up a fight. Now he was wondering if that had been the right play.

"I'm really sorry if I overstepped," Tess said, knotting her fingers together and looking worried.

"No need to apologize, I was just thinking," Mac mumbled. "Why don't we change the subject? Tell me about what you're going to do in Spain."

Tess's lips turned up in a smile. "El Camino Santiago," she said, her accent very precise and her tone very dreamy.

"You're going to Spain to buy a car?"

She gave a musical little laugh at that and slapped his arm playfully. "No! It means The Way of St. James. I'm going on a seven-day spiritual hike in Northern Spain. It's a pilgrimage, a time of prayer and discipleship and reflection. I'm giving myself fully over to God before I fall into my studies at UIC. I don't want to lose sight of Him in that critical time, so I'm sort of stockpiling some time in His presence. I'm not sure if that makes any sense..."

Mac gave her a vague nod. He had never been a religious man, had always been too busy seeking after worldly pleasures to bother much with church or God. Tess made it sound very romantic, but beneath her thirst to explore a foreign country, Mac could detect a deep maturity. Her faith was youthful and fresh but not naïve. It wasn't as off-putting as he might have expected it to be.

"I'm not sure it totally makes sense to me," he admitted. "But it sounds very nice." He looked up then to see the flight attendant nearing with the beverage cart. All at once, his throat went very dry again. He'd been waiting for this. He'd fully intended to purchase an alcoholic drink when the time came, but now he wondered if Tess might not approve. She was not his wife or his daughter of course, but he'd begun to value her opinion of him. He knew all Christians weren't teetotalers, but he wasn't sure he ought to risk it. She had an optimism and a spirit about her that was refreshing after so many months of depression and foreboding, and he didn't want to disrupt that. And then of course, he had the meeting of his life this afternoon. He knew all too well how one drink to calm the nerves soon became six to drown out the sorrow and pain of the day. So he asked for a coffee instead.

Tess simply asked for water and spent the next several minutes sipping quietly and munching on her complimentary pretzels. Mac thumbed through the seatback pocket and pulled out what he expected to be the *USA Today*, but it seemed he would have to make do with the *Des Moines Register*, something left behind by an earlier passenger apparently. He found the financial section mildly entertaining for a while, and circled a few interesting stock prices, but found himself glancing over at Tess every now and then. Unlike most girls her age, she didn't seem to have a phone with her to play with, and while she wore an expression of calm, it seemed a bit forced. Several minutes later, when the trash from their little snack had been collected, Tess seemed ready to burst if she didn't speak, so Mac pocketed the newspaper and asked her to tell him more about her upcoming trip.

For most of the remainder of the flight, the two studied a paper map Tess had brought that showed the sixty miles she would be covering over the next week. Mac listened to her itinerary and asked questions about what would happen with her luggage and where she would sleep. It amused him that though the nature of the pilgrimage seemed to be a return to old-time methods for travel and one-on-one communion with God, each night was spent in a nice hotel or bed and breakfast along the route, and most of her meals were to be prepared by high end Spanish chefs.

It wasn't until the plane was beginning its initial descent that Tess brought up Misty again. She wasn't pushy about it, just simply asked about their first meeting. Mac was happy to relay that story, when he'd first seen her on the steps of a beautiful Chicago manor house. The setting sun had turned her golden hair a molten coppery color and he'd fallen in love with her right there.

"That sort of love can fade out," Tess said wisely. "It burns bright and fast and if you don't fan those flames, they can die. But I can tell that you still care for her. I don't know what pushed her away, but you owe it to yourself to fight for her."

Mac grinned patiently. "And what do you know about bright, burning love?"

She gave him a sweet smile. "The Bible teaches about all the different kinds of love. I'll be ready when the right boy comes along."

"I'm sure your dad can't wait for that!"

Tess laughed for quite a while at that one. When the plane landed and she was retrieving her bag, she brought his document tube down for him and handed it over. "Are you sure there aren't any secret plans in there?" "I'm afraid not," Mac said. "Maybe one day you'll see a chic little office building in New York designed by the rich and famous Gerald MacNamara III, and it will be our little secret that you knew him back when he was poor."

"Oh, Mac. Poor is an attitude, and one that you don't have," Tess assured him. "I'll say I knew you back when you were broke and on the outs with your wife. How about that?"

"I think that sounds pretty great. Take care in Spain, Tess."

"I will. Good luck today!" And she melted into the crowd, leaving him to walk down to the cab stand alone. Mac took a deep breath, tasting the subtle difference in the way the New York air felt in his lungs. It wasn't the cleanest feeling in the world, but it was full of promise. As he waited his turn for a taxi, he thought that regardless of how his meeting went today, maybe it was time to give Misty a call. In fact, he thought perhaps a call was long overdue.

STAPLE HERE

INSERT TEXT HERE

BOARDING PASS

PASSENGER RECEIPT 1 OF 1

Narong, Patesh

LGA-LAX

Chapter Three

Global Air

SEAT NUMBER

19F

Date and Time

JUNE 09, 2017 11:57 AM

Destination: ATL

Chapter Three

LGA to LAX (Dr. Narong)

Dr. Patesh Narong sat patiently in his window seat 19F, reading the latest *Journal of American Medical Association* about an emerging strain of the Ebola virus. He had co-authored the article, and was pleased with the clarity of the details and the effectiveness of the charts and graphs. The article was even featured on the cover of the magazine, which was a quite a coup. As a researcher, Dr. Narong had been very successful in developing and testing vaccines for some of the more challenging diseases of the 21st century.

In fact, it was that success that had led to today's flight. The CDC in Atlanta had learned of his latest research, and had read an advance copy of the article. They begged him to come to the CDC to head up their Ebola project, and offered prestige and notoriety that was hard to refuse. He had packed up his office in Manhattan, shipped his meager belongings to a storage facility recommended by his real estate agent, and boarded the plane to Atlanta where he was told he would be participating in a press conference soon after arriving at the airport. This sure was a long way from his humble beginnings in a poor village in India.

He was born the third of nine children (but the oldest son), and life was very hard for everyone in his family. Food and water were often scarce, and Patesh never believed that his dream of becoming a doctor could ever come true. But one day while he was attending the local missionary school, a special visitor from the US spoke about a medical school in Chicago that was offering full scholarships to students who were willing to train in the US and promise to remain in America for ten years, practicing in poor inner city areas or entering specialties such as research or pathology. Patesh talked to his parents about the idea later that night, and within a few months he had flown to Chicago to begin his studies. He spoke virtually no English at the time, and felt very isolated from most of the students. He studied hard and excelled in his classes, but was quite lonely and spent most of his time alone in the library. Graduation and residency followed, and then a research position at a top hospital in New York City. He had been able to take a few short trips back to India to see his family, and felt the culture shock of the extreme poverty of his village versus the excesses of the Big Apple. He did send as much money as he could to help things out at home, but never felt that it was enough. He felt guilty for this success and for their struggles.

When his ten years of obligation were over, his family had urged him to return home to help solve the various health crises brought on the crushing poverty. He struggled with the decision for quite a while, but then decided that his skills could be better utilized in a facility with top-notch funding and equipment. Of course, any vaccines or drugs that he developed would be of a benefit to everyone, including those in India. His family did not understand his decision, and a silent rift grew between them.

"Son, you have a duty to come home. You are the oldest son and have a responsibility to your family. Your people need you. Your family needs you. How can you justify your lavish lifestyle when you spend more money each day for your coffee than we do on food the entire week?" His mother pleaded with him to return to India and work with the government to help solve the poverty crisis.

The years passed, and Patesh's reputation as an impeccable researcher continued to grow. He had taken English lessons in his spare time, and had become quite proficient with the language. He worked doubly hard to lose most of his accent that he felt would stereotype him and hold back his career. Of course, his family disapproved and felt he was becoming too westernized.

He was quite handsome, in the dark and brooding sort of way typical for those of his heritage, and at 5 feet 11 inches, he was a bit taller than his father. Although he was a naturally shy and reserved young man, his long hours in the lab prevented him from having much of a social life. One of his co-workers, a long-legged blond named Stephanie, had tried in vain to get him to notice her for more than her expertise with a microscope, but Patesh seemed blind to her charms. He lived in a tiny efficiency apartment within walking distance of his office, but spent very little time there. The walls were bare and the tiny loft contained few clues as to the personality of the person who lived there. He actually had very little to pack once the call from the CDC came.

The plane began to fill, but both seats beside him remained empty. How nice to have three seats to himself! He smoothed a few stray wrinkles from his slacks and adjusted his tie. He wanted to look impeccable for the cameras at the press conference.

Just as the doors of the plane were about to close, a young man in his middle to late 20's came rushing in and hurried down the aisle to stop at row 19. Tossing a small bag into the overhead bin, he sank into the aisle seat. Almost immediately, the plane pushed back from the gate. "Wow, just made it!" he exclaimed in a thick southern drawl to no one in particular. He turned to Patesh and said, "My flight from Maine was late and I was just sure I would miss my connection!"

Patesh smiled politely in his direction, and turned his attention back to the article. It was as if all of his life had been in preparation for this moment, this position of importance with the CDC. Not bad for a poor kid from the dregs and lowest caste (the Shudra) in India. He was mentally practicing his comments for the press conference, trying to quell his nerves a bit. Even though he knew all the facts of his research by heart, he reviewed them over and mover, making sure of every last finding and statistic. He was never one for the spotlight, and had made few public speeches. The anticipated sea of TV cameras was a bit intimidating to him.

"So, where are you going today?" the young man asked Patesh. "I've been in Maine on a business trip – I'm a marketing rep for a trucking company, and we have a BIG client in Portsmouth who was threatening to go with a different company, someone more local. It was all I could do to try to save this big account, but I'm glad to be going back to Atlanta. Two days is way too long for me to be away from my wife and kids. Twins – age 3. What a handful!"

Patesh knew there would be no peace and quiet on this plane today. Mr. Chatterbox here was going to see to that.

"Gina – that's my wife – she stays home with the kids all day and I usually try to help in the evenings so she can have a break and a little time for herself. She's been alone with the twins for over 48 hours now, and is climbing the walls! Here's a picture she sent me just this morning." He put his cell phone on airplane mode to show Patesh a picture his wife had emailed to him earlier. "It's a picture of the kids eating breakfast today, with cereal on their heads and milk all over the table! What a mess!"

Patesh quietly closed his magazine and slid it into the seat pocket in front of him, alongside a newspaper someone on a previous flight had left. Perhaps if he made a point of reading the newspaper this guy would be quiet and leave him alone?

Pulling the *Register* from the pocket, Patesh saw that it was open to the financial section, and many of the stocks were underlined or circled. Someone sure had been very interested in the stock market today. Patesh turned to the health section, and was distressed to see a report of a new epidemic predicted to sweep Southeast Asia in the coming months. This virus was a mutation of a strain that Patesh had worked on a few years ago, but had somehow become resistant to the standard antivirals being used. If he was still in the clinic in New York, perhaps he would be able to shift his focus to include this new virus, or seek funding for hiring additional researchers. But now his hands would be tied with the Ebola research for months and maybe years to come.

"What? Oh, I'm sorry," Patesh finally answered. "I am on my way to Atlanta to work for the CDC doing research on viruses.

"Wow, that sounds important! You must be quite a famous guy, right?"

"No, not really. Or maybe just in my small circle of researchers.

Not many people know what we do or really care. They just want vaccines to protect their kids and grandparents. They have no idea what all is involved before the vaccines or other medications hit the shelves."

"I suppose. My name is Andy, by the way. Have lived in Atlanta all my life. You can probably tell that by my accent. Do you have someplace to live?"

"The HR people from the CDC have arranged for a corporate apartment for me for a month or two until I find something permanent. Since most of my time will be spent in the lab, I just want something close where I can walk or take the bus."

"So, no wife and kids to come with you? Or are they already in Atlanta waiting for you?"

"No, no wife or kids. I have been much too busy for that kind of distraction."

"Tell me about it! Sure has been hard to climb the corporate ladder when your wife is expecting twins and then they are born three months early. Or when they both come down with the chickenpox at the same time. I even had to pass up a promotion because it would have meant moving to Phoenix and all of our family is in Georgia. Plus, we are really involved in our local church. So, where is the rest of your family...... parents? Brothers and sisters?"

"My father passed away last year, but my mother and my siblings still live in a small town outside of Delhi, India, where I was raised."

"India? Wow, you sure are a long way from home. Sorry about your dad. You must get really lonely being so far from home......"

Patesh shifted his weight in his seat a bit, and looked down at the newspaper. This stranger, this ANDY person, was getting way too personal and digging into places that Patesh had not wanted to look for a very long time. Yes, he was lonely. Much more lonely than he wanted to admit to anyone, especially a stranger on an airplane. From the time he was in medical school and did not know enough English to make many friends, he had retreated to his books and lab experiments as a way to push that loneliness away. Even after learning English, he had remained a loner. But now this guy was ripping that wound open, and his constant chatter was like pouring salt into it. How was he going to get this guy to change the subject? Or stop talking altogether?

His reprieve came in the form of a frazzled flight attendant passing out drinks and offering granola bars for sale. Patesh's request for a cup of hot tea was met with a frown and a roll of her eyes that told him he should have asked for a coke instead. He finally got a cup of hot water and a tea bag, but was hesitant to ask for some sugar and a little milk. He unwrapped his snack and sipped the hot drink, letting his mind drift back to the streets of India and the ever-present crowds and squalor. How different his life would have been if he had never left. So why the nagging thoughts now, of all times? Why was he feeling so unsettled? He was on the verge of something more important than anyone had ever dreamed of. Should he leave it now to return home? Where could he do the most good for mankind? Was there really a way to balance his demanding career and find a little peace and happiness for himself?

Andy finished his snack and started chatting again about the best places to visit in Atlanta and his season tickets to the football team, but Patesh was not really listening. Each minute brought them closer to Atlanta, closer to this amazing opportunity. Closer to this new chapter of his life.

Patesh let his mind wander back to his first airplane flight. He was 17 and on his way to Chicago to start his medical studies. Two young men from his village were in the seats beside him. None of them spoke much English or had been more than a few miles from home. They barely spoke or moved from their seats the entire long flight from India. When the plane touched down in Chicago, they stood in awe, staring at the people and the sights of the big city. The director of the medical program was at the gate to meet them, along with an interpreter. They were escorted to the dorms and introduced to a few other foreign students. Patesh truly was a stranger in a strange land. He had immersed himself into his studies, always feeling the burden of responsibility and duty to his family and his country.

The flight attendant asked them to put away their carry-on items and to prepare for landing. Patesh was still looking for some sort of sign, something that would help him make the right decision. He looked again at the cover of *JAMA* and saw his name in print. He knew his family would be so pleased to get the copy that he had mailed to them. As the plane approached the airport, he looked at Andy and said, "I'm sorry, what did you say?"

"I said I really admire you and your dedication to your work. Not everyone could give up so much to devote their lives to serving others like you do. But anytime you want a home-cooked meal or to watch a game or something, give me a call. Here's my card – I know my wife would love to meet you. And she would be the first to let you know that her older sister Gloria is a nurse at a local hospital and SINGLE. I really think you two would have a lot in common."

"Thanks, Andy, that means a lot to me. I don't have a new card with me, of course, and will be very busy for a while. But I appreciate the offer."

After a moment or two of silence, Patesh turned to Andy and asked, "Do you ever regret your decision to put your family ahead of your career? Do you wonder what things might have been like if you had moved to Arizona?"

Andy did not hesitate with his answer. "No, I'm so glad I put my family first. The career will always be there, my wife and kids may not be. I would not miss the chance to watch my twins grow, and Gina is the love of my life. So, I'm not making as much money as I could have, but at the end of the day, I'm one lucky guy."

Patesh turned his gaze toward the window and watched the Atlanta skyline come into view. He strongly wished he felt better about the decision he was about to make.

The landing was rather bumpy and the plane came to an abrupt stop on a runway far from the terminal. The pilot came over the loud speaker to tell the passengers that there had been a mechanical problem with the plane at their gate, and that they would be delayed for a few minutes. Andy turned on his cell phone and called Gina to tell her he would be a little late getting home.

"Wow, you should have heard the commotion in the background," Andy said when he hung up the phone. "She sure sounded exhausted. The twins are just getting over the stomach flu and everyone is pretty irritable."

Patesh turned on his cell phone and saw that he had a text message from the CDC Director, telling him that the press was waiting for him to deplane. Even before he could respond, the plane began to move and they taxied toward their gate. When it was finally their turn to leave their seats, Andy retrieved his bag from the overhead bin and said, "Good luck to you doctor. I know you have an important job ahead of you, and millions of people are counting on you."

"Thanks, Andy. I just hope I am up to the task. It has been a pleasure talking with you."

With that, the doctor walked off the plane and into a waiting throng of TV cameras and reporters. Andy stood off to the side and watched in amazement as Patesh took his place at the podium and began to speak.

"Thank you all for being here today. My name is Dr. Patesh Narong, and I am pleased to stand before you today to make an announcement. My journey to Atlanta and the CDC began almost 30 years ago in a small village in rural India...."

STAPLE HERE

BOARDING PASS

BOARDING PASS

PASSENGER RECEIPT 1 OF 1

Sullivan, Joel

ATL - DFW

Chapter Four

Global Air

SEAT NUMBER

19F

Date and Time

JUNE 09, 2017 02:07 PM

Destination: DFW

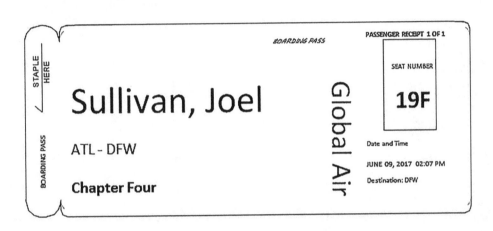

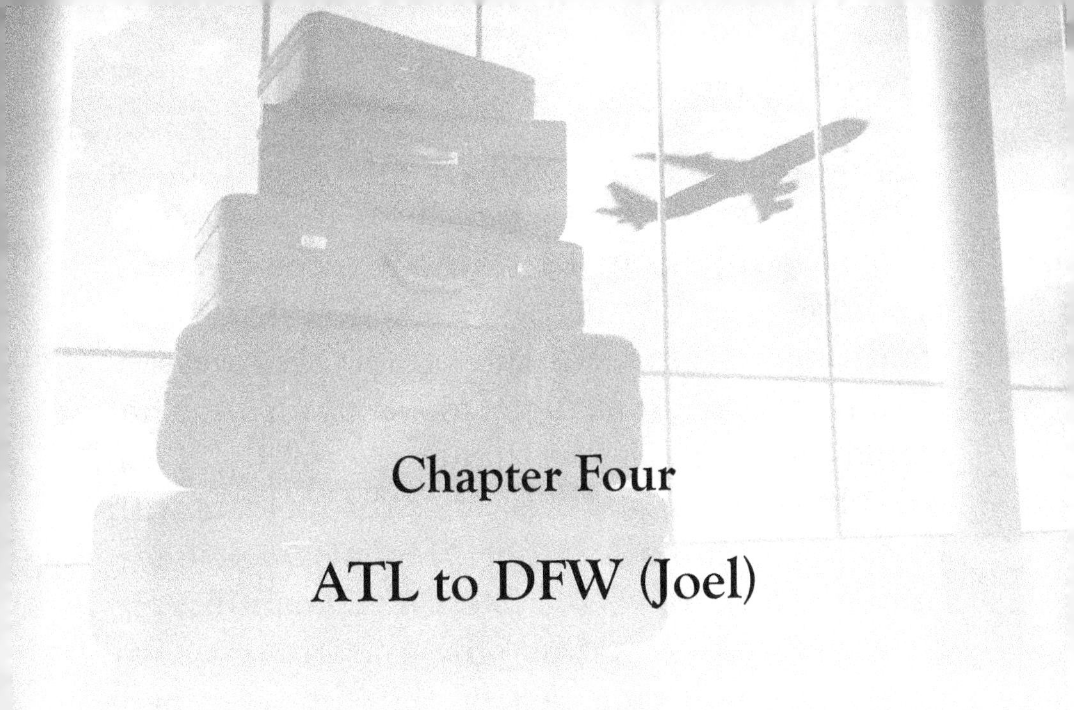

Chapter Four

ATL to DFW (Joel)

Women just love a man in uniform. This fact had always rather embarrassed Joel, whether back in his jock days or now as a soldier. But he couldn't deny that it was helpful today.

The female cab driver had refused to let him pay for his quick jaunt from the Army base down to Columbus. The woman at the Greyhound station had "accidentally" forgotten to charge him for his last-minute ticket to Atlanta. And the lady at the airport check-in had obligingly put him on the 'first available' flight to Dallas, after he'd heard her tell the couple in front of him that nothing was heading anywhere in Texas until later that night.

He fidgeted with anxiety as the woman printed up his ticket. The change in his plans went against his very un-spontaneous nature, but it had been necessary. It had been impossible to sleep last night on the base for three reasons. First, he was ridiculously jet-lagged. The hours from Baghdad to Georgia were nearly reversed, making it uncomfortable to lie down at what would normally be his noon. Secondly, sleep brought dreams, and ever since the incident with Pete...his dreams had not been pleasant ones. And lastly, there was Kristen. The beautiful girl he'd left back home was only a few hours away from him now. Being back on the same continent had made him restless. To be back in America, lying on his back in bed, and not feeling her resting on his shoulder—it was just wrong. As sleep evaded him, he'd stared at a photo of her, trying to find comfort in her wide green eyes and her tumble of chestnut hair. But her smile made him impatient.

So he'd bailed early, refusing to wait until tomorrow night when she arrived. She'd be so surprised! Her face would light up even brighter than the woman's behind the counter, whose brown eyes had gone all sparkly since he'd smiled at her.

Yes, women were naturally drawn to him in his fatigues, following him surreptitiously with their eyes as he moved with innate confidence, which was only partly for show. He had a good face, clean cut and honest. He was a poster boy for the young American hero. Women would moan and groan about not needing a man to take care of them or rescue them, but they gravitated to heroes. It was some bizarre genetic response.

It seemed that the only female who hadn't responded favorably to Joel was the girl sitting next to him in seat 19E. But she was a freak. Well, okay, that's not totally fair, but she certainly *looked* like a freak. She and the nondescript businessman in 19D had shuffled aside to let him into the window seat, and he'd had a hard time not starting at her. After the utterly foreign quality of war, he found it amusing that a young girl, eighteen years old at best, could startle him. She was of average height, willowy, and had probably been pretty once before dyeing her hair a jet black so severe, it was nearly indigo. Her eyes were heavily outlined in black liner and shadow, standing out harshly against her luminous pale skin. Dressed all in black, with a spike of metal through her left eyebrow, she was terrifying. Joel was uneasy sitting next to her, and ignored her thoroughly as the plane taxied and took off.

He opened his book, trying to sink back into the words he'd been reading on the bus, but they wouldn't take. His eyes kept migrating to Kristen's picture, which served as the bookmark for the battered paper- back. Her sweet face, so unlike the stranger's next to him, gave him peace and butterflies all at once.

He gave up on the book after a few minutes, rifling through the seat pocket and finding an Iowa newspaper, left by some previous passenger. It seemed totally random, but then again, everyone flies these days – even corn farmers. He amused himself for several miles with the small town baseball scores, finding it hard not to reminisce back to easier times when a clear blue sky meant excellent baseball weather and wasn't about visibility from enemy spy planes. To try and quell the unpleasant thoughts, he worked the puzzle in the back of the in-flight magazine. Someone else had started it, but he was pleased to add a few answers of his own. Each person on this plane seemed to be adding a bit to the puzzle, much like life, he guessed.

He nursed a soda when the refreshment cart came along, gasping at the revelation of having ice in his glass. How many months had he guzzled eighty-degree water and been grateful for it?

It was after he'd munched the last of the ice cubes that he be- came aware that the girl next to him was angled slightly toward him, staring at him. From the corner of his eye he watched her gaze move from his large hands to his fatigue pants tucked into standard issue boots. Up to his suntanned face and closely buzzed sandy hair. From the book he'd tucked between his right thigh and the wall of the plane then up to his face again.

He turned his head toward her slowly, eyebrows raised expectantly. This was the mute equivalent of saying "What are you staring at?"

He waited for her pale cheeks to flush, or for her to turn away in embarrassment, but she surprised and terrified him again by keeping her blue-violet eyes trained on him. Long seconds ticked on and she simply cocked her head to the side as though studying something of interest under glass.

Hating to break first, Joel gave a resigned sigh. "Was there something you needed?" he asked tightly.

She watched him for another long stretch of seconds before flicking her eyes to his left wrist. "What's with the rubber band?"

His right hand went automatically to his wrist, fingering the thick rubber band that he wore like a bracelet. The skin beneath was bright red. He smirked, wondering why he felt compelled to explain this bizarre little detail to a stranger. But she had noticed it, and commented on it before asking all the basic questions that normally come up when a civilian sits next to a soldier.

"It's to keep me from swearing," he said rather sheepishly. "Hanging around a couple dozen guys who use the worst language imaginable...it rubs off after a while. And my parents are real salt-of-the-earth type of people. When I came home from boot camp sounding like a sailor, they nearly tossed me out. So I'm training myself to quit cussing. Every time I swear, or feel like swearing, I snap myself." He demonstrated for her, pulling the rubber band back an inch or two and then letting go, feeling his raw skin sting again.

The girl's lips turned down and she nodded her head, as though digesting whether his story was believable or not, and deciding that it was.

"So, you're coming back then?" she asked, and he nodded. "Where from?"

"Iraq," he said simply. Not even his own mother had known the exact city.

"Did you kill anyone?"

His head snapped to the left and he stared down at her sternly. The words were so bare, so naked in their simplicity, it was almost as if he'd imagined them. The girl could have been asking him if it was hot in the desert.

"What?"

"I'm just wondering. It's a part of war. So...did you?"

"No," he lied smoothly, turning his face forward again. "It was actually pretty boring most of the time." He closed his eyes, but after only a second of peace, images of blood and pain flashed behind his eye- lids, so he opened them again.

"So, now that you're back, what college are you going to? That's what happens next for you, right?"

He turned his face to her again, surprised at the presumption. "What makes you think I'm going to school? I'm a soldier, not a scholar." He gestured at his uniform, which she was apparently impervious to.

"Oh, please," she replied, looking vaguely insulted. "You're not a lifetime soldier." When he looked bewildered, she plunged on. "First, you lie and lead me to believe that it wasn't totally crappy over there in that godforsaken desert, and then your eyes get all defensive. You're reading a well-worn copy of *Slaughterhouse Five*, so you're not a dummy. And your bookmark is a picture of a pretty girl I'm assuming you left back home. You love her. I can tell by how often you keep turning to look at it. So you clearly had other options. You took the Army route because it pays for college, something the parents couldn't afford, and maybe your jock scholarship fell through. I had you figured out before you had your seatbelt buckled. I'm just wondering what school the government will be paying you to attend."

Joel felt his brow furrow, and he bristled at her wild assumptions. He'd been in a company with plenty of other young men who were pretty smart and had other 'options,' but had foregone them. His officers were the same way. Sometimes you just choose to be a solder. Or it's something you're meant to do. This girl was so far out of line to assume that he wasn't one of those, however much she might be correct. He had indeed chosen not to re-enlist, a decision made so recently not even his parents or Kristen knew. They were expecting to welcome him home for a visit, and he couldn't wait to see their faces when he told them the truth.

His seatmate watched on in amusement as his face registered defensive irritation and then faded to concession. She'd judged him at first sight, and unlike his quick assessment of her, she was right on the money. Her perceptive manner had been highly unexpected when he'd labeled her as a freak. Freaks didn't have such laser-sharp intuition.

"The University of Texas," he said eventually, an air of resignation in his tone.

Her face lit up with a smug smile. "Majoring in...."

"I want to be a large animal vet," he said slowly, thinking of his horses back on the farm in Boonesville, Texas. He missed them almost as much as his missed Kristen. The weather report had been favorable for the weekend, and he couldn't wait to get back in the saddle. Literally Bears?"

The girl's face was confused. "Large animals like what? Polar

He laughed, and it felt good to do so. "No, like horses." "Oh," she said, cringing slightly. "I don't like horses."

"Nobody dislikes horses," he rebutted, trying in vain to think of anyone in Boonesville that would disagree with this.

"Well, I don't. They're too tall. I'm scared of heights."

Joel laughed again. He'd rappelled down a hundred feet from a moving helicopter before. The five or six foot fall from a horse was the least frightening thing he could imagine. And then her words took on a different meaning.

"You do realize that we're...um....flying right now?"

The girl closed her eyes and turned away from him. "Yes, soldier, I do. Why do you think I've been chatting at you? You're distracting me."

Joel smiled. "Well, then, perhaps it's my turn to ask irritating questions."

She grinned, still keeping her eyes closed. "Shoot." "So what are you doing once you get to Dallas?" "Nothing," she replied. "Changing planes."

"Where are you going then?"

"Kansas City. I'm going to the Paramore concert."

"To the *what* concert?"

She turned to face him, her oddly colored eyes turning a purplish shade of bewilderment. "Oh, come on! Paramore? The greatest female-fronted rock band in the history of *forever*?" When he still looked perplexed, she reached for the bag at her feet. "You've been off the continent too long, sir."

He watched on as she dragged a heavy looking canvas satchel into her lap. It was black, of course, but decorated with handwritten lyrics and cartoons in what looked like a white-out pen. She emerged a moment later with an mp3 player, which she switched on quickly and cued up, handing him one of the earphones.

They leaned close together and listened. The lyrics were a bit angry for Joel's taste; he had been raised on classic country and Baptist hymns. The girl was singing something about putting all of her faith in a boy, only to have him cast her aside. It reminded him uncomfortably of a fight he'd had with Kristen when he'd enlisted in the Army, but the singer's voice was pretty – powerful, while still remaining young and vulnerable.

He looked over at his neighbor, whose eyes were closed again. Her lips were moving along with the words, and a crease had formed between her eyes. She nodded in time to the driving beat, looking as though she were in deep prayer. The angst-heavy lyrics moved her deeply, like pages stolen from her own personal diary.

Joel grinned as he handed the earphone back to her. He could still hear the beat in his head and made a mental note to pick the CD up the next time he found himself in a Wal-Mart – another novelty he'd missed while hiking through the fiery sand.

"Great, right?" the girl asked, beaming.

"Yes, ma'am," he replied, pleased that he hadn't needed to lie.

"Ugh, don't call me ma'am. It's creepy." She reached her hand out. "I'm Charity," she said, grinning.

Joel took her hand, smirking. Half an hour ago, he wouldn't have been able to imagine a person less worthy of the name Charity. But she was just one of those books whose cover is incredibly misleading. He gave another smile as he looked down at her fingernails, which were very short for a girl's, though pained with shiny black polish. "I'm Joel," he said.

Just then the plane dipped a few feet, responding to a rogue pocket of air. Charity gripped Joel's hand fiercely, slamming her eyes shut and sucking in a sharp breath. She uttered a rather vicious curse word, and Joel laughed.

"Maybe you need a swear bracelet, too." He pried his fingers out of hers and patted the back of her hand gently. She had yet to reopen her eyes, though she'd given a little smirk at his attempt at a joke.

"I just need to keep talking," she said decidedly. "Tell me about your girl, the one in the picture you keep staring at."

"Kristen," he said fondly, feeling the way he said her name like a prayer.

Charity leaned back in the seat, forcing her body into a calmer posture. "How did you two meet?"

Joel thought back. "I can't even remember. We were probably in strollers next to each other. We grew up together. She was my high school sweetheart. Love of my life."

"Let me see the picture again," Charity mumbled, breathing deeply and fighting to relax over the little tremors of turbulence that continued to shake the plane. Joel obliged, letting her see the photo- graph that had been taken last year at his farm. By some miracle, it had come out looking almost professional. The sun was pushing through her dark hair, turning it nearly auburn, and little sunspots gleamed from her eyelashes and across her smile. She was breathtaking. Even Charity, whose conceptions of beauty seemed a bit skewed, was forced to concede. “She’s pretty. Let me guess....cheerleader?”

Perceptive as always. “Yes,” Joel admitted.

“And you were a jock, I assume.” She looked him up and down once as though deciding which sport better fit his body. “Football? No wait, you were reading baseball scores earlier.” Her eyes missed nothing.

“Both, actually. I’m from a small town. You can play every sport there is if you have the stamina to go to all the practices.” He preferred baseball, truly. The sport carried less prestige than football in Texas perhaps, but it hurt a heck of a lot less. And he hated seeing the worry on Kristen’s face on Friday nights when he limped away from a vicious tackle.

“So, I was right about the sport scholarship?”

Joel gave a bitter laugh. “As it turns out, being the best corner- back in Boonesville, Texas earned me fourth string for the Longhorns. I would never have taken the field on a Saturday. And though you were right about me not being dumb, I’m not exactly much of a student. The little bit of scholarship money I got for my academics didn’t make a dent in the tuition. I’d nearly bankrupted my parents after the first semester. So, I found a recruiter and enlisted.”

"You don't love it though." She didn't ask this; she just said it like it was fact.

"What's to love?" he muttered, feeling strangely at ease admit- ting this. He'd never before hinted that serving his country wasn't the ultimate achievement. "It's overcrowded on base, and yet you're always alone. You get homesick, and then you just get sick. The food is crap, and the hours are terrible. You get to build your muscles up and play with weapons, but then they ship you over to this foreign planet that feels it was built on the sun. And then....it's not play anymore. Everything is real, and yet nothing feels real at all. It feels like this hot, sweaty dream that never seems to end."

Joel turned to see that Charity's eyes were wide with surprise. He cringed, realizing how dumb his rant would sound to a stranger. It would sound dumb to pretty much anyone.

"Sorry. That was lame of me to just babble on like that. Maybe I need a bracelet for when I talk too much." He smirked and gave himself another snap with the rubber band.

Charity punched him on the arm. "Quit it," she said with a smirk. "I asked you to talk to me. And you shouldn't feel ashamed of what you feel."

Joel frowned, not wanting this to get all serious. He wanted to focus on going home to Kristen. Maybe he'd go home first and ask his parents for a loan. Then he could buy Kristen the ring she wanted, and they could get started on all of their dreams.

But when he thought of those dreams, he could only see how he'd put them on hold to serve his country. He could only see the hurt in Kristen's eyes when he'd explained how many more years it would take before they could get married and start a family. And then there was the numb horror in her eyes when Joel had been deployed. She hadn't cried. She hadn't screamed or thrown anything or stormed out. She'd just been frozen, her emotions locking her into place.

Joel frowned again, and Charity gave him another whack on the arm. "Are you beating yourself up mentally, soldier? It's not good for you. Keep talking to me....remember, I'm a very nervous flier and you're the type that can't keep from helping a woman in need."

He cut his eyes over to her and she was grinning faintly. He could see the shred of fear in her eyes still, but it was clear that he was the one in need between the two of them. He sat back heavily in his seat, feeling his eyes finally begin to burn from tiredness. It had been ages since he'd slept properly.

"We don't have to talk about Iraq," she continued. "We can talk about anything. Tell me about your home and your horses."

Joel smiled, and began to prattle on about his white mare named Shadow and his big black gelding named Faust. He tried his best to ignore the twist of disgust on Charity's face when he mentioned how he loved to take Shadow for a blazing gallop through his parents' acreage. No matter how he explained the thrill of all that big wind in his face and all that powerful animal underneath him, he couldn't get her to budge on the issue. "Not even a little trot?"

"Drop it, soldier," she replied tightly, and he help up his hands in surrender.

"Well, aside from going out of state for concerts, what do you like to do?" he asked, stretching and feeling the bliss of relaxation finally stealing over his body.

"I read," she said, and it was one of the least surprising things she'd uttered since they'd met. He'd seen a slew of books in her satchel when she'd dug it out earlier, but he would have pegged her for a prolific reader anyway. Especially after she'd opened her mouth and started handing out five-dollar words.

"And what are you reading right now?" he asked, trying to draw a bit more out of her. As much as he didn't really want to admit it, he enjoyed talking with her.

"*Slaughterhouse Five,*" she replied tightly. The plane had gone back to jostling just a bit, which was plenty for Charity's nerves.

Joel chuckled at her joke. "Seriously."

"Well, I've emptied the bookstore's selection of angsty teen novels, so I moved on to the classics. I'm reading *The Picture of Dorian Gray.*"

Joel raised his eyebrows. It was such a classic that he'd never heard of it, not that he would ever doubt her about such things.

She seemed irritated that he wasn't following, however. "Oscar Wilde?" Her face was lit up and she didn't seem to register the next few hiccups in the planes' trajectory.

"Oh, I've heard of him," Joel said, wracking his brain. "Isn't he the gay one?"

Charity gave a sharp intake of breath, a wicked gleam appearing in her strangely colored eyes. "Oh, is that all you know about him? Wonderful. Do we get to have a scintillating debate about gays in the military now? Please say yes!"

The businessman on the aisle, who had shot them confused looks now and again, shifted uncomfortably in his seat and stared determinedly at his laptop. Joel rolled his eyes hugely. "No, we are not. I'm certainly sorry I brought it up."

Charity pretended to be incredibly disappointed. "It would have been a good debate, I bet."

Joel answered with a laugh. He didn't doubt that in the slight- est. Intent on corralling this conversation, he turned to face the seatback ahead of him, nestling into the seat. "When you're not reading, what else do you do?"

"Um," she replied, picking at a fingernail. "I don't know. I write, I guess."

"Poems about death and pain?" he jabbed, chuckling.

"Good Lord, Joel, you might be the most stereotypical person I've ever met!"

He closed his eyes, feeling the lovely sensation of calm even as he laughed with his neighbor. "I'm just giving you a hard time. But you have to understand that your...*look* affects the way people see you. It's no different than my uniform."

"People see your uniform as a sign of heroism and bravery. They see my clothes as a sign that I'm some delinquent that's depressed all the time and thinks about suicide."

"So, why do you dress like that?" he asked, still keeping his eyes closed. The questions were coming slower as something like sleep threatened on the horizon.

"I'm expressing myself. I'm being an individual." It was her standard reply, and he could tell that she knew it wasn't ringing true just now.

"By dressing like everyone else your age? Yeah, that's so brave and unique of you." He gave another chuckle, retreating into the darkness behind his eyelids.

When she replied, her voice was softer and more thoughtful. Though he didn't look, he imagined her brow was furrowed in concentration as she took the billions of words she'd read and the words she'd written, trying to arrange them into a pattern that fit this question perfectly. "I started dressing like this because I was rebelling against my parents. I kept dressing this way because people leave me alone. They give me a wide berth, and I like it that way. I don't really like talking to people."

"Could have fooled me," Joel said, his words slurring out on the edge of sleep. Peace was maybe thirty seconds away. As it was, Charity's reply was lost in the fog, her words turning into marshmallow clouds.

But something was wrong. Those clouds were familiar, and be- fore Joel could blink himself awake, he was stuck back in the place he hated most lately: his nightmare. It was that same day, of course it was. The clouds were so puffy and innocuous, no one would have expected anything to go wrong.

He was in the second of three Humvees in their convoy, running the same strip of sand that they ran three times a week. Joel was to the point where he could recognize the shrubs and other scrubby bushes that lined the roadway. He was bored. And so was Pete. Joel hadn't known Pete until their tour here. Pete was the top bunk and Joel was the bottom. When Pete started to snore in the night, Joel would kick under his mattress. When Joel would moan and whine about Kristen too much, Pete would punch him or hide his picture of her. They were friends. They wouldn't have been close had they grown up together perhaps, but none of that mattered in the sandbox.

Joel shifted in the dream. He knew all of this had already happened, and no matter what he did now, it couldn't be changed. But he would try. He always tried. He turned to Pete. Pete's eyes were the same color as the sky that supported those marshmallow clouds.

"Pete, don't get out of the truck." Joel had a hand on Pete's arm. "No matter what, okay buddy? Stay here!"

"You worry too much, Joel," was Pete's reply. That was always his reply. Joel swore, and then reached for his bracelet, but there was nothing there. He hadn't started wearing it yet. No point. He swore again.

That's when the gunfire began. The first rounds took out the truck behind them. The heat from the fireball was intense. Joel had forgotten that things could be hotter than the Iraqi sun. The second set of rounds missed destroying any vehicles, but the driver of the first Humvee was clearly dead when the smoke cleared. The truck began to drive off the sandy road as the other soldiers in it tried to regain control of the situation.

"Don't do it Pete," Joel whispered as Pete turned his sky-bright eyes on him.

"I'm gonna jog up there and make sure everything's alright," Pete announced, leaping out without another word.

"Of course you are," Joel replied tiredly. This is the part where he began pinching his skin, punching the dashboard, anything to wake up, to get out of here. It never worked, but he would never, ever stop trying. Even something as simple as keeping his eyes closed was forbidden here. He would have to watch every second in high-resolution.

Pete wasn't ten feet in front of the truck when the shot hit him. Some vicious high-caliber round that was designed to shred him from the inside once it penetrated the skin. The force of the impact shot him back to where he collided with Joel's truck, taking half of his body through the windshield. Joel prayed for the thousandth time just for the ability to close his eyes. But instead, he saw his friend, drenched in red, his chest smoking from the heat of the bullet. He saw the sky-colored eyes blink rapidly and then stop. And he saw the last liquid breath of the guy who shared a bunk with him at their camp.

Something sharp was stinging his left wrist, and suddenly he was soaring upward through the puffy clouds and landing with a jerk in seat 19F of an airplane bound for Dallas. Charity was leaning over him anxiously, her fingers pulling back on his rubber band bracelet, poising for another snap.

"What?" Joel asked with a groggy voice.

"You were swearing in your sleep," she chastised. "Rather fluently, actually. Dude next to me was getting nervous. And making people nervous on a plane isn't a smart play, soldier."

"I'll keep that in mind," he snapped acidly. He could see that his tone hurt her feelings, but was too raw to care.

"Fine, fine. Go on back to your little post-traumatic stress dream you were having there," she said tightly. "But you should know we'll be landing soon." She turned away from him with a huff, but not before snapping him once more with the rubber band.

Joel stretched. He'd slept longer than he'd thought, longer than he should have, which was not at all. Charity had a valid point about exposing his crazy sleep-taking nightmares to strangers on an airplane. And if they were landing soon, he didn't want bad blood between then. Though they had only just met, Joel found her opinion of him very important for some reason.

"Listen, Charity, sorry I snapped at you there. You were right about the bad dream." He gave a shrug. "I wanted to thank you. You made this plane trip a thousand times more interesting than it could have been." He gave his most winning smile and she returned it with a sarcastic grin.

"Alright, alright. You helped me out, too. Without you here to talk to, I would be chatting *this* guy's ear off. And I can't image he'd be as nice as you about it." She jabbed her thumb in the direction of the businessman on the aisle, who couldn't hide behind his laptop any longer. He gave a wince that he was even being discussed by such a scary girl, and seemed a bit too fascinated by the back of the seat in front of him.

Joel gave a rousing laugh as the plane touched down and Charity seemed surprised. "Normally I throw up right before the landing," she mused, and Joel made a face at her, but still kept a healthy distance in case her nausea was delayed.

They filed out into the terminal and reached the hallway where Joel would head toward baggage claim and Charity would go find her connecting flight to Kansas City. They paused, searching for appropriate parting words. As the seconds passed, Joel noticed that people were making strange faces at the two of them together. He smiled at the fact that he had the pleasure of knowing the girl under the scary clothes and makeup. At least a little bit.

"Enjoy your concert," he said, and she nodded, looking just as hesitant to part ways.

"Enjoy your girl. You should marry her. Well, you should ask her, at least." She smiled at him.

"I think I will," she said with a grin. They were moving apart now, waving as they stepped backwards into the flow of traffic.

"I hope you find some new angsty teen books to read," he called. "I hope you don't fall off your horse!" She had to yell to be heard.

He laughed, and when he turned, her dark head had vanished into the sea of commuters. Turning back, he broke into a run, more anxious than ever to fall into the arms of the girl he loved. And because of his uniform, the crowds parted easily to let him pass.

STAPLE HERE
INSERT TEXT HERE
BOARDING PASS
PASSENGER RECEIPT 1 OF 1
Miller, Jean
DFW – STL
Chapter Five
Global Air
SEAT NUMBER
19F
Date and Time
JUNE 09, 2017 04:00 PM
Destination: STL

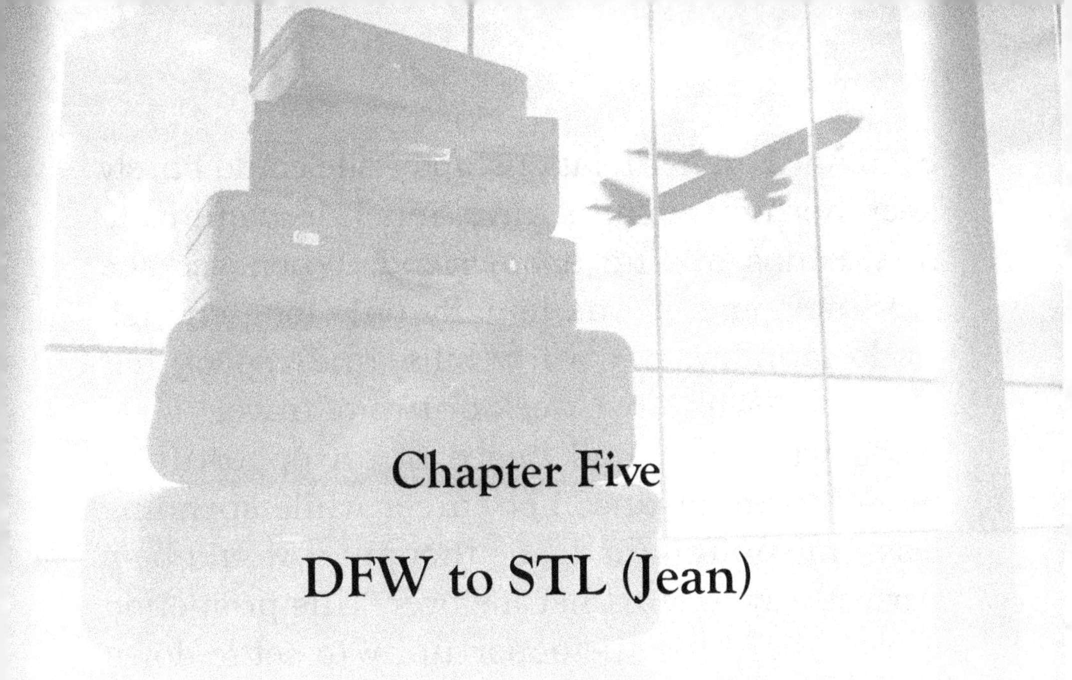

Chapter Five

DFW to STL (Jean)

What a lousy way to spend her 50th birthday. Instead of celebrating a successful job interview in Dallas, Jean found herself jammed into the window seat on a crowded and delayed flight back to St. Louis, sweltering in the 105 degree Texas heat. Her black pinstriped interview suit clung to her sweaty body in a most uncomfortable manner, and her feet were swollen and tired.

Jean had been feeling that her life was at a crossroads for quite a while now. Seventeen years as a travelling pharmaceutical sales rep had left her tired and discouraged. She was often on the road 15-20 days per month, and spent more time in airports and hotel rooms than in her own small apartment. This hectic travel schedule had been hard on her relationships – she could barely keep her houseplants alive, much less cultivate friendships or find a boyfriend. Whenever she WAS at home, it was usually only long enough to do laundry, pay a few bills, and repack her suitcase for another week or two of travel.

So when she had heard of an opportunity in Dallas to advance her career while spending less time on the road, she thought it would be a perfect way to start her life over. This promotion would afford her the opportunity to settle down into a routine where she would make friends and even join a church. Over the past few weeks she had sailed through two rounds of phone interviews and was excited to be one of final three candidates invited to the headquarters in Dallas for product testing and a tour of the corporate office. Who could have guessed it would turn out so badly? From the moment she walked in the door early that morning, she knew taking this job would be a huge mistake. The people were rude and the corporate culture was hostile and intimidating. The interview did not go all that well, and Jean felt that about half way through she must have said the wrong thing, because she could feel the air go out of the room. They took her to a testing area and told her she had as much time as she needed to take the online test. The test was very complex, and everyone knew it was going to take several hours to complete. But every half-hour or so, the secretary would interrupt her and ask if she had completed the test because they wanted to call a taxi to take her back to the airport. When lunch time came around, they acted annoyed to have to go to Subway to get her a sandwich. She finally quit the test early, knowing that she did not finish and would get penalized. But she was certain that she did not want the job anyway – in fact, she could not get out the door fast enough. The taxi took her to the airport and she rushed to the check-in counter to see if she could fly standby on an earlier flight. Her frequent flyer status helped her get one of the last available seats on this flight, and even though she preferred to fly in business class, she rushed down the jet bridge and sank exhaustedly near the window, in seat 19F. She hated sitting next to the window, often feeling trapped into a small space by strangers who may or may not let her up to stretch her legs or go to the restroom. Ironically, this was much the same way she felt trapped by her life and a lifetime of questionable decisions.

"I am sorry Miss Miller," the ticket agent had told her, "but the best seat available is 19F."

"Nothing else?" Jean asked dejectedly. "I have tons of airline miles I will gladly give you if you can find anything else."

"No, nothing in Business Class or even on the aisle. Just a few window seats and a dozen or so in the middle."

"OK, I guess it's 19F for me. No offense, but I just really want out of Dallas ASAP."

The plane continued to fill and Jean watched in dismay as family after family joined her in the crowded airliner. Everyone seemed to be going on vacation, and were taking huge carry-on bags with them. As a seasoned road warrior, Jean carried virtually nothing with her onto the plane. Do these people not understand that space is limited in the overhead bins? Somewhere behind her a baby started to wail, and Jean's mood sank even further. This was going to be a long flight for sure.

Finally everyone was on board, including an elderly couple who sat down in the aisle and middle seats next to her. They struggled with their seatbelts and the wife wanted to hold her giant purse in her lap in- stead of putting it under the seat in front of her. The husband, who was seated next to the aisle, was having trouble getting settled and it was obvious that neither had flown in quite some time. They studied the safety information card and looked for the nearest exit. All Jean wanted to do was to get home and cool off – why was this plane so hot? She adjusted the air vent above her, but nothing but warm air was pumping out. Soon the flight attendant made the announcement that Jean had been dreading....there was an electrical problem with the air conditioning, but the mechanics were working on it and they hoped to be in the air within 30 minutes. The plane had been heating up while sitting on the tarmac in the hot Dallas sun, and was getting warmer by the minute. Jean struggled out of her suit jacket as sweat started to trickle slowly down her back. She saw her flushed reflection in the window, and was saddened at how tired she looked. Her once flaming red hear was starting to gray, especially around her face. The same thing had happened to her mother, but her dad had loved it, calling it her "halo." Jean felt her halo drooping a bit today, and there were dark circles under her pale blue eyes, along with frown lines on her brow. Beads of perspiration glistened on her forehead and cheeks, and a ring was pooling at the base of her neck.

Jean grabbed the safety information card from the seat pocket in front of her – after all the flights she had been on, she had it memorized, but knew it was sturdy and would make a good fan. While waving it back and forth with her left hand, she picked up the in-flight magazine with her right. Realizing she had thoroughly read it during her flight to Dallas yesterday afternoon, she started to put it back. Her eye noticed something sticking out of the magazine - it was a boarding pass for someone named Lisa Davis who had been in this seat on a flight from Des Moines to Chicago earlier this morning. Also folded neatly in the bottom of the seat pocket was a *Des Moines Register* from this morning, open to the sports section.

The small child seated behind Jean was getting restless and started kicking the back of her seat. Jean began to think about Lisa Davis – "Who was she and why had she been in this seat? Where was she going so early this morning? Is her life any more fulfilling than mine? Did she spend her 50th birthday jammed into a crowded plane full of strangers, or did she celebrate with friends and family?" Jean's mood continued to deteriorate as the child behind her climbed up the back of her seat and pulled her hair. She shot a stern glare back toward the child's mother, but the mom was busy reading a book and did not notice. Soon the child started to cry in earnest and Jean closed her eyes in exhaustion. She listened to the couple next to her fretting about the delay.

"George, what are we going to do if we miss the connection in St. Louis?" the wife asked, almost in tears. "You know how important this trip is!"

Finally the air conditioning was fixed, and the plane pushed back from the gate. Jean checked her watch and found that they were leaving nearly 45 minutes late – almost the exact time she would be boarding her originally scheduled flight where she would have been flying Business Class in an aisle seat and with working air conditioning. So much for her brilliant idea of flying standby and getting home earlier. The flight attendants made their usual safety speech, and Jean found herself quoting it along with them in her head. The elderly man and wife next to her nervously followed every word, and were concerned about turning their seat cushions into flotation devices. They were obviously fearful of flying and wondered how to work the oxygen masks. In all of Jean's travels, she had never needed a flotation device or an oxygen mask. But there was always a first time for everything, she guessed. Just not today, please God, not today.

Jean stared out of the window and reflected back over the past several years. Her small Illinois family became even smaller when both of her parents passed away last summer – first Mom from cancer and then Dad just a few months later from heart failure (and probably a broken heart as well). They had been married one week short of 59 years when Mom succumbed to her breast cancer. Jean glanced down at her wrist to the pink bracelet she wore in her Mom's honor, and said a short prayer. One of the few commitments Jean was able to make the past few years was participating in the *Komen Walk for the Cure.* But losing both of her parents back-to-back like that had left Jean feeling pretty lost and lonely.

She was not very close to her two older brothers Mike and Tom, or to her much younger sister Liz. They were all married and had kids and grandkids of their own. Never having married or even seriously dated, she usually felt out of place at family gatherings. Perhaps that is why she chose a life on the road – it was less painful to be lonely in a hotel room in a strange town than at home where she could see everyone else so happy. This past Christmas had been particularly difficult, since it was the first one since their parents' deaths. They had all gathered at Liz's home on Christmas day, and the grandkids spent the day playing with new toys and video games. But it was painfully obvious that there were two empty chairs at the dinner table, and Jean found that she did not have much of an appetite.

After taxiing around DFW for another fifteen minutes or so, the plane took its place in line, waiting to take off. The captain announced that they were 10th in line and Jean watched as the planes ahead of her took off to places unknown. She could not help but wonder where they were going, and if their air conditioning worked betters than hers did. Finally they were in the air, and plane began to cool a bit. Jean rested her head against the window and tried to ignore the screaming children behind her, while wondering what to do with her life when she got home. After about half an hour in the air, the child behind her had finally cried himself to sleep, and Jean was trying to drift off to sleep as well. Suddenly, there was a commotion beside her as the woman next to her decided she needed to get something out of her bag that was in the overhead bin. Jean used this chance to climb out into the aisle and head to the back of the plane to stretch her legs. Even thought she was barely five feet tall, Jean found the confines of a window seat quite confining indeed. Plus, she had read somewhere about the dangers of blood clots in the legs if you sit too long. She spent the next few minutes pacing the aisle, trying to ease her troubled spirit as well as her cramped muscles. She got a cup of ice water from one of the flight attendants, and studied her 100+ fellow passengers who were in various stages of flight fatigue. She knew that feeling all too well.

She overheard the flight attendants discussing the usually long day their aircraft was having. Usually, a plane of this size would make five or six flights in a 24-hour day. However, the

NTSB had found a defect in the landing gear of several planes, and a huge portion of the fleet had been grounded. This plane was one that had been called to pick up the slack, increasing the number of flights to eight today. Jean hoped the old bird was up to the task, and that they could land safely. She really was not in the mood for any more excitement.

After a few minutes, she returned to her seat and looked for something interesting to read. The airplane took an unexpected lurch as it hit a bit of turbulence, and the older woman next to her let out a gasp. Jean instinctively turned to her and said, “It’ll be OK, just a bit of bumpiness here and there. No cause for alarm.”

“You travel a lot?” the woman asked nervously.

“Yes, almost every week. Have been doing it for years. This is nothing to get worried about, trust me.”

“You really fly EVERY week? For business? This is the first time we have flown since 9/11 – things sure have changed!”

“Yes, 9/11 changed everything for all of us. I’m a pharmaceutical sales rep, and travel to different hospitals and physician clinics all across the country. I’ve been doing it for so long I hardly remember doing anything else.”

“Wow, that sounds so exciting. My husband George and I are retired now, and usually the only travel we do is with our RV. But we are on our way to our grandson Peter's college graduation in Michigan. We have five children and 12 grandchildren – have not missed a graduation yet!"

"Well, that's pretty amazing, too. Sounds like you guys keep busy. I don't have any kids, but lots of nieces and nephews. I don't make it to many graduations, though."

"Oh, but I'm sure you go to so many exciting places and see so many wonderful things."

"Actually, most of what I see are airport terminals and hotel rooms. I spend most of my time working or writing reports until late at night. I really don't get much time to go sightseeing."

"Oh, that's too bad. You should take some time off for yourself and actually see this wonderful country of ours!"

Jean returned to her task of finding something to read. Unfolding the *Register* from the seat pocket, she quickly dismissed the sports news and headed instead to the human interest stories. Not finding these rural Iowans very interesting, she tried the employment section instead. "Maybe I should give Iowa a try?" she thought. "St. Louis is sure not working out for me." She turned the page and was amused to find a story about starting a new career as a *mature* adult (over 50). Well, she qualified for that as of today, so she read suggestions from employment specialists and HR executives. They stressed the need to work with a passion, doing what you love. One section in particular seemed written just for her:

> *"Another thing that older workers struggle with these days is the fact that they are working longer and postposing retirement until age 70 or later. Gone are the days of working at one job until age 62 or 65 and then sitting on the porch in a rocking chair, living off a corporate pension. Most baby-boomers have changed not only employers but whole careers numerous times by age 55, and are feeling burned out and burned up. They worry about the economy and the fear that they have not saved enough for retirement. Many are concerned about dragging through their final work years in jobs that offer little satisfaction or fulfillment. The trick is to find something that will not only pay the bills but offer these experienced workers a chance to make a contribution and feel valued by the organization. And if they can also be doing a job they love, all the better!"*

She tore the article from the newspaper and returned the rest of the paper to the seat pocket. She read the article again and again, trying to re-evaluate her goals and ambitions. She knew she was tired of the constant air travel, but what should she do with her life? She still had almost 20 years to work before she could retire, and needed to make as much money as possible to fund her golden years. As a single female with no children, she was facing those golden years alone, and right now they were not looking so shiny.

She closed her weary eyes and tried to envision what the "perfect" life for her would look like. Sadly, she just kept coming up with mostly questions and few answers. The article said that she should do what she loved, but what is that? What would it feel like to have a job she actually enjoyed going to each day? Having something that she felt passionate about, instead of something that just paid the bills? Having a job with a regular schedule so that she could actually *plan* time with family and friends? Actually having friends?

She folded the article to put it into her purse, but noticed a picture on the reverse side. It was an advertisement for a local TV talk show telling of a middle-aged Iowa woman who self-published a book that had become the newest literary sensation. It had been on top of the *New York Times* best seller list for several weeks and had gotten rave reviews. The author was to be on the local talk show next week to tell of her journey from school secretary to successful author. She had written the book in her spare time at home, and did not have an agent or publishing firm backing her. She had found a way to self-publish the book, and printed only a few copies at a time. She gave a few away as gifts, but urged everyone she knew to order the books online – she even had an electronic version and was considering an audio book! She used social media to promote the book, and eventually word got around. The rest was history!

Jean thought about how much she used to enjoy writing, and how her friends and teachers always said she had potential for a great novel. She had tinkered around with it a bit as a college student, working on the school newspaper and entering poetry contests. With all of her recent travels, she certainly had enough material to write something interesting. Pulling a scrap of paper and a pen from her purse, she started to jot down a few ideas. She had been to 47 of the 50 states, and even to Europe twice. She had flown on hundreds of flights over the years and met thousands of people. What kind of story could she write? Romance? Mystery? Thriller? And where should it be set? California? New Hampshire? Italy? The ideas started tumbling around in her head and out onto the paper. She was so focused on writing that she no longer heard the crying babies or felt the heat and claustrophobia of the crowded airplane. She glanced again at the boarding pass for Lisa Davis and again wondered about her life. She turned the small piece of paper over and over in her hands, almost willing it to tell Lisa's story. She quickly lost all track of time, and the next thing she knew they were taxiing to the gate in St. Louis. She tucked the boarding pass and her notes into a pocket of her small carry-on, thanked the pilot for a safe flight (as she always did), and headed to the gate area. There was quite a crowd of people waiting to board the plane (since the flight had arrived almost an hour late) and she almost tripped over a young boy sitting on the floor listening to his IPod.

Finally in the main terminal, she passed a newsstand and glanced at the books for sale. Perhaps she would see HER book there someday! With the first smile to grace her face in quite some time, Jean's pace quickened as she headed toward baggage claim and then into the summer afternoon heat.

Happy Birthday, Jean!

STAPLE HERE

INSERT TEXT HERE

BOARDING PASS

PASSENGER RECEIPT 1 OF 1

Evans, William

STL - MEM

Chapter Six

Global Air

SEAT NUMBER

19F

Date and Time

June 9, 2017 06:24 PM

Destination: MEM

Chapter Six

STL to MEM (Will)

Was there any possible way to make it more obvious to everyone in the airport that he was an unaccompanied minor? Will Evans stared in dismay at the large blue plastic pouch hanging around his neck. His mother had just left him in the care of a flight attendant to be escorted down the jet bridge for his short flight to see his dad in Memphis. He was only a few weeks short of his 10th birthday, but to this stupid airline, he was still too young to fly without an escort. Good grief! Because he had gone with his mom on several of her business trips, he'd been on more airplane flights than many of the people in this place, but rules were rules, and everyone continued to treat him like a baby. He even had to wait next to the gate and be MONITORED by some old lady who insisted on hovering over him. The incoming flight had been delayed – again– and in frustration, he flopped down next to the wall and pulled out his IPOD. He closed his eyes to listened to the angry rap music that seemed to be such a big part of his life these days.

Will was tall for his age, slender and long-legged. His mother complained that he could grow an inch in his sleep, making his jeans too short overnight. His pale eyes and slender face were framed by a mop of curly brown hair. He was wearing a Superman t-shirt and his long legs were stretched out in front of him. He kept a nervous hand on his backpack – not wanting to take the chance of losing it.

The flight attendant firmly shook his shoulder and said that the incoming flight was finally about to reach the gate. From the look on her face, he could tell she had been calling his name for a while. Obviously, the sound had gotten lost behind the thud of the bass in his ears.

The gate agent announced the arrival of the flight from Dallas and once everyone was finally off, the old lady escorted him down the jet bridge to the plane. They stopped at the door of the plane, and Will was formally handed off to the flight attendants on board. They checked his paperwork again, and a young girl in her early 20's escorted him down the aisle to his seat. He kicked his small backpack under the seat in front of him and fastened his seatbelt.

Officially in his place next to the window in seat 19F, Will watched as the baggage handlers loaded the suitcases into the cargo area of the plane. He was always fascinated by the inner workings of the airport, and how they could keep all of the bags on the right planes. He often thought he would love to work in aviation somehow. Relieved to see his Memphis Grizzlies duffle bag on the conveyer belt, he relaxed a bit. Nothing would be worse than a long weekend with his dad and not having his own stuff. This visit was going to be bad enough without losing his luggage as well. Plus, his dad had sent that bag to him for Christmas a few years back, and it meant a lot to him.

His mom and dad had been divorced almost five years now, after another five years of friction and discontent. Will could not remember a time when they had been a happy family. After the divorce, Will and his mom had left Memphis and moved to St. Louis to be closer to his maternal grandparents. He could count on one hand the number of times he had seen his dad since then. Out of sight, out of mind, as the saying goes. So when his mom told him that an email from his dad had arrived a week ago, Will was shocked, but secretly excited. Then he read the email, and could barely contain his anger and disappointment. His dad wanted him to come for a visit now that school was out for the summer, but not because he missed him and wanted to spend time with him. NO, he wanted Will to meet his new wife and three new step-children.

The other passengers started to board and plane, and Will silently said a prayer for the seat next to him to remain vacant. He really did not want anyone that near to him right now. Much to his dismay, an older Hispanic woman sat in the seat next to the aisle, and gave him a curious glance. Her hair was completely gray and in a way it reminded him of his own grandmother. "Is no one sitting here?" she asked as she pointed to the middle seat. "Are you alone?" She seemed genuinely concerned, but Will was not in the mood.

"No, no one is sitting there, and yes, I am alone," Will answered, trying hard to be polite but barely hiding his frustration. He pointed to the 'unaccompanied minor' badge around his neck and then turned back to the window.

"Oh, dear, I'm sorry you have to travel alone," the woman gushed. "I just hate to see young folks flying by themselves – so many things can go wrong! I certainly hope whoever is picking you up on the other end knows we have been delayed almost an hour already."

"Yes, ma'am," Will answered sweetly, while uttering a few choice words under his breath. "My dad knows we'll be late."

"Oh, I feel so bad for young kids growing up without their dads. Such a sad sign of the times, I guess."

Will really did not want to get into this conversation with a strange person. He was trying hard to keep these feelings buried, where they had less power over him. Turning away from the woman to hide the slight tear that was fighting to slip from his eye, he pretended to be interested in the other planes outside his window. That woman had no idea how hard it has been for him without his dad.

Will had enormous respect for his mother and how hard she worked to provide for them during the past five years. He was old enough now to understand the fatigue in her voice at the end of her 10-hour shifts at the local casino where she worked in the back office. She also traveled to other casinos in the Midwest for training. She was taking online classes at night, studying business management and hoping to climb the ladder at work. Will came home from school each afternoon to an empty apartment, but his grandparents lived just down the street so he often went there instead. Grandma always fed him a snack and helped him with his homework.

Sometimes when his mom came to pick him up, they would stay for dinner as well. Grandma seemed to know when they both needed a little extra attention. Just last night she had fixed his favorite dinner of spaghetti and garlic bread. She and Grandpa were happy about this trip to see his dad.

"Will, I am so glad you have this chance to spend a few days with your dad," his grandma had said over dessert of angel food cake and strawberries, another of his favorites. "I know it will be a little strange having other people in your old house, but I'm sure you will be fine. And flying by yourself – wow! When did you get so grown up, young man?"

"So, what do you guys have planned?" his grandpa had asked between bites of cake.

"I'm not totally sure. Gonna get some good ribs, that's for sure!" Will really missed the Memphis barbeque. St. Louis ribs were fine, but not as good as what he used to eat as a little kid. "And there is a new 3-D Disney film at the IMAX that the girls want to see. Other than that, the weekend is fairly free, I think."

"Well, whatever you end up doing, I know it will be fun. Now, how about a game of skip-bo before you leave?"

Will knew that they meant well, but he could not help but be apprehensive about meeting his dad's new family. Was it really possible to stop caring about one family and start over with a new one?

He was just beginning to understand the friction between his parents, although his mother tried hard to hide it. His dad rarely called, and had visited only a couple of times since the divorce. He had gotten behind with his child support payments once, and the tension had really escalated then. But now that he had been gone so long, Will and his mom had settled into a kind of strange routine where his dad was seldom mentioned.

But Will thought about him all the time. As much as he loved and respected his mother, he really missed having a dad around. When he was at the mall or church and saw boys his age sitting with their dads, he felt a pang of loss and jealousy. And he could not help but feel that dad's absence was somehow his fault. Had he done something wrong that would make his dad not care about him anymore? Maybe his dad would have paid more attention to him if he were smarter? More athletic? He knew that he looked a lot like his dad had when he was a young boy – a crooked smile and dimples that everyone thought were so cute. He had one family picture that had been taken the last Christmas they were all together before the divorce. He was fairly oblivious to the tensions then, but now he could easily see the stress on everyone's faces. He did remember the fights – the yelling and crying behind closed doors. Although they had tried to shield him, he knew something was wrong.

The captain came on the intercom to announce that the plane was ready to leave the gate. He apologized for the delay but said that he hoped they could "fly fast" and make up as much time as possible. Since the flight from St. Louis to Memphis was only scheduled to be about 40 minutes, and they had been delayed almost 60 minutes, just how fast was the pilot going to fly anyway? Will was not sure he wanted to know the answer, but he adjusted his seatbelt just to be safe.

The flight attendants gave their usual safety speech about oxygen masks and finding the nearest exit. Will wasn't crazy to be sitting so close to the rear of the airplane, but at least there was an exit back here if he needed it.

He pulled the wrinkled email from his dad out of his pocket and tried for the umpteenth time to read between the lines, to understand why his dad would contact him, now of all times.

> *Hey, Billy…I hope you are enjoying your summer. I have big news! I got married last month to a nice lady named Lily*

and she has three little girls: Emma, Colby and Sophie. They have moved into the house and are busy getting settled in, but I would love for you to come for a few days to meet them. I'll have a ticket waiting if you can come next weekend – miss 'ya buddy. Love, Dad

Will had talked to his mom about it, and she did not want to keep him from going, if that was what he wanted to do.

"Of course you can go," his mom had told him. "If you want to, that is. This is totally your decision. Swimming lessons don't start for about a month, and the church camp-out is in August. Actually, this would be a good time. But it's up to you."

He had called dad later that night only to find out that two of the girls had moved into his old bedroom and already painted it princess pink. There was no place for him to sleep except for on an inflatable mattress on the floor of the office, and for some reason that really bugged him. Not that he expected his dad to keep his old room like it was in the old days, like some sort of shrine or something, but pink? Three little girls? He replaced me with three little girls? And it had been so long since they had talked, his dad did not even know that he went by the name "Will" now...no one called him Billy anymore!

The flight attendant stopped by to check on him and make sure he was securely buckled in. She then presented him with his "junior flight wings." Will carefully folded the email around the wing-shaped pin and slipped them into his pocket. As much as the words from the email frustrated him, it was one of the few communications he had from his dad, and in some strange way he wanted to protect it. He wondered how it will make him feel to see his dad with the new family, treating another woman nicer than he ever saw him treat his mom. And did he know more about these little girls than he did his own flesh-and-blood son?

Shortly after the plane took off, Will felt an intense pain in his left ear. Ever since a severe infection when he was seven, he had trouble with pressure building in his ear during flights. He reached into his backpack to pull out his favorite double-bubble chewing gum, and saw a strange envelope in a side pocket. Curious, he opened it to find a letter from his mom.

> *Hi, Will. By now you're on the plane and headed to your weekend with your dad. I just wanted to write a short note to let you know that I'm so proud*

of you and the fantastic young man you are becoming. I know that growing up without your dad in the house has been really hard on you, and I've seen you struggle with frustrations and loneliness that I have not been able to fix. As your mom, I've tried to shelter you from pain but also give you the wings to learn and grow and develop the amazing potential we all know you have.

Your dad and I were very young when we first got together, and since he had grown up without a dad of his own, I am not sure he really understood what it meant to be a father. I'm not making excuses, just trying to explain. I know you were really little when you dad and I separated, but I am sure you know that things had been rough between us. But he did love you – DOES love you – and I don't ever want you to forget that.

You know that he and I don't talk very often, but when I heard about the marriage and the three little girls, I was surprised, yet hopeful that he had finally gotten his priorities in order and was ready to settle down and be a family man. And the fact that he contacted you right away is a good thing – I suspect that he sees now what he has been missing by not being near you, and this is his way of reaching out and making amends. Is he the perfect dad now? Probably not. And will this make all of the hurt of the past several years go away? Doubtful. But I think it's a step in the right direction and I hope you will accept his gesture and see if things can be better from here on.

I did love your dad very much, and there are so many of his better qualities that I see in you now. Not just your cute smile and those killer dimples (sorry!) but his tender side and passion for life. You got his outgoing nature and optimism for the world that I don't always possess, and while he and I were not meant to be together forever, I am so thankful that we were together long enough for you to join this world. You are truly a blessing to me and to your grand-parents. I hope that as you spend more time with your dad, you will find a way to have the type of relationship I had always wanted for you.

Enjoy your weekend. I will miss you, of course, but am so proud of you and love you more than you will ever know. Love, Mom.

Will stared at the letter and tried to understand what his mom was telling him. Maybe his dad's absence had more to do with him than with Will? He thought back to all the missed ball games, school programs, and church outings where he had secretly hoped he dad would appear unannounced and cheer him from the stands or sidelines. Many times he scanned the crowd, hoping to see him slip in the back door at the very last minute. But that never happened, and the hurt still burned deep. He as not sure that one letter from his mom, and one very short weekend with his dad and new family, was going to make any of that go away. But maybe mom was right –maybe dad was just too young back then, but had seen the error of his ways? Maybe he really should give him a second chance?

Will carefully folded the letter to put it back in the envelope, when he noticed something else still inside. He pulled it out and one of the tears that had been welling in his eyes for the past couple of days finally spilled out onto his cheek.

In his hand was a picture he had never seen before, one of those taken at that funny photo booth at the mall. He was just a tiny baby in the picture, only a few weeks old from the look of things, and his dad was holding up in front of the camera with a cheesy grin on his face as he peeked out over Will's shoulder. The resemblance between them really was striking – same nose, same chin, same dimples. But yet will could see how he looked a bit like his mom, too, with her curly hair and pale eyes. He truly was a combo kid, but what he could not get over was the look of love and pride on his dad's face. On the back, written in his dad's handwriting, were the words MY SON! The pride – the joy – all conveyed with that exclamation point. His dad did love him. Really loved him. The shell around Will's heart cracked a bit, just a tiny bit.

After an announcement that it was safe to use electronic devices, Will reached into his backpack for his IPod, more for the isolation than for the music. The Hispanic grandma on the aisle had just come back from a trip to the restroom and was trying in vain to start a conversation. He found a newspaper in the seat pocket and flipped to the entertainment section. Not finding much of value in the hick Des Moines paper, he shoved it back into the pocket. He closed his eyes and let the hypnotic 'thump-thump-thump' of the music lull him into that special place he of- ten retreated to when he we was sad or lonely or confused. The emotions that the letter and photo had stirred were too painful to fully process right now.

Soon the flight attendants were in the aisle, passing out pretzels and drinks. “Would you like some milk Will? Or some juice?”

Will pulled one earbud out of his ear and said in his most sarcastic voice, “I don’t like milk, and had juice at home. Thank you anyway.” He shoved the earbud back in, closed his eyes, and leaned against the window. Hardly two songs had completed when the flight attendant touched his shoulder and asked him to put his IPod away since they were about to land. Wow, the pilot was not kidding about flying fast! She then informed him that he was to wait until all the other passengers had gotten off the plane and then she would escort him to meet his father. If there had been anyone around him who did not know he was an unaccompanied minor before, they sure did now. Lovely. Why did everyone insist on treating him like a child? He had been forced to grow up a lot these past few years. The fact that he was only about five feet tall did not mean he was a kid on the inside.

Once the plane was on the ground and taxiing toward the gate, Will gathered his belongings and tried to prepare himself mentally for meeting his dad and the new family. What was he supposed to call this new woman – mom? No way! Lily? That sounded too informal and strange. Mrs. Evans? No, that just sounded weird.

Will waited impatiently while the rest of the passengers deplane, the smell of Memphis barbeque floating down the jet bridge and into the plane. Will's stomach growled at the familiar smell, and he could not wait to get a taste of heaven for himself. One of his favorite childhood memories was when his mom and dad had taken him out for ribs and burnt ends. Even as a small child, he had devoured a rack of ribs by himself, sauce dripping down his chin. The Hispanic grandma reached over and patted his hand, wishing him a fun visit with his dad. If she only knew. Once everyone was off, the flight attendant signaled that it was his turn to leave. She walked up the jet bridge with him, verifying again who was to pick him up. Once at the gate, he saw his dad right away, scanning the passengers and looking anxiously to see him emerge from the tunnel. Will was overcome with a mixture of joy and apprehension. His dad gave him a big hug and marveled at how much he had grown. After showing some ID and signing a couple of forms, they left the gate area and headed toward the baggage claim, where Lily and the girls were waiting. His dad talked non-stop, asking questions about school and summer camp, telling him about the changes at the old house and a surprise the girls had for him. He did not seem to notice that Will was silent or only answering in one or two word phrases. But when they got to the escalator that would take them down to the baggage claim, his dad stopped and looked into his eyes.

"You seem really quiet, Billy. Is everything ok? Or are you tired? Was the flight ok? I know you were delayed a bit, and it's been a long day I imagine."

"Well, dad, first off --- no one calls me Billy anymore. I go by Will now. I'm almost a man now, you know."

"Well, of course you are," his dad said with a smile. "The girls will call you Billy because that is what I call you when I talk to them about you. But we can fix that right away."

"You talk to them about me?"

"Of course! You are my number one son, and I will always be proud of you and your accomplishments. It's only natural for me to talk about you all the time. Oh, there they are!"

Will looked down the stairs to see a pretty lady with three cute little girls, all of them waving and the littlest one was jumping up and down. "I see Billy!" she squealed, and Will had a hard time concealing a smile. The middle girl and Lily were both holding bags of his favorite barbeque. “I guess this will be OK” he thought to himself, feeling less nervous than he had anticipated. “But did they have to paint my old room pink?”

STAPLE HERE

BOARDING PASS

BOARDING PASS

Rodriguez, Ana

MEM - DFW

Chapter Seven

Global Air

PASSENGER RECEIPT 1 OF 1

SEAT NUMBER

19F

Date and Time

JUNE 09, 2017 08:00 PM

Destination: DFW

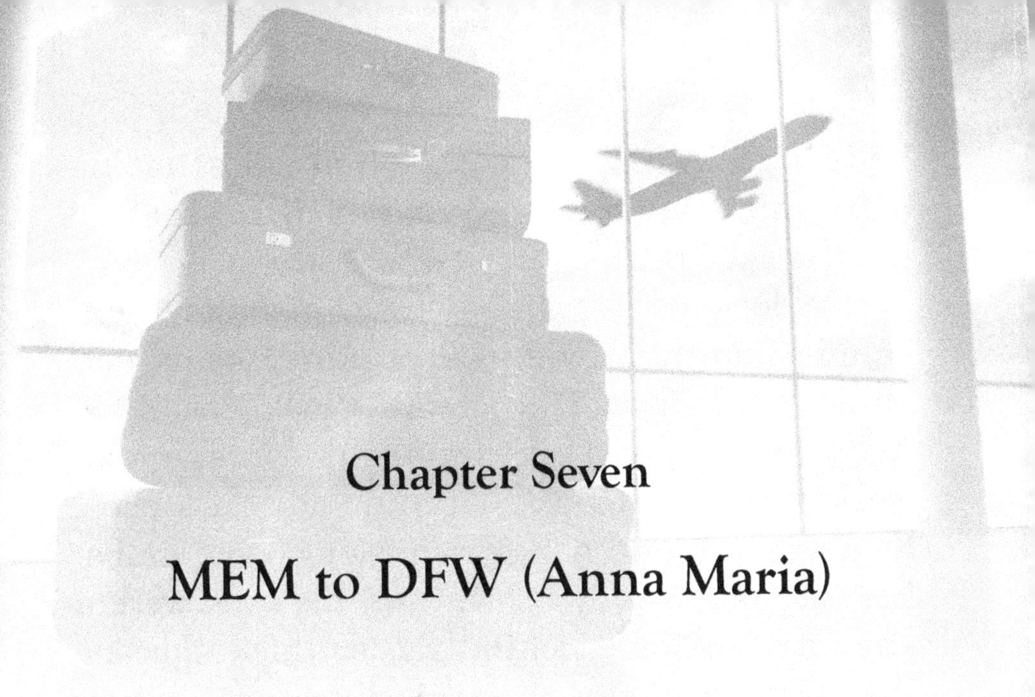

Chapter Seven

MEM to DFW (Anna Maria)

Ana Eppstein. Ana Maria Eppstein. Ana Maria Rodriguez-Eppstein. Oh, good grief. The pen would run out of ink before she got all of that written out!

She'd been married for almost twenty-four hours, and she was still struck by the novelty of her new surname. Along with the novelty came the uncertainty though. *What is my name now? Who am I now?*

When she ended her broadcast stories for Channel Five in Memphis, the words always came naturally: "This is Ana Maria Rodriguez with Eye-Witness News 5." How long would it take to make the change? Or should she take her producer's advice and continue to go by her maiden name? There was no law that said she had to go by Eppstein. Kyle had said that he didn't mind, but men are so much more sensitive than they appear.

She looked over at her new husband then, smiling faintly at the look of barely contained panic on his face. They couldn't look less alike. Ana was short and curvaceous, brown-skinned, with long, silky black hair and wide dark eyes. Kyle was tall and gangly with long, pale limbs. His hair was sandy brown and his eyes were a shy shade of blue behind rather thick glasses. But beyond their physical differences, their respective body language was like night and day. Ana was folded neatly into her window seat, radiating comfort and excitement to get into the air and on the way toward her honeymoon. Kyle had his long arms crossed over his narrow torso, trying to take up as little space as possible. He was anxious, wound tight enough to snap at any second.

Ana smiled wider, reaching over to cover his tense fingers with her own. It was cruel really that the honeymoon had to come so soon after the wedding. If you think about it, you don't really know a person until you travel with them. Is it really the best idea to test a marriage so soon? As a young-ish and attractive female anchor, Ana always got the top news stories, the ones that required her to travel frequently. Taking a plane was just as comforting and familiar as taking a cab or a bus. If it weren't for the leftover adrenaline from her wedding, and if it weren't for having Kyle next to her radiating anxiety, she would already be asleep, lulled into dreamland by the soothing hum of the jet engine.

This was Kyle's third plane ride ever. The two prior to this had taken place before the attacks on September 11th, so he was naturally a bit high strung, although he did seem to relax minutely at the feel of his new bride's hand on his own.

"Was I whimpering or anything embarrassing out loud?" he asked in a choked whisper.

Ana shook her head and gave him a fond grin. The plane had begun to taxi away from the airport and Kyle's eyes kept focusing beyond her to the window and then back.

"Would you like to see?" she asked kindly, flattening herself back into the cushions. "Or I can close it if you'd rather not."

Kyle's response was a jerky twitch of his chin from left to right. "No, if we're going down, I suppose I'd like to see it coming."

Ana did look at him sternly this time when she noticed the older woman on the other side of Kyle give him a panicked glance. "We're not going down. Everything is going to be great. We will be in Dallas in less than two hours, and Houston a couple hours after that and then we'll be on our way to the dock to get on a gorgeous cruise ship, and before the sun goes down, you and I will have the salty breeze in our faces and a cocktail in each hand."

Kyle smiled at last, showing that one of his incisors was endearingly crooked. "No," he said. "Almost all of that sounds great, except for one thing."

"What?" Ana asked, feeling the plane pick up speed. She wanted to watch the world fall away outside her window, but for the moment Kyle seemed to be relatively calm and she didn't want to disrupt that.

"I can't possibly have a cocktail in both hands, because I'll have at least one of my hands full with one of yours."

Ana giggled and felt a rush of heat in her cheeks. She wasn't normally a giggly girl, but so much had changed in her life so quickly. It hadn't even been a year since the first time she and Kyle had exchanged hesitant but flirty online banter, barely six months since their first phone call. Her friends and family thought she had lost her mind when she agreed to meet him, and many of them wrote her off completely when she announced their engagement just weeks later. But while Ana wasn't usually prone to giggles, she was prone to making decisions and sticking with them. The first time she'd seen Kyle in person, had seen his slight clumsiness and his undeniable charm, well, she hadn't been able to stop herself from falling in love right then and there.

"Oh, Mr. Eppstein, you do say the sweetest things," she murmured. "Only the truth, my dear Mrs. Eppstein," Kyle replied grandly, giving her a little bow. But then his face tensed as gravity tried to keep them on the ground while the plane rose up into the air. For a moment, Ana lost his attention as he stared out the window. Fortunately, when he did look back at her, he looked more relieved than frightened. "I think I like calling you Mrs. Eppstein," he announced.

Ana gave a half smile. "I was just thinking about that actually. I like it, for my driver's license and all of that. I'll probably keep my maiden name for work though."

As soon as the words were out of her mouth, she wanted them back. Kyle's expression dimmed and his posture slumped as though someone had pulled the plug on him. "Oh," was all he could say.

"I mean, I haven't decided for sure," Ana said, backpedaling quickly. "I'm mostly worried that I'll mess it up, since I'm so used to saying Rodriguez."

"That's understandable," Kyle said, but his tone was a bit flat.

"Nothing has to be decided now. Although I'm sure it would be easier for my audience if I kept it the same. And it would save the station from having to rebrand everything."

Kyle's expression was more than a little condescending then. "It's a small local station that I'm sure has enough turnover that rebranding wouldn't be an issue. And change is inevitable. I mean, it's not like we'll be in Memphis forever."

Ana gritted her teeth and focused on her wedding ring. It wasn't large but it was so new and shiny, it dazzled her, even though the thin veil of tears that had just welled up in her eyes. She and Kyle had hit it off so completely that she had never questioned being in love with him or wanting to marry him. But their brief romance hadn't been completely devoid of argument. Perhaps their biggest disagreement involved their future residence. Despite being well traveled, Ana loved Memphis and had no desire to leave. And even though Kyle didn't care for planes, he had seen most of America through a bus window, and found little use in being sentimental over places or things. He could pick up and leave at any time, carrying most of his belongings on his back if need be. Ana hoped that their marriage would show him the appeal of having roots and traditions, but it was hard not to see that he found her profession unimpressive.

Kyle was a writer, and a good one. It was his clever words that had ensnared her in the first place. But Ana wondered now if her career of "reading the news" would ever be good enough for him.

For a long while, Ana stared out the window, watching streaks of clouds rush by. She wasn't having doubts exactly. It only took a few moments of calm thinking to see that Kyle hadn't meant to hurt her feelings. They were different people with different ideas and goals. If they were too much alike, surely one of them would be redundant. So Ana made the conscious effort not to be offended as she scraped around for a change of subject.

It didn't take long at all to forget her moment of annoyance. Kyle's quick humor and almost childlike amusement at the in-flight snack options made Ana laugh out loud. She was really starting to see herself spending the rest of her life with him, but then something happened that had Kyle convinced they wouldn't even make it to Dallas in one piece.

After their empty drink cups had been collected by the flight attendant, Kyle's energy dropped a bit and Ana encouraged him to take a quick nap. They had been rushing around with wedding plans for days now, and it seemed like he was finally ready to crash. While he folded his arms across his stomach and closed his eyes, Ana dug in the seat-back pocket for something to occupy her mind. She found a newspaper that must have been left by a previous passenger, someone from Iowa. One quick glance at the front cover made her wonder what was going on at home. While she wouldn't exactly call herself a workaholic, she did love her job immensely, and the few occasions she'd actually taken vacation time, she had fretted about what news stories she was missing. While Des Moines was clearly not quite as action packed as Memphis, Ana found herself absorbed in the story of the upcoming state fair, when her stomach gave a sharp jolt.

She hadn't noticed at first how the sky outside her window had darkened, but it was obvious now. And the jolt in her stomach hadn't been homesickness or nervousness about her honeymoon. It had been the result of the plane dipping several feet and then stabilizing.

Ana held perfectly still, hoping that the bump hadn't woken Kyle, but the next thing she knew, he was jerking into consciousness beside her with a gasp. She might have been able to convince him he was only imagining things if that had been the only bump, but soon the fuselage shook with mild turbulence as they passed through a storm.

"Oh, Jesus," Kyle whispered, which always made Ana laugh, since he was Jewish. She smothered her smile when she saw the panic in his face and reached for his hand.

"It's totally fine, sweetheart," she assured him. "Just a little turbulence. Nothing to worry about."

He was shaking his head frantically, disagreeing with her but unable to make the words come out of his mouth. Ana could feel the plane changing its trajectory slightly, trying to slice through the clouds at a different, smoother angle. It worked a little, but not for long. With a *ping*, the fasten seatbelt sign came back on, and Kyle's eyes dilated in fear.

"Hey…hey look at me honey," Ana said soothingly. "Focus on my eyes and my voice."

"Oh, we're going down," he muttered tightly.

"Nope, not at all," Ana replied in her gentlest tone. "Planes want to stay in the air. It's just a little bumpy. She put her hands on Kyle's face, trying to hold him steady both literally and figuratively. As he forced himself to breathe and be calm, she let her thoughts wander a bit. She'd watched him shave his face this morning at the hotel, but could already feel the prickles of stubble under her fingertips. It was something she had never noticed or thought about him. "Have you ever grown a beard?

"What?! You're asking me that now?" Kyle said through clenched teeth.

"I was just curious," she replied, keeping her voice as calm and even as possible. "I can feel a five o'clock shadow already."

"Yeah, I'm a hairy guy," he said distractedly.

Ana frowned as she considered this. They'd been together such a short time, and he'd always been clean shaven and well groomed. She'd given no thought whatsoever to what he would look like with facial hair, or once his hairline began to recede, or if he put on weight in middle age. She'd given no thought to any of it.

Suddenly, Kyle wasn't the only one panicking. "Hey, are you okay?" he asked when Ana had turned abruptly toward the window.

"Fine," she choked out. "It's fine." But inside she was far from fine. She was thinking back to that first day they'd met face to face. He was almost five years her junior, but she hadn't cared because he was steady and serious and mature. He was Jewish, but she hadn't cared because being Catholic didn't really mean much to her besides the occasional Christmas Mass or fancy wedding. He was a bit of a nomad and a loner, but she hadn't cared because he was so content just to be with her and to make a home wherever she was.

Despite all of their differences, they had been a perfect fit for one another, but Ana hadn't thought any of it through. It was as if she expected that glow of togetherness to carry them off into the sunset, but what did that even mean? As the plane jostled and dipped, she knew that reality had always been coming for them, ready to remind them that there would be trials in their marriage as they learned to balance and to compromise with one another. She had fallen in love with Kyle so quickly, had fallen in love with the idea of a wedding and a honeymoon, that she hadn't given nearly enough thought to what it meant to be a wife or a partner. It was surely going to be a lot more than comforting him during turbulence on a plane or agreeing to use his last name at the end of her broadcasts.

"Ana Banana," he said gently, touching her knee and coaxing her to face him again. He still looked nervous, but apparently, the nonchalant attitude of the dozing woman beside him was helping, and he was able to see past his anxiety.

"I'm sorry, babe," Ana whispered. "I just had a little moment there."

"Talk to me."

"It's weird… I just felt your beard coming in and I realized I'd never seen you with a beard. And then I realized I've barely seen you at all. Just a handful of times really. I mean, I fully believe that I know everything I need to know. I love you and I'm always going to love you. But just because I know what I *need* to know doesn't mean I know everything... Does that make sense?"

"Totally," Kyle replied, his eyes warm and kind now. "There's plenty more I'd like to know. Like last night, when you braided your hair after your shower... What was that all about?"

Ana chuckled and pulled a long strand of her hair over her shoulder. "My hair is bone straight normally. When I braid it while it's wet, it helps make waves like this."

Kyle gave a little hum of understanding. "Well, now I know that. And just so you know, my dad has always had a beard, so I think I avoided it because I associated it with being old."

They both laughed then. "I think you should try it at least once," Ana suggested. "Maybe don't shave on our trip and we'll see if we like it."

"I'm telling you, I'm a hairy guy. It will only take a day or two." "I can't wait."

"Thank you," Kyle said quietly after a moment. "For what?" Ana wondered.

"Oh, for so many things. Thank you for loving me and marrying me. But, most currently, thank you for distracting me from the turbulence. I appreciate it."

Ana gave a quick glance out the window and saw that the sky had cleared again and the sailing was smooth. "It was nothing," she said sweetly.

"No, it wasn't nothing at all," Kyle insisted, and he squeezed her hand. She wasn't used to wearing a ring yet, and it pinched a bit, but she kind of liked it. "I know we are very different people," he went on. "I know we come from different backgrounds and have different expectations for what life and happiness really means. I know we're going to fight and disagree. And maybe it sounds crazy, but I'm really looking forward to that."

She grinned. "I don't think that sounds crazy at all."

"So what should we fight about next?" he asked, his smile wide and challenging.

Ana opened her mouth to reply, but just then the captain's voice filled the cabin, advising them that they would be landing in Dallas in just a few moments. "We can fight on the next flight," she promised, tucking the newspaper from Des Moines back into the seat pocket. "For now, let's act like we like each other."

Kyle laughed loudly and gave Ana's hand another squeeze. When she leaned against his shoulder, he rested his head on top of hers, and when the plane hit the runway with a bounce, he barely flinched.

STAPLE HERE

INSERT TEXT HERE

BOARDING PASS

PASSENGER RECEIPT 1 OF 1

West, Kristen

DFW - MSY

Chapter Eight

Global Air

SEAT NUMBER

19F

Date and Time

JUNE 09, 2017 10:30 PM

Destination: MSY

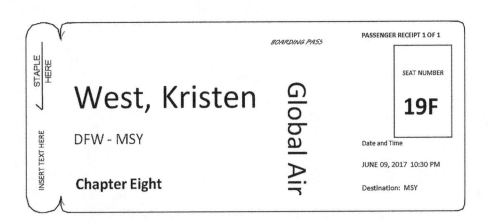

Chapter Eight

DFW to MSY (Kristen)

She was crying before the plane had started taxiing. Spontaneity wasn't her thing; she always planned things thoroughly. Not that she hadn't planned taking this flight. She just hadn't planned on doing it alone.

For years she'd imagined soaring through the skies from Dallas to New Orleans, but the destination was to be a honeymoon vacation, not a hiding place. She didn't like to run from things. But the last twenty-four hours had changed her, threatened to shake her apart completely, leaving her to put the pieces back in any way they would fit.

The large stocky man in his forties next to her was eyeing her nervously. Like most men of his generation, something genetic was buried within him, triggering a nervous response to a woman crying. And she wasn't some average woman. She was young and beautiful,with wide liquid eyes that just radiated with vulnerability. She was the type of girl that didn't have to try for anything at all; it was just handed to her. And yet she didn't seem to know the power of her own pretty face. Her beauty was the rare and humble type, and the man beside her in seat 19E was practically forced to respond to her.

"The name's Bob Gardner," he said, thrusting a meaty hand toward her. "I always like to introduce myself when I fly alone. That way, if we go down, I wasn't surrounded by strangers."

She turned her eyes to him slowly, blinking back a new set of prickling tears. She wondered if that line was meant to calm her. It was a crummy attempt, and she couldn't help but notice that he wasn't trying to introduce himself to the rather frumpy woman in the aisle seat. But she forced a small smile and reached out to take his hand.

"I'm Kristen," she replied, deliberately leaving off her last name. Bob didn't appear to be the stalker-type that would look her up later, but you never can tell these days. She turned and faced the seatback in front of her, blinking rapidly to keep from disintegrating again.

"So, what's got you headed for the Big Easy?" Bob went on, trying to angle in the seat to face her more directly. Kristen tried not to shrink into the wall. “Business or pleasure?” His face was so genuine that she had to answer.

“Neither,” she admitted. “I’m....I’m running away.” And the tears built up again.

Bob’s face paled slightly and he reached to put his hand on her arm, then pulled it back quickly when he noticed her tense up. “Running away from what, darlin’?”

Kristen leaned her head back against the seat and stared up at the display for the light and air controls. A stream of icy air dried out her tear ducts for a moment. “Joel,” she whispered.

Bob’s genetic makeup kicked into overdrive again, and his mind seemed to be grinding away in search of a response. “Boyfriend? Did he... hurt you?” Kristen watched his eyes moved over the bits of skin that weren’t covered in clothing: wrists, neck, face. The bruise on her heart wouldn’t be visible.

“No,” she said quickly, not wanting to lie. “Joel’s a great guy. The best guy. He’s a real hero. He’s served in Iraq.”

“A soldier? Wow.”

“Yes,” Kristen agreed with a sigh. Whenever she told someone about Joel’s enlistment in the Army, she always got that sort of reaction– awe and pride. It made her feel even guiltier, like she was un-American to hate everything about his devotion to the military. And she didn't really hate it. She was proud of him, of course. But she'd had plans. From the tender age of fifteen, when Joel had first kissed her, she'd known that he was the one. All through high school she'd watched him, searching for a flaw, for a reason to look elsewhere, but they were soulmates through and through.

After graduation, he was supposed to go to UT on a sports scholarship—hopefully baseball. Watching him play football made her queasy. She would work around the clock to save up money. And after he got his Bachelor's degree, they'd get married and honeymoon in New Orleans like they'd always talked about. He'd go on to vet school, and she'd set up house and start having babies, and it would be a small town fairy tale. A dream come true.

But he didn't make the UT baseball team. And his football scholarship didn't pay much. His folks were dead broke after one semester, on the verge of having to sell some of their acreage to keep him enrolled. He did the "right thing." Kristen began to tear up again at the memory.

She could recall it perfectly. It doesn't snow very often in Boonesville, Texas, but it was snowing that day. Huge, puffy flakes of the stuff were floating down onto him where he paused on the porch, sticking in his hair, clinging to his eyelashes. He was breathtaking, but his eyes were strange. They glittered with purpose and with resolution, and for one heart-stopping moment, she thought he was going to propose.

But no. He told her that he'd joined the Army. He was leaving in a week for basic training. And all the plans they'd made were forced to shift.

At first, it really wasn't so bad. She kept working, which was part of the original plan. And she didn't see him much, but she hadn't while he was away at college, either. So they missed each other, but it could have been a lot worse.

But then it actually got worse. In August, they deployed him to somewhere in Iraq. She only vaguely remembered that announcement. Her whole body had gone numb with fear and with grief, as though she already expected him to come home in a body bag. She hadn't cried then, not until after he was gone. His mother had screamed in agony; his father had clenched his jaw and patted his son bravely on the shoulder. But Kristen had been silent, her mind sluggishly trying to rewrite her future, praying that it could still have a happy ending.

She blinked when Bob put his hand on her arm again. The refreshment cart was parked in the aisle. Kristen didn't even remember the plane taking off.

"Are you thirsty, honey?" the Flight Attendant asked, her eyebrows so high on her forehead they threatened to disappear into her hairline. She'd clearly been standing in the aisle for a while, waiting.

Kristen flushed and ordered a ginger ale to soothe her nervous stomach. She barely tasted it, except to notice that it was cold and wet.

"I didn't mean to pry before, doll," Bob Gardner was saying in his drawling voice. Kristen blinked again. She was having a lot of trouble staying in the present. "It's just that a man hates to see a girl upset. He hates seeing a pretty girl cry, especially over some dumb boy."

"He's not a dumb boy," she retorted, drawing her body slightly in upon itself. "He's a wonderful young man. I'm going to marry him someday."

Bob's eyebrows mimicked the Flight Attendant's from earlier, and Kristen almost smiled at this. He wouldn't understand it, right? How could he?

"Are you married, Bob?" she asked.

"I'm on my third wife, actually. I really like getting married." He guffawed and Kristen really did smile then.

"So you understand what it feels like when love makes everything else seem small and inconsequential. That's how Joel makes me feel... *made* me feel."

"What changed, doll?" he asked her, leaning in like he truly cared.

Her skin crawled a bit at his proximity and the fact that he treated her like a doll, but after all, he was the only one listening. Julie had listened enough and had finally broken her. It was really her fault that all of this had come about.

"Julie," Kristen muttered.

"Julie?" Bob said, confused. "She's not...um, the other woman, is she?"

Kristen couldn't help but laugh at that. It had been far too long since she'd even chuckled; nothing seemed funny to her anymore. But the idea of Joel and Julie, who was thirty-seven and married with six children, being anything other than passing acquaintances made her almost giddy with laughter.

"No, no. She's a coworker of mine," Kristen sputtered. "She's not exactly happy in her marital situation, and she got a little tired of me whining about my perfect boyfriend off defending his country from all enemies, foreign and domestic." There was a sardonic note in her tone as she recited part of Joel's pledge to the Army. Another twinge of guilt flooded over her, and it took Bob's expectant face to remind her that she was in the middle of a story.

"She asked me what I liked most about Joel," she said, and the conversation came rushing back over her like it was yesterday, because it had just been yesterday. Amazing how lifetimes can be lived in just one day.

◇ ◇ ◇

Kristen had gone all dreamy in the face when Julie had asked the question. She thought about what to say. He was beautiful, but that was obvious, not to mention shallow. He was kind and generous, but that wasn't specific to her. He was an amazing kisser, but she felt embarrassed to tell Julie this. No, there was really only one answer to this question.

"When I'm with him, I feel complete. We were made for each other."

But instead of Julie going all soft and giggly with her, she turned stern and cold. "I was afraid you'd say that," the older woman replied.

"What's so wrong with that?" Kristen had argued. "Is it a crime to be a romantic?"

"No," Julie mused. "And it's not a crime to be young and dumb, either, although it ought to be."

That stung. Kristen had considered Julie a good friend, despite the fact that they had almost nothing in common except work at the diner. She didn't try to hide the sadness and anger on her face.

"It happens, once out of a million times, I suppose, that two people love each other equally, and there is a happily ever after down the road," Julie preached as she filled salt and pepper shakers with a practiced hand. "And for all I know, you and Joel are that one couple. But more often than not, there is an imbalance. When you realize that it's worth working through that imbalance, you have a relationship that survives. When you can't, well, you become one of the majority that get divorced. Heck, tons of couples aren't even getting married anymore. They're just shacking up to save the drama when it ends. Not that you could get away with that in this small town and still expect to show your faces in church on Sunday." She laughed, and Kristen felt herself blush and then glow with irritation. What did this woman know about her and Joel? How could she just assume that they were not perfect for each other? What had happened to her that she was so cynical and jaded?

"Look, I love him, okay? And we are that one in a million. We're perfect together and we're going to get married and have babies, and everything's going to be great."

Julie stopped her work for a second and leveled a hard glance at her young coworker. "Can I ask you something personal?"

"You're going to anyway," Kristen retorted, stacking packets of jelly into the metal holder. She always made a point to separate the jellies from the jams, not that any of her customers would know the difference or care.

"What is something that you want to do with your life, something that doesn't involve Joel?"

Kristen made a face, but the honesty in Julie's expression made her actually consider the question. Every avenue of her plans had Joel at the heart of them, and that was the point, right? It apparently took her too long to answer, because Julie was looking smug.

"My point exactly. You've wrapped your whole future around that kid, and I'm certainly not going to say he's not worth it, because he's a doll. I love him, you know I do. But here's the deal, honey. Marriage is tough, and even if it works out, it not always perfect. It's rarely perfect, actually. You get a few top notch vacations or anniversaries, a few great memories, and then it's all about the kids and what they're doing and where they're going to school. And then it will be about *their* kids. You never get to be just you. This is your chance to be you, and I worry that you're wasting it."

"I know this may sound backward to you, but I don't want anything for myself except to be Joel's wife and to have his kids and keep his house. I've known that since I was fifteen. That's who I am."

"I'm not trying to be mean, Kris, you know that." Julie insisted. "I just want you to really think. Is there nothing that you wanted to do, something that was just for you? Did you ever want to take a class, or learn an instrument, or take a trip by yourself, just because you wanted to go? Maybe I'm just cynical because my mom was a single parent, and she taught me not to rely on a man, to be able to stand on my own two feet. It's why I work here, even though I don't have to and Lord knows I don't have time for it, what with the kids and all their sports. But I hate when young girls go on and on about how a man completes them."

"But he does complete me," Kristen argued. "We match up perfectly. We were meant to be together."

"I don't doubt that you're supposed to be together, honey. I've seen the way you look at each other. I know if anyone's got a chance to be that one in a million, it's you two. But you have to be complete on your own! You have to know who you are, to be able to do what you want to do, just because it makes you happy. Now, I'll ask you again, is there nothing you ever wanted for yourself?"

Kristen said the first thing that popped into her head, the only thing she'd ever really wanted. She wanted to go to New Orleans. Born and raised a small town girl, she'd never had the urge to go anywhere. Content to read about other places in books, no other city or state or country had ever called to her. Except for New Orleans. She couldn't explain it to anyone, because she didn't really understand it herself, but she'd seen a documentary on television when she was about thirteen, all about Mardi Gras. She didn't truly understand the whole drunken revelry or the beads in exchange for nudity, but the colors were so overwhelming.

Boonesville is vast and brown for the better part of the year, and vast and greenish-brown during the late spring and early summer. The French Quarter on the documentary had shone like a Christmas tree in April, bursting with color like ripe fruit. Something tangible had awoken inside of her upon seeing that, and ever since, she'd been obsessed with the city. She'd even convinced Joel that they would honeymoon there. She'd found the best hotels and restaurants for them to hit while they were there. He'd imprinted on her dream, bit it had been hers alone once.

As Kristen gushed to Julie about her desires, she began to finally see what Julie had told her. Life before Joel was a hazy inconsequential memory to her. Except for this one thing. This trip, this place was the one thing she had that was her own.

The seed was planted. She had excitedly packed her bright pink camouflage suitcase, and she was ready to go to Atlanta to meet Joel. He was due back stateside anytime now. After months of lonely separation, he was coming back to her. And all of the sudden, she felt trapped by his return.

◇ ◇ ◇

She looked with her big, panicked eyes at Bob, who had listened to her story with rapt attention. "So you see, after all those months of wishing for the clock to move faster, suddenly I was out of time. I know that I could still go to New Orleans with him after we were married, but who knows when that will be? We've had to keep pushing the date because of his tours being extended. And who wants to be married to a man who's never home, who's off getting shot at every five minutes?"

Bob looked on mutely, trying to emote with only his face because he didn't seem to be able to trust his words. Kristen realized that her questions were mostly rhetorical anyway, and plunged ahead.

"So, I had this crazy idea to just go to New Orleans. Now. By myself. Have that thing that's mine. And maybe I come back and maybe I don't.

I was almost decided; I almost had decided to come. And then he called me."

Bob watched as her face glowed and her whole frame seemed to relax. "His voice...oh his voice on the phone, and not some crappy international connection that's bouncing off nine different spy satellites. I could hear him breathing, smiling. He was mine and he was home. I forgot all about New Orleans. I went to the airport so that I could go to Atlanta and get him. Bring him home with me for however long he can stay."

"But something happened," Bob guessed, seeing as how she was most definitely not on a plane to Atlanta right now.

Kristen's face contorted and the tears pooled again. Bob tensed and apologized with this eyes for setting her off again. "It was a Marine and his wife at the security station. He had two daughters with him. They were all crying and hugging, but the little girls were so brave about it. You could tell they'd done this before. Daddy was headed off to the front lines. Again. Even after he'd settled down and gotten married, he'd stayed in the service. He kept putting himself in harm's way. And I get that it's noble," she said quickly before Bob could retort, though he probably wouldn't have. "I get that it's unbelievably brave, and that someone has to go, but I don't want it to be Joel. And worse than that, I don't want to be that woman left behind here, with children, wondering every day if she's going to get a phone call from him or if it will be from some faceless person telling her that her husband is dead. Even if he keeps coming home safe, I didn't sign on to be a soldier's wife. No one asked me if I wanted that. He just did it. To help us get the future we wanted, yes. But I would have changed my dreams, maybe. If it would have kept him safe *with me,* I would have changed my dreams."

She put a shaking hand to her face and pushed away a couple of tears that managed to fall past her eyelashes. She sniffed once.

"But I watched that woman walk away from the gate, looking like she had been beaten, she was so torn up. And her little girls, for all of their bravery, they were crying. And I just knew I had to get out. Out of this stupid boring state. Out of this fake future that's never going to happen because Joel will never be home to enjoy it. I marched up to the gate and changed my ticket. And now I'm here. With you. Crying all over you, I'm so sorry."

"That's alright, doll," he said quietly, not quite truthfully perhaps. "You'll like New Orleans. It's just as colorful and loud and exciting as you think. You missed Mardi Gras, of course, but there's always a party going on somewhere."

"Thank you, Bob," she said with a sniff. "Thank you for listening."

She turned away from him and began to rifle through the seat pocket in front of her. Amazed, she felt the tiniest hint of a smile working its way up within her. Even though her cheeks were still damp with tears, she felt lighter, as though just speaking her fears and her frustrations had lifted weights from her shoulders. She still didn't know the answers. She still wasn't remotely sure that taking this random trip was the right thing to do, but for this next half hour or so, she didn't feel the need to dwell on it. There wasn't a whole lot she could do about it at 30,000 feet, anyway.

The Sky Mall catalog amused her for a few minutes, but the gadgets all began to blur together for her, none of them holding her attention. Kristen managed to waste another few minutes pawing through a tattered newspaper that turned out to be from Des Moines, Iowa. She didn't really read the thing; she only pondered how something that had been printed on a press overnight in Iowa had travelled so far in just one day. Feeling poetic, she imagined the parallel between the newspaper's journey and her own over the past day – some sort of random, crisscrossing trek from one extreme to another. Instead of putting the paper back, she tucked it into her purse, not entirely sure why she was doing it.

The only thing left to occupy the last few minutes of the flight was to strike up more conversation with Bob. Or else work the crossword puzzle in the in-flight magazine. She stole a glance at her neighbor and found him buried in a John Grisham novel, so she opted for the crossword instead. To her dismay, most of it had been worked by previous passengers, many of them judging by the varied handwriting and pen colors. It was just as well – she was almost sure she did not have a pen of her own handy.

On the verge of closing the magazine and attempting to grab a nap, something caught her eye. She couldn't quite explain how she noticed it, but one small character stood out. The letter Z, crossed through the middle like some people do. Like Joel does. The ache she'd felt earlier welled up like a slap in the face, and she had to lean back and slam her eyes shut just to keep from whimpering at the pain.

But the hits just kept coming. Breathing in deeply, she realized that she could smell him. Someone wearing Joel's cologne was close by, or had been here recently. The sharp scent triggered so many memories. Kristen opened herself up to the dizziness and kept breathing it in, kept feeling him. And she was right back to the way she felt when she'd heard his voice yesterday.

That same fuzzy sensation that made her smile at just the thought of him.

Panic followed swiftly after. She was going the wrong direction. Joel would be waiting for her in Atlanta, and she was only moments from New Orleans. Just thinking about the sparkling city added another layer to her confusion. She could feel the streets of the Lower Nine beckoning her with their ghost stories. Could Joel's hold on her be stronger than that of her one childhood dream?

"Bob!" she said suddenly, and the big man jerked in surprise.

He used a thick finger as a bookmark and turned to her expectantly. "Sorry to scare you. I'm just trying to work out a little internal drama. Will you answer a question for me?"

"Of course, doll," Bob replied, his voice having transformed from intrusive to comforting over the length of the flight.

"Do you think I did the right thing? Do you think me going to New Orleans is the right thing to do?

He winced briefly, wanting to answer anything but that, but then he laughed good-naturedly. "Well, my dear, you have to understand that I'm a serial monogamist. When I fall in love, I fall hard and I commit. Until she leaves me for one reason or another." He chuckled, showing just a touch of sadness in his eyes. "So, I'm always in favor of love winning out. It's a gamble, sure. But it's so worth it. So I think you play around in the city for a few days and remember that time before all of your decisions took your soldier into account. Have time with you and the city lights. And then you go on home to that boy and tell him to make an honest woman out of you. Tell him what you told me, that you'd move heaven and earth to be with him, but that he's got to *be there.* If that's what you want, if *he's* what you want, then you need to tell him. That way, even if he does deploy again, he'll know for sure that you're the one. He'll put aside anything that keeps you two apart. I know that's what I'd do, if a pretty girl said those things to me." He smiled sheepishly at her and she turned away, letting the tears fall helplessly.

"Thank you, Bob," she whispered.

"Don't mention it," he replied gruffly. Just then, the plane began its descent.

Kristen let the next several minutes spinning out in a sort of recap of the last day. She heard Julie's words, and Bob's. She recalled the Marine parting ways with his family. She basked in the memory of Joel's voice on the phone. Everything felt obvious, like the right decision was directly in front of her. At the same time, no plan seemed to be better than the other.

Bob patted her lightly on the shoulder when they'd emerged into the terminal. He trotted off toward the baggage claim area, leaving Kristen standing in a sea of commuters. They parted around her as though she was a rock in a swift stream, no one really bothering to wonder why she looked so sad, so confused.

She was in New Orleans, but it just looked like another airport, nearly identical to the one she'd left just hours before. Joel was in Georgia, probably too anxious to fall asleep, assuming they'd be together soon. The desire to go and find him made her take a step forward. But the call of her old dreams wouldn't let her go any further than that. She couldn't say how long she just stood there.

"Can I help you find something, dear?" a guy in a uniform asked her, startling Kristen from her thoughts. She turned to look at him, taking in none of his appearance except that he wore a polyester vest and a nametag that reflected the fluorescent lighting in an authoritative way. "The baggage claim is up that way," he gestured, his thick Cajun accent twisting the words charmingly. "Or I can point you to your connecting gate."

"No, no, I've got it. I know where I want to go. Thank you."

And she began walking, smiling, as she became more confident of her decision with every step.

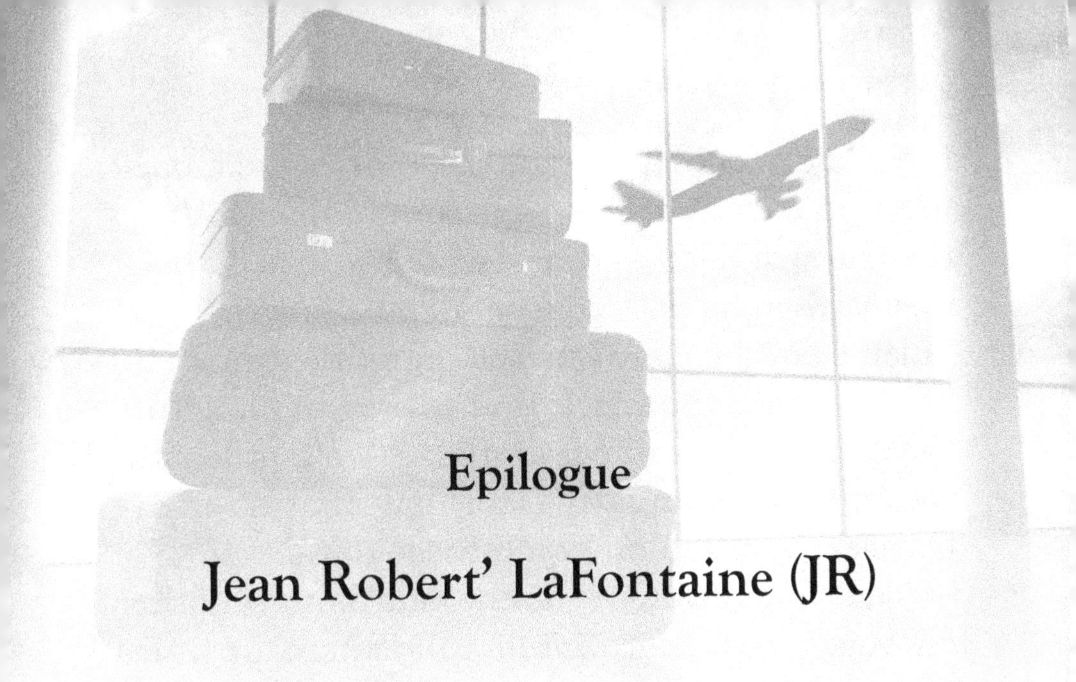

Epilogue

Jean Robert' LaFontaine (JR)

Jean Robert' leaned back in his chair in the baggage handlers' lounge, his long legs propped on the lunch table. There was just one more flight to unload tonight before his shift ended, and then he could head home to his wife and five kids. He was scheduled to have the next four days off, and was anxious for some rest and relaxation. Most everyone was already gone from the 3-11 shift, but he and his buddy Manny had volunteered to stay and offload the late flight from Dallas. When the radio squawked to let them know the plane was within range, JR grabbed his knee pads and headgear and stepped out onto the tarmac.

Manny climbed up into the belly of the plane to put the bags onto a conveyor belt that led down to JR's truck. JR waited on the ground to stack the luggage onto a cart and then drive them back into the terminal. The bags were unloaded from the plane quickly and he was ready to head back inside when he noticed a small pink bag that had fallen from the conveyor belt onto the tarmac. He hopped from the truck and tossed the bag into the back. Hot pink camouflage? Well, at least it was not the standard black bag that so many travelers insisted on using these days.

The bags were quickly put onto another conveyor belt that would take them upstairs to the waiting passengers. After clocking out and saying goodnight to Manny, JR chatted with the staff coming on shift and reviewed his schedule for the following week. Still bragging about having the next four days off, he walked across the parking lot towards his car. Noticing something white on the ground, he stopped to pick up a newspaper that someone had dropped, and tossed it into the nearest trashcan. His eye caught the masthead – *Des Moines Register.* "That's pretty unusual, finding a paper so far from home. Bet it's had quite a day," and he walked off into the intoxicating New Orleans night.

FUTURE FLIGHTS

Second Installment of
The Boarding Pass Trilogy

BETTY GOSSELL

KAREN PICKENS

Other Books by Betty Gossell and Karen Pickens

- *The Boarding Pass* - 2017

Excitement for a Sequel to "The Boarding Pass"

"I loved the first book but kept wanting to know 'the rest of the story' so I'm thrilled that a sequel is in progress!!" Mary B.

"Anxious to see where the journeys end. Suspense of the return. Didn't put the first book down till I finished it." Susan H.

"I loved the first book but now I desire to be 'a fly on the plane' to see where the story goes!" Julia P.

"I'm SO EXCITED to hear about a sequel! I couldn't put *The Boarding Pass* down – I can't wait to read more!" Sarah B.

"The first book peaked my imagination on what these people in 19F did when they reached their destination. Ready and anxious to find out the rest of the story!!" Mary Sue R.

"I can't wait for the sequel! It's like hearing your favorite new show is coming back for another season!" Karen H.

"So anxious! My library needs it!" Wanda G.

"I loved this book. I'm excited for the sequel!" Patty E.

"I thoroughly enjoyed the first book and can't wait to read more about each passenger. I haven't been reading much over the years due to some vision problems, but I sure enjoyed *The Boarding Pass.*" Lorri M.

Dedication

I certainly never dreamed we would be here again, finishing our second book together. Writing may be a solidary endeavor, but it's much more pleasant when done with the blessing of those most important to you.

To my family and friends, whose excitement and support for the original *Boarding Pass* exceeded all expectations, and whose encouragement helped so much with this sequel. Thanks for always being there for me, pushing me and loving me;

To my co-workers (past and present) with whom I share a love of travel and infinite travel stories - your support and encouragement mean the world to me;

And to my amazing daughter Karen, who continues to inspire me daily with your talent and enthusiasm. I have enjoyed sharing so many journeys with you – both in the air and through life, and now through our words. Thanks for always being the light of my life. I love you more!

Betty Gossell

This time around, I have to thank my friends and family who supported the first book and begged us for more. I was all for leaving the endings open for personal interpretation, but our characters did have more to say, so I'm thankful that you wanted to listen;

To my husband Chris, who is grounded while I'm up in the air - you somehow manage to be steady and surprising all at once, and I love you for that. Thanks for holding things together while I'm lost in my writing. Your support means the world to me;

To my precious Lilah Joy - I borrowed a little bit of our story for this book, so I hope you don't mind. Never forget how special you are to me, and how happy I am that God chose you to be mine;

And of course, to my loving mother - you've taken this little idea of ours and really given it life. While I was dreaming and procrastinating, you were making those vague ideas real, and I couldn't be more grateful. I love you more!

Karen Pickens

Foreword

The funny thing about stories is that they don't always end the way we would like, or on the timetable of our choosing. Some situations wrap up rather quickly, while others take years to come to fruition. And what may look like an ending to some, is actually a beginning to others. Answers to our problems often come in bits and pieces, and it is up to each of us to recognize which is a resolution, which is just a stepping stone, and which is a detour. We may have it all figured out in our heads, knowing the answer we are looking for, but life has a way of springing surprising events on us, forcing us to choose a path different from what we had originally planned.

Looking back, however, we are often able to see where the path took an unexpected turn, where one seemingly insignificant choice affected the outcome more than we ever could have imagined. Real living is a series of thousands of small decisions, each one adding a new line onto the story of our life.

- Betty Gossell

Contents

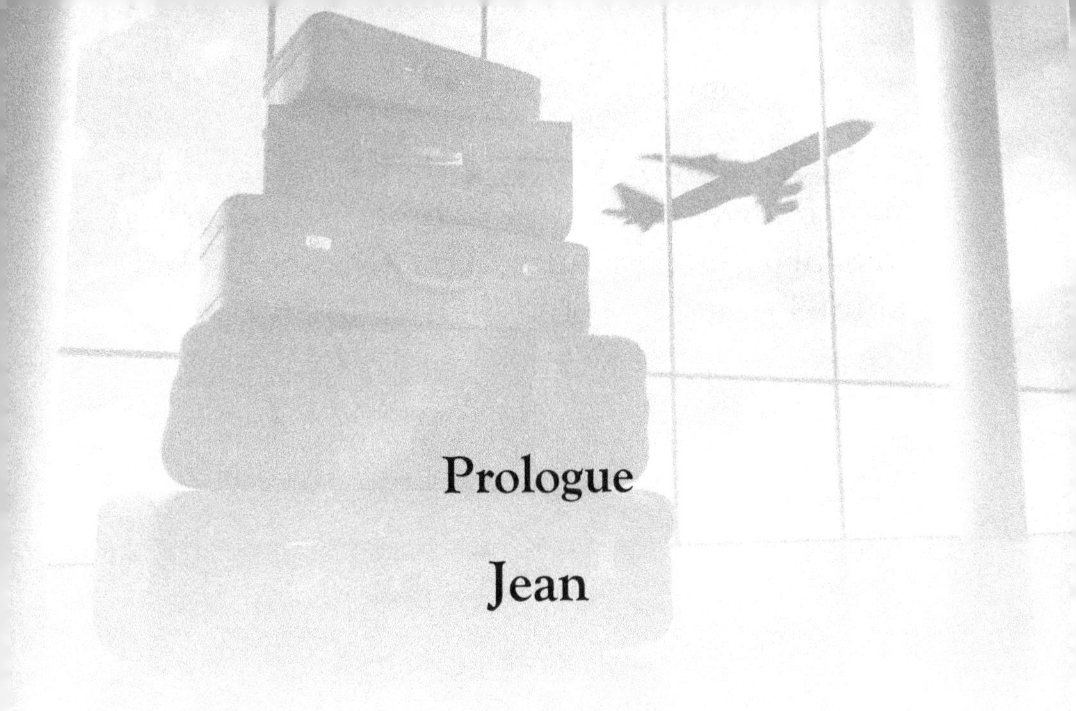

Prologue

Jean

Sitting in her First Class seat and enjoying a warm cup of coffee, Jean gazed out the window at the tarmac of DFW airport. She watched in dismay as sleet and freezing rain pelted the side of her plane, and she thought back to another flight long ago when she was feeling hot and miserable; so unhappy with her life and her life choices. It was hard to believe that flight was less than two years ago - so much had changed in her life since then.

She was now living in a new city, working at a job she loved, and going to school on the weekends. Her hand touched the sapphire necklace resting at the base of her throat and she giggled like a young girl. Glancing at the romance novel in her lap, a broad smile spread across her freshly-painted lips. Who could have imagined that she would be here today?

STAPLE

INSERT TEXT HERE

BOARDING PASS

PASSENGER RECEIPT 1 OF 1

Sullivan, Kristen

ADD to FRA

Chapter One

Global Air

Sullivan, Kristen

SEAT NUMBER

12B

Date and Time

APRIL 16, 2026

10:30 AM

Destination: FRA

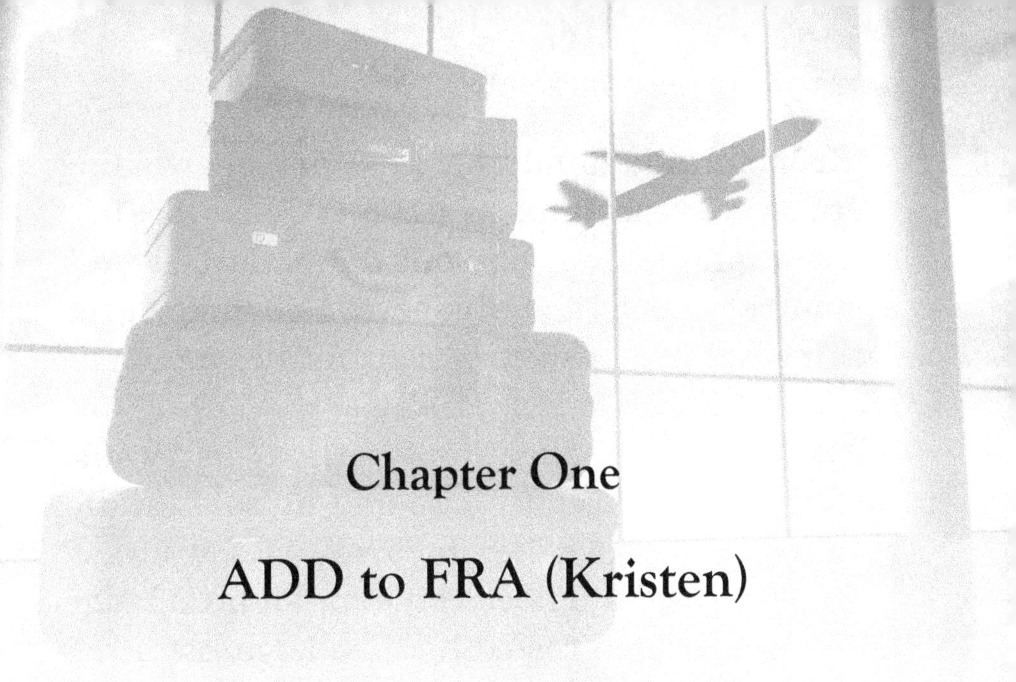

Chapter One

ADD to FRA (Kristen)

Kristen Sullivan reached up and twisted at the air vent above her. Just as it had been the last three times she'd checked it, it was maxed out. The flow was strong and cool against her fingertips, but by the time it reached her face, it just wasn't sufficient to soothe her clammy skin. A wave of nausea rolled over her, and she fought to keep her breath steady.

Beside her, in the aisle seat, Kristen's husband Joel reached up to aim his own air vent in her direction. She grinned at him gratefully, trying not to let on that it wasn't much help, but as always, he could read her easily.

"Still queasy?" Joel asked in his sweet baritone voice.

Kristen ran a hand over her stomach, wishing there was some kind of pain to press against rather than just the nebulous discomfort. "I can't seem to shake it," she whispered, slurping at the melting ice in her cup, which tasted vaguely of ginger ale.

"I would have thought that the last flight would be the one you'd be nervous on," he said kindly, running a hand over her forearm. "I know I was!"

They shared a tender smile and a little laugh then, and Kristen rested her head against Joel's shoulder. He had a very valid point. The last flight they'd been on had featured them both in a state of extreme anxiety that had little to do with the storms that had chased them from their layover in Frankfurt, Germany to their destination in Ethiopia. Even Joel, no stranger to international travel, had been stressed on that trip. He'd told her that none of his deployments in the Middle East had prepared him for flying to a distant African country to meet his future son.

Kristen closed her eyes and marveled as she often did about the beautiful twists and turns her life had taken. Once upon a time, she had been afraid to marry the boy that everyone assumed that she would marry. She'd actually tried to run away to New Orleans before coming to her senses. There had been a time when she had been worried that her life would be too predictable.

Well, Joel was a near perfect husband and life partner, but that was about the only part she could have predicted.

All of her visions of the future had included a house full of children, but the only pitter-patter of little feet came from their two dogs. Joel had never been quite as keen on having lots of kids. He was an only child and was happy to pass his name on to one or maybe two little ones. As the years had passed, Kristen began to accept that one or two might just be all they got.

Just before their fifth anniversary, a pregnancy test finally came back positive, and the entire town of Boonesville, Texas, was delighted at the news. The entire town also stepped up to mourn with Joel and Kristen a few months later when that happy dream was shattered by miscarriage.

That had been an impossible time. Every day of her pregnancy had brought new aches and pains and weird symptoms. The sudden abdominal cramps had seemed like just another thing she would have to endure. But it hadn't taken long to learn that something was very wrong. It was over so quickly. She hadn't had time to think of names or wonder about gender or daydream about nursery decorations of baby shower themes. She had just begun to get comfortable with the idea of being a mom-to-be, and then that title was taken from her.

Although they were both devastated, Kristen had researched that miscarriage was shockingly common, and not usually a sign that all dreams of children had to be abandoned. It took Joel a little while to get back on board, but soon they were trying again, and after an endless eighteen months, Kristen found herself holding another positive test. She told Joel right away, but they agreed to keep it to themselves for a while this time. Not even their parents were told, although they suspected the truth when only about seven weeks into the pregnancy, Kristen miscarried again. She didn't leave the house or even her bedroom for days, and Joel could not console her.

If the first time had been impossible, there were no words for this time. She tried to hold fast to her faith and to the science that assured her she could still try again, but she lost her grip over and over again. The future was hazy and bleak and she wanted nothing to do with it. She felt like a failure. People called it the miracle of life, but so many other women performed that miracle so casually, even unintentionally. It was unfair that she couldn't be like them.

Accepting that there must be something physically wrong with her, Kristen saw a doctor and went over all the options. Drugs. Surgery. IVF. Surrogacy. For weeks, the couple clung together, praying fiercely for the wisdom to find the right path amid all the pamphlets and websites they researched. Joel made decent money as an equine veterinarian and Kristen was now a part-time bookkeeper for a local farm equipment manufacturer, but even with their combined salaries and insurance benefits, they didn't have enough to cover expensive medical procedures, especially since the outcomes seemed so uncertain. The chances of success were not inspiring, and though Joel did agree to try whatever it took, Kristen just couldn't find peace in her spirit about any of it.

The answer came to her in a dream some weeks later. She imagined that there was a bundle in her arms, a baby, squirming gently but hidden from her sight by the way the blanket was wrapped. She'd had this dream so many times that she almost cringed away from it. It brought her too much pain. But her curiosity got the best of her and she had to pull the blanket away.

In her arms was a tiny baby, eyes closed against the bright world, miniature fingers grasping at the air. Kristen's heart squeezed as she looked at the child, realizing that even in her dreams, she'd never seen anything so beautiful. This baby's skin was as dark as night, and there was no feature upon its face that suggested she or Joel had any influence on its genetic makeup. But the sense of possession that Kristen felt, the rightness--it made her realize there was an option to grow her family that she had not yet considered.

The next day, with a nervous but convicted heart, she broached the subject of adoption with Joel. He was logical at first, noting that the expense involved would stand a better chance of seeing a return when it came to adoption. He recited all of the correct lines about how there were surely so many children in need of good homes and families already. Kristen could see that he was warming to the idea, but she knew she would have to put the question to him plainly and not make assumptions. She'd asked him outright if he could truly love a child that was not his own, if he could honestly be nurturing and affectionate to a baby that he had not created.

To his credit, he hadn't just blurted something out to appease her. He'd been thoughtful for several minutes, and Kristen had been able to see him imagining the scenario. "I can see you holding him or her, can see you loving them despite not having been made by your body," he'd said. "But that's easy--you were born to be a mother. I'm less sure about me in that regard. But if I couldn't love and care for a child just because it didn't look like me, didn't carry my DNA, then isn't that just the height of vanity? I don't want a child because it would carry on my genetics. I want a child because I want to be a dad. I want you to be a mom. The things we could pass on to a kid are much more important than our genes."

It had been the perfect answer, one that had warmed Kristen's heart all the way through, and ignited the true peace she'd been waiting to feel. And it seemed that the universe had been waiting for them as well. After all of the lost time and the disappointment and the tears, suddenly things were going at lightning speed. The couple attended adoption seminars and filled out mountains of paperwork, and were soon made aware of a local missionary who was seeking support for an orphanage in Ethiopia. God opened one door after another; it was impossible not to see divine influence as useful contacts were found around every corner.

In less time than it would have taken to carry a child to term, Kristen and Joel had been matched with an infant who'd lost his father to political violence and his mother to a swift and vicious disease. Over the past week, they had visited the African orphanage where they held him and prayed over him and filled out still more paperwork. In another month, they would come back and finalize everything with the courts, although things had been finalized in Kristen's heart from the very first sight of the little boy.

It had pained her to leave the baby there in the orphanage, but she and Joel simply couldn't afford to be out of work and live in Africa for a month. And after all, there was so much to be done at home. After so much waiting, there suddenly wasn't much time at all. Kristen wondered if this anxiety was what had her feeling so nauseated, but it seemed like something deeper. When she'd chewed up all the ice in her glass and slurped the last hint of moisture from the plastic cup, she gave up and asked Joel to let her out to use the restroom.

In the moment that they stood together in the aisle, he looked down at her with tender concern, stooping over to make his hazel eyes even with hers. Kristen always loved when he did that, when he dropped the posture he'd adopted as a soldier and put himself on the same level as her. When he put his big hand against her face, she leaned into it and smiled as encouragingly as possible before heading to the lavatory at the back of the plane.

The space was uncomfortably tight and loud, and splashing her face with water offered her little relief from the queasiness or the prickling sweat that covered her. Kristen stared for a moment at her wan reflection before realizing there was now a new problem. The soap she'd used to wash her hands had made them very dry. Hauling her purse up onto the tiny counter, she went in search of some lotion.

She'd never been one to carry a fancy handbag. This one had been chosen for its extensive number of pockets inside, something that was proving frustrating now as she couldn't remember which one held the little lotion bottle. Her hands closed on everything from tissues to a flattened granola bar before they settled on something she hadn't expected to find. It was a pregnancy test, still sealed, leftover from the days when she would impulsively check to see if the miraculous had taken place. Staring at the white and pink wrapper, she almost didn't notice when the plane gave a little dip, knocking her against the door. Her stomach had dropped, but it had nothing to do with the turbulence.

It can't be. Now? It couldn't possibly be happening *now*!

But it all fit. Over the next paralyzing thirty seconds, Kristen had catalogued all of her symptoms and compared them to the times before. The nausea and the headaches and the weird sensitivity in her skin. With chagrin, she realized that in the hectic run up to this overseas trip, she'd failed to notice that her period was now several weeks late. She stared at her ashen reflection in the little mirror until there was a polite tap on the door, breaking her reverie.

She opened the door to see a nervous mother trying to keep hold of a little girl who was dancing urgently on the spot, desperate to get in. Kristen hurried out of the way, hoping she didn't look too shell shocked. She wanted to giggle at the little girl, who was struggling with her overalls as she rushed into the tiny bathroom, but her mind was reeling too quickly. On numb legs, she walked back up the aisle and gave Joel a tap on the shoulder.

He popped up at once and smiled at her. "Feeling better?" he asked, though he must have been able to see how pale she was. She could only give a half smile and shrug as she pushed past him into the middle seat, waiting until she was safely buckled before daring to meet his worried gaze.

When she opened her mouth to speak, there was a dinging sound and then there was an announcement from a flight attendant saying in German, French, and then English that they would be landing soon. Kristen waited as Joel obediently buckled his own seat belt before turning his eyes on her expectantly.

"Babe, I'm not at all sure how to say this," she whispered through dry lips. "But I don't think I'm airsick. I think I might be pregnant."

STAPLE

BOARDING PASS

BOARDING PASS

PASSENGER RECEIPT 1 OF 1

Rodriguez, Ana

ATL – JFK

Chapter Two

Global Air

Rodriquez, Ana Maria

SEAT NUMBER

1D

Date and Time

AUGUST 1, 2019

07:15 AM

Destination: JFK

Chapter Two

ATL to JFK (Ana Maria)

The sun was still an hour or so from rising, but Ana Maria had been awake for what felt like days. She had no fear of flying, but this was different. This wasn't the hurried hop to a faraway city to cover some breaking news story. It wasn't an excited excursion toward a long, sunny vacation. This was a nerve-wracking step into the unknown.

She was alone, and she hadn't quite reached the point where she was glad about that. There had been days when she felt close, but most of the time, being alone just felt lonely. Her love affair with Kyle Eppstein was something that she wanted to look back on fondly, as a learning experience just as much as a cautionary tale. She wanted to think of him and remember the good parts, the sweet parts before everything became sour. But it was too soon for that. Everything with them had happened too soon.

In less than thirty months, she had gone from not knowing Kyle existed to being his ex-wife. Even though she wanted to claim responsibility for her part in all of it, Ana couldn't help but see him as some kind of whirlwind that had swept in and overturned everything in her life, taking her from a confident news reporter to a frustrated divorcée.

He had never really respected her career, her dreams, or her desire to stay in her hometown of Memphis. These were crucial arguments that had weakened them from the very beginning, and would have probably finished them even without all the other nitpicky things. Ana liked a low roar of activity at all times, usually watching the news on TV while surfing and scrolling social media on her phone. Kyle had demanded utter silence when he was writing, which was most of the time, and this drove him to the back bedroom for hours until he only came out for mealtimes, where he would judge her on her admittedly limited cooking skills. By the end, even Ana's choice to wear contact lenses during her broadcasts instead of glasses was a source of argument between them. He accused her of pandering to society's beauty standards, and of course he'd never forgiven her for keeping her maiden name as part of her sign-off.

Ana had truly loved Kyle. She was sure of it. But by the end of their brief marriage, she didn't even think she liked him. During one rare, sweet moment, she'd told him of her dream of becoming a field reporter for *The Today Show*. Having a home base in New York City, while jetting around to cover the beat in Washington or wherever the news was—it was a fantasy that had never fully left her. Naturally, Kyle had found fault in this plan. In one breath, he made her feel silly for hanging on to such an unlikely goal. And in the next moment, he made it seem like the entire field of broadcast journalism was a joke and beneath her. He'd been especially savage about the New York part, demanding to know how she expected to survive in such an expensive city when her aspirations inevitably fell through.

This last part really stung, because once their divorce had been finalized and Kyle was free to go back to his nomadic roots, his first stop was none other than the Big Apple. This had infuriated Ana, making her feel like her dream city was now off limits. But today, she would change this. Today, she was flying to New York City, and this afternoon, she had an interview at *The Today Show*. It was a long shot, but it felt like a step in the right direction. Or it would be once the plane started moving. She glanced nervously out the window, hoping last night's thunderstorms hadn't caused any delays.

The rain had slowed to a mere drizzle a few hours before, but everything was still slick and shiny, reflecting the various blinking lights that marked the edges of the jet bridge. Ana was sitting in her favorite place, the window seat just over the left wing. There was something calming about watching the wing's slats and flaps as they went through their last minute tests before pushing back.

It wasn't a full flight, and Ana was just beginning to hope that the middle seat beside her would remain empty, but just as the flight attendant was moving to lock the door, a tall Asian man rushed on board and was soon wedged between her and the middle aged woman on the aisle. Ana made herself as small as possible, tucking into the curved wall of the plane and resting her head against the cool windowpane. It was still dark enough outside to see her dim reflection, so she closed her eyes. She didn't want to see herself this way: tired and anxious and lost.

For the entire taxi and take off of the plane, she kept her eyes shut, experiencing it all by sound and vibration. Her sense of smell also felt heightened in compensation, and she realized belatedly that she had turned her whole body toward the young man in the middle seat, drawn unintentionally to the rich scent of his rain-dampened leather jacket. She snapped her eyes open, ready to apologize, but the words died in her throat.

The man couldn't have noticed her reaction as his own eyes were closed. One bright tear slid slowly down his cheek and then splattered down onto his leather collar. Ana felt her stomach tighten with concern and curiosity. Judging by the rest of his body language, he wasn't crying out of fear. His hands were calmly folded in his lap, not gripping the armrests. His ankles were casually crossed and his jaw wasn't clenched. So he wasn't scared, just unbearably sad.

Ana retreated back to her corner, but she couldn't seem to stop watching him. One more tear joined the first, but then there was the *ding* of the intercom, and he abruptly opened his eyes and wiped at his damp cheeks.

A flight attendant announced that electronic devices could now be used again, and Ana made herself small and unobtrusive as the young man grabbed for the backpack he'd shoved under the seat. He didn't pull out a laptop or tablet though, but rather a small notebook and a pen. Spying shamelessly out of the corner of her eye, Ana saw to her dismay that she couldn't read a word of what had been scribbled there. She knew enough to know that he wasn't writing in any language she was fluent in, but the characters reminded her of something. After about five minutes, she realized that she'd seen similar writing all over the photos from the last Winter Olympics.

It's Korean! she exclaimed internally, but she'd actually snapped her fingers as the solution had come to her. This of course drew the attention of the man she'd been spying on. He looked over at her, one eyebrow slightly raised.

For a moment, Ana was a bit speechless. Not just because he was quite handsome, but because when he raised a hand to push his hair back from his forehead, she noticed his skin was almost the same cinnamon shade as her own. He had dark eyes and dark hair as well, and it looked like he might even have one dimple like she did. But that's where their similarities ended. His hair, still a bit wet from the rain, was close cropped while Ana's dark tresses fell past her waist. His frame was long and gangly while she was short and generously curved. And his eyes, puffy from crying and the early hour, were hidden beneath long sloping monolids, while Ana's eyes were wide and round.

The young man blinked those exotic eyes and looked pointedly at Ana's fingers, which had just distracted him with their snapping, and she gave an embarrassed gasp. "Oh, I'm so sorry! I didn't mean to interrupt you!"

The young man made an attempt at a smile. "I'm not usually so easy to distract," he said, and Ana realized his English was perfect, bearing only the slightest hint of an accent. "I'm having a hard time focusing today." The plane gave a little shudder then, and the man's pen skated in a jagged line over the page. He winced and flipped to a fresh sheet.

"Are you working on a love letter or a speech?" Ana asked boldly, and then immediately wished she hadn't. The hollow look that came into his eyes was like a punch to the gut.

"Um, I suppose you could say it's both," he said sadly, flipping back to the scribbled page and running his hands over the letters. "It's a eulogy."

"Oh," Ana said, kicking herself for her inquisitive nature. "I'm so very sorry for your loss." The next words tumbled out even as she tried to swallow them down: "Was it a friend? Family?"

The man cleared his throat and stared into space. "My sister."

Finally, Ana was able to stop running her mouth. She was too stunned to go on. This man couldn't have been thirty years old yet, not so far off from her own age. Far too young to lose a sibling, at least to natural causes. Ana's mouth stayed quiet, but her face drained of color and her brain reeled as she imagined deadly illnesses or violent accidents that could have led to this achingly sad moment.

To Ana's surprise, the man's face lifted into something almost adjacent to a smile. "I can always tell whether someone else has a sister, based on their reactions," he said in a remarkably pleasant tone. "People without siblings react differently, and so do those with only brothers. Those with sisters, like you and me, we just feel things differently, don't we?"

"I suppose we do," Ana said, a bit breathlessly. "How could you tell?"

The man gave a little shrug and the leather of his jacket squeaked. "Something about your eyes. You were sad for me, but you couldn't help imagining if you were in my shoes. Do you just have the one sister?"

"Yes. Marisol," Ana replied, unable to keep the ache out of her voice.

"I'm guessing she is younger." At Ana's nod, the man went on. "Ji-yeon was older than me by a year and a half, but she was a mile ahead of me in absolutely everything. She is...*was*...the better musician, the better student, better at sports, and way better at public speaking. She would have loved giving my eulogy, no matter how sad it made her. She would have excelled at it. Even if I can decide what all to say, I'm sure I'll stumble over the words when it's time to say them."

Ana couldn't imagine having to speak at any funeral, let alone Marisol's, despite being a pro at speaking in public. If something tragic ever happened to her baby sister, she would likely be comatose for weeks afterward. She couldn't even seem to speak now, but the young man beside her filled the empty space easily enough.

"Ji-yeon had an aggressive tumor behind her left eye," he said quietly. "One day she had a bad headache and then two weeks later, she was getting chemo and radiation. She fought hard for a year, but she was just too much for this world. Too bright, too brilliant."

Ana was finally able to pull herself back into the conversation enough to give him a sad smile. "I'm so very sorry for your loss," she said again, hating how insufficient those words felt.

The young man bowed his head in thanks. "If only it was just my loss. She was such a gift to the world—the youngest ever interpreter for the U.N."

"Wow!" Ana said. She was passably fluent in Spanish thanks to her Puerto Rican grandmother, but she couldn't imagine interpreting when global policy was at stake. "That's really amazing."

"I know," her neighbor replied. "I wrote down everything here about her time at NYU and the two years she spent in Seoul, but it all reads like a résumé. I don't want to just list her accomplishments, but there will be important people at her memorial, and I don't think they'll care about how we played together as kids."

Ana grinned. "Well, I know we're total strangers, but if I was Ji-yeon's coworker, I would want to know that stuff, the human stuff."

"I don't consider us strangers anymore, but it is a bit funny that we know our sisters' names and not each other's." The man held out a hand. "I'm Jae-won. Just call me Jae. Atlanta-based software developer on his way to his sister's funeral."

"Ana Maria," she replied. "Or just Ana. I'm a broadcast journalist from Memphis, who decided while visiting some cousins in Atlanta to be brave and chase my dreams. I'm hoping to nail an interview with *The Today Show* this afternoon."

For a moment, they just grinned at each other, and then Ana tapped the paper with the eulogy written on it. "Let her coworkers talk about her work history, or leave that to the obituary. You should focus on your personal relationship with her. Don't worry about the so-called important people. This day isn't about them. It's about you and your parents and Ji-yeon's friends. You loved her best and will miss her the most. Surely there's a memory that stands out..."

After a pause, Jae gave a quiet little chuckle. "It's strange the things that stay with us over the years," he said. "Before Ji-yeon discovered her affinity for languages, she wanted to be an orchestra conductor. She was always waving her arms around, conducting the songs on the radio or even during television commercials. I always felt a bit sad that she changed her path. She had the most graceful hands. But then I realized that she never really stopped. The last time I was in the car with her, I remember watching the way she turned the steering wheel. She managed to turn something so simple into this beautiful dance." Jae smiled and looked down at his own hands.

"I think that's lovely," Ana replied softly, and she watched as Jae scribbled a few lines onto his page. She looked out the window at the stunning sunrise and tried not to think about Marisol. Or Kyle. It didn't work. She found herself rubbing at the place on her left hand where her wedding ring had been. She'd worn it just long enough to get used to it, and its absence still distracted her.

"You said before that you were visiting cousins in Atlanta," Jae said after a long session of writing. This startled Ana for a moment, but after she nodded, Jae asked: "So where is home for you?"

"Memphis," she replied proudly.

"Oh, I love it there. Good food. Great music."

"It's the best," Ana agreed.

"But you got an idea to go to New York while visiting family, and you're not going home first?" Jae wondered.

Ana grinned awkwardly. "I didn't want to give myself time to chicken out," she admitted. "The last time I did something reckless... It didn't work out so well. I knew I'd talk myself out of this opportunity, so I just left on the first flight out."

"That's impressive," Jae said. "I can't remember the last time I was spontaneous."

"It's feeling less spontaneous and crazier at the moment," Ana admitted. She was beginning to feel a bit nauseous.

"No, I think it's great. It's brave." Jae smiled thoughtfully. "It's what Ji-yeon would have done."

Ana laughed. "I didn't know her, but that honestly makes me feel a lot better."

"Glad I could return the favor," Jae said softly, closing his notebook and holding it close to his chest.

They were beginning their slow, spiraling descent into the city now, and this peculiar meeting was drawing to a close. There wasn't much pressure to fill the silence though. They each retreated into their own thoughts and didn't speak again until they'd landed with a double bounce at La Guardia.

"I think you'll make a brilliant *Today Show* employee," Jae said, handing Ana her carry-on bag from the overhead bin. "You're a good reporter. You got a good story out of me."

"I got a *great* story out of you," Ana replied with a bright smile. "And I think your speech will be perfect. I'll keep your family in my prayers."

"Thank you," Jae said, shaking her hand earnestly. "Good luck to you, Ana." And then he melted into the crowd flooding into the busy terminal.

She stood there alone for a few moments, getting her bearings and convincing herself not to jump onto the next plane headed home. Then she looked up at the nearest television and saw that of course *The Today Show* was on, and she knew she was exactly where she needed to be.

STAPLE

INSERT TEXT HERE

BOARDING PASS

Evans, William

MEM – STL

Chapter Three

Global Air

PASSENGER RECEIPT 1 OF 1

Evans, William

SEAT NUMBER

10B

Date and Time

JUNE 14, 2017

06:24 PM

Destination: MEM

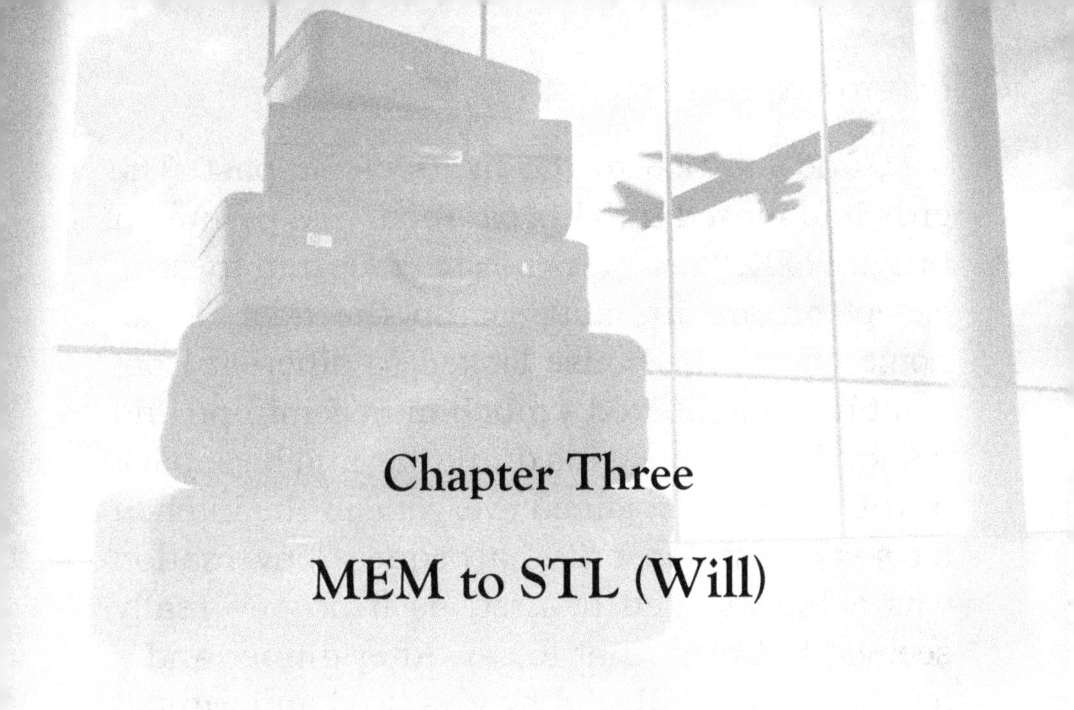

Chapter Three

MEM to STL (Will)

Just like his flight a few days ago, Will once again found himself an unaccompanied minor. But this time it did not irritate him as much as it did then, since he now had other more important things on his mind. And he was not even upset to find that he was in a middle seat between a teenaged girl and a stuffy businessman.

Just five days ago he had gone to Memphis to see his dad with his new family – Dad's new wife Lily with her daughters Emma, Colby and Sophie. He had been full of resentment towards his dad for abandoning him and his mother, and for the seemingly easy way they had been replaced.

When they all came to meet him at the airport, he was worried about feeling out of place, in the way, and too tied to the hurts of the past. The girls had moved into his old room and painted it bright PINK. There was nowhere for him to sleep except on an air mattress on the floor of the home office. The house looked so different from what he remembered – much more feminine and homey. Will dropped his duffle bag and back pack in the office, then joined everyone in the kitchen for some of his favorite barbeque. Conversation was a bit strained at first, as if no one really seemed to know what to say. After dinner and a quick shower, Will said he was tired and wanted to turn in early. But he didn't fall asleep for quite a while – instead, he laid on the office floor and listened to the easy banter between his father and the others. "Why is it so easy for him to talk to them and not to me?" he asked himself over and over.

Eventually he did fall asleep, but was troubled by restless dreams while struggling to be comfortable on his temporary bed. When he opened his eyes around 8 AM, he again heard voices coming from the kitchen, along with the comforting smells of coffee and freshly-cooked bacon.

"How long do you think he's going to sleep?" Lily asked. "The girls are getting really hungry, but I was hoping we could have breakfast together as a family."

"I honestly don't know," his father said. "But I can't imagine it will be much longer. Maybe I should go wake him up?"

"No, let me do it!" Sophie enthused, and she scampered down the hallway. Will closed his eyes again and pretended to be asleep. There was a timid knock on the door, and then she opened it just a crack. She tip-toed over to him, and put a gentle hand on his shoulder.

"Billy.....I mean, Will.......are you awake? Mom wants to make pancakes and bacon and I just love pancakes and bacon, but we can't eat until you get up and I'm starving!"

Will opened one eye to see an adorable 4 year old girl in a *Frozen* nightgown peering down into his face. How could he resist her, and pancakes and bacon? He smiled at her and let her lead him back to the kitchen.

After a great breakfast, they all gathered in the living room to discuss plans for the day. Will's dad had a few things planned – Mud Island and the ducks at the Peabody Hotel – and the girls wanted to see the new Disney movie at the IMAX and then go to the zoo. Lily had heard about a paddleboat dinner cruise that sounded like fun, but the only thing Will was really interested in was spending time with his dad. Just his dad, without Lily or the girls. Was it wrong of him to want some time alone with him, just the two of them? He had missed his dad so much over the years, and was hoping for some time to get reacquainted.

It took several days, but they were able to accomplish most of the things on the list. The dinner cruise was amazing, and Will imagined that he was Tom Sawyer, floating up and down the Mississippi. Yesterday they stopped at the mall and Will's dad insisted on getting some new school clothes for him. The girls gave style suggestions, which he accepted with a smile, as Emma described what would make the girls notice him. He ended up with several new pairs of jeans and a couple cool new shirts. Plus a new Memphis Grizzlies hoodie, since he had outgrown his old one. Will observed that their conversations slowly became more spontaneous and less strained, and he found that he liked having other kids to talk to and be around, even if they were a bit younger, and girls. They played board games in the evenings, and Will taught them how to play Skip-Bo with the cards he had brought from home.

He was having a good time, but continued to struggle with what to call his dad's new wife..... Lily just seemed too familiar, and Mrs. Evans was too formal. And there was *no way* he would ever call her 'mom.' On their second afternoon together, Lily took him aside and said, "I know all of this is a bit strange for you – new people living in your old house, new relationships competing with old memories. But I have an idea – I know that calling me 'mom' is something uncomfortable for you, and I would never push you into calling me that. You have a wonderful mom, and I could never take her place, nor would I want to try. You may not know this, but I am part Cherokee, and I thought maybe you would like a word that is special for just you and me. 'Mom' in Cherokee is 'Etsi' – pronounced EET-see. Do you think that is something you would like to do?"

"You are part Cherokee? That's really neat! I had no idea! Yeah, that might be kinda cool – like a secret code between you and me? Etsi – I like it!"

"Sure – and I would love to teach you more if you are interested. No pressure of course."

"No, actually I would like that. I've always been interested in history, and this sounds like fun!"

After lunch on their last day together, Will was packing his bags and getting ready for his evening flight back to St. Louis. He discovered that his duffle bag did not have enough room for all the extra clothes he had picked up shopping the other day, and he went to the living room to see if there was a bag he could borrow from his dad.

"Hey, Will, can you sit for a minute? I have something I wanted to talk to you about," his dad asked, looking uncomfortable and nervous.

"OK, dad," Will answered, feeling like something unpleasant was about to happen. Surely he hadn't done anything to make his dad mad, had he? And he had tried so hard to get along with the girls and Lily, err, *Etsi*. What had he done to disappoint them?

"I hope you enjoyed your time here these past few days.....I know I have, we all have. The girls adore you, and Lily is impressed with how mature and polite you are."

"It's been great, and getting to know the girls has been fun. But I have to be honest, dad, I'm ready to go home and see mom. I really do miss her. And my own bed, my own things."

"That's what I wanted to talk to you about. Lily and I have been discussing something important, but I really need your opinion. What would you think about staying here longer? The girls are just getting used to having you around, and you are such a good influence on them. It has been such a joy for me to get to spend so much timc with you, too. But five days is just not enough. I know you need to fly home tonight, but maybe you could come back for a longer stay – maybe a month? And maybe....just maybe......." and his voice trailed off.

Will looked at his dad, trying to figure out just what he was saying. A whole month? Yeah, this visit had been fun, but a month? Where would he sleep? Camping out on an inflatable mattress on the office floor for a few days was one thing, but not for a whole month!

Almost as if he was reading Will's mind, his dad said "I know sleeping on the floor is not ideal. Lily and I are already discussing the need to expand the house a bit as the girls get older. We've decided to add a master suite and another family room onto the back of the house, and will let the girls have our room with its own bathroom. It's plenty big enough for the three of them, and it is on the opposite end of the house so they would have their privacy. Your old room would be vacant again, and perfect for you after we get rid of the pink paint, of course. And you wouldn't have to share the bathroom with a bunch of pre-teen girls! I know this is a lot to take in all at once, but what I am hoping is that maybe you would consider moving here permanently."

"MOVE here? Leave St. Louis and mom? And my grandparents? My school? My friends and my church? Wow – that's just..........wow."

Will sat there for what seemed an hour, just staring at the floor, his thoughts racing. Part of him was thrilled at the thought of being with his dad, finally having him in the stands cheering for him, going on scout campouts, teaching him all the guy things that his mom would never be able to. But to leave his mom? And all his friends back home? That was an awful lot to ask of him after such a short visit. His dad had continued talking, but Will had trouble hearing any of it.

Eventually, Will went back to his room to finish packing. He sat on the edge of the air mattress, his head in his hands, his mind reeling. There was a light tapping on the door, and Lily peered into the room hesitantly. "Is it alright if I come in?" she asked.

"Of course, *Etsi*," he said carefully. "I'm just making sure everything will fit into this bag dad let me borrow."

"I guess your dad talked to you about coming back for a longer visit? How do you feel about that?"

Will was surprised at how comfortable he had become with Etsi, how easy it was to talk to her.

"A longer visit would be nice, but then he talked about MOVING here, and I'm just not sure how I feel about that. My WHOLE LIFE is back in St. Louis – my mom, my grandparents, my friends, my school. As much as I want dad to be a part of my daily life, that's an awfully big change and a lot to give up."

"I understand – it's a HUGE decision. How about this........you go home and think about it, and we make plans for you to come back later in the summer for another visit. We will be starting the construction on the addition to the house anyway – it's something we need to do whether you move here or not. Maybe after you have a chance to talk to your mom, you will have a better feeling of what you want to do. I hope you don't feel like we are pressuring you in any way, or that your dad will be upset if you decide against it. Disappointed, of course, but not upset. He totally realizes that you have a life and friends back home."

"I just don't want him to be mad at me if I say no," Will said softly, as he turned his head away, afraid the tears that were welling up in his eyes would escape down his cheeks. Lily softly patted his shoulder, and quietly left him to his thoughts.

After a while, Will's dad appeared at the door to tell him it was time to leave. Everyone piled into the van for the short ride to the airport. The girls chatted away, asking Will all sorts of questions about St. Louis, and wondering when he was coming back. But he was so distracted by his own tumultuous thoughts, he had little to say back to them.

Lily and the girls stayed in the car in the parking garage while Will's dad walked inside with him to check in. After verifying that the flight was on time and signing a release form, Will said goodbye to his father and then found himself alone at the gate, waiting for his turn to board.

It was only a few minutes before the inbound plane arrived and the passengers exited. Once the plane was tidied up a bit, the flight attendant escorted him to a middle seat close to the front of the plane. She gave him the same instructions that he had heard the week before – that he needed to wait until everyone else was off the plane in St. Louis before leaving to meet his mother. He kicked his backpack under the seat in front of him, and closed his eyes. Was this really happening to him?

Soon the other passengers were allowed to board, and Will found himself seated between a pretty girl not all that much older than himself and a businessman who sat on the aisle and was totally focused on finishing his phone calls before the plane took off. Neither one spoke to him, which was perfectly fine.

Will noticed very little else during the short flight. What in the world was he going to tell his mother? How could he tell her that he was not only going for another visit later in the summer, but that he was considering moving there? She would be so disappointed, and so lonely without him. After all she had done for him over the years, raising him on her own, how could he break her heart this way? And all his friends at school and church – he would miss them so much! But what about his dad? Spending more time with him was all he had ever wanted – was he going to pass up this opportunity?

Sometime during the flight, the flight attendants passed out drinks and snacks, and presented him with another pair of flight wings. He sipped on a Sprite and ate his small bag of pretzels, barely tasting either. Soon the trash was collected and the captain announced that they were making their initial approach to the St. Louis airport. If anything, his thoughts were more confused than when he got on the plane just an hour earlier.

The plane taxied to the gate, and Will waited while everyone made their way off the plane. The flight attendant motioned to him, and he grabbed his backpack and shuffled up the aisle. Somehow, he felt that if he walked as slowly as possible, he could postpone the decision that he needed to make.

As he reached the top of the jet way, he saw his mother standing at the desk. He quickened his pace and almost sprinted into her arms. He had no idea how much he had missed her until now – he loved the way she hugged him, the smell of her perfume that filled his mind with memories of their years together. She signed a few papers and they walked toward baggage claim. He told her that he actually had two bags this time, since he had all the new clothes his dad had gotten for him. She asked lots of questions about the visit, and he gave short answers with limited details. He was so conflicted – how was he supposed to choose one parent over the other?

After they got his bags and headed toward the door, he said he needed to stop at the restroom. But once inside, all he did was stand at the mirror and look at his reflection. Who was he now? He had changed so much over the past week, but was he really in a position to make this kind of life-altering decision?

Eventually, he washed his hands and face, and took a deep breath. He looked in the mirror once more, suddenly feeling older and more mature. His eyes seemed to show a depth of wisdom they did not hold before, wisdom with a hint of sadness. He walked outside toward his mother; the decision had been made, and now he had to face the reality of breaking someone's heart.

STAPLE

INSERT TEXT HERE

BOARDING PASS

Miller, Jean

DFW – CVG

Chapter Four

Global Air

PASSENGER RECEIPT 1 OF 1

Miller, Jean

SEAT NUMBER

3B

Date and Time

FEBRUARY 13, 2019

04:00 PM

Destination: CVG

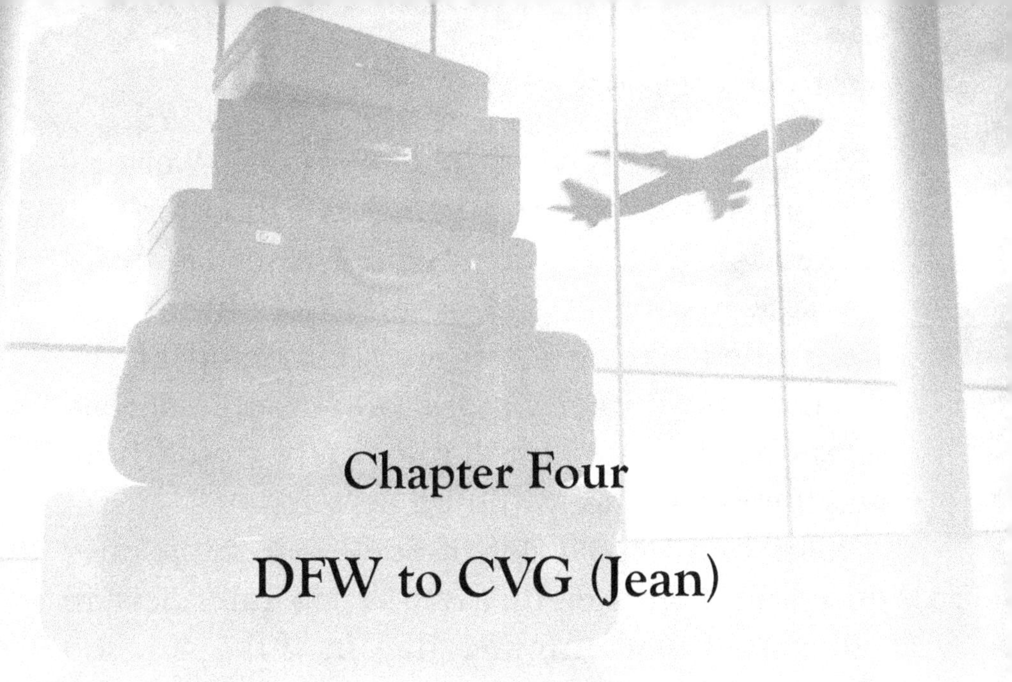

Chapter Four

DFW to CVG (Jean)

Coffee, glorious coffee. It wasn't until she had her first sip of the airline coffee that she realized just how tired she was. Jean had been running on nervous energy for the past several days, and only after settling into her First Class airplane seat did the fatigue start to sit in. Plus the cold – oh, it was SO cold outside, and inside the plane as well.

She looked out the window at the tarmac of DFW airport and watched in dismay as sleet and freezing rain pelted the side of her plane. She thought back to another flight so long ago when she was horribly hot and miserable, unhappy with her life and life choices. It was hard to believe that flight was less than two years ago - so much had changed in her life since then.

She was now living in Cincinnati, working at a job she loved, and going to school on the weekends. Her hand touched the sapphire necklace resting at the base of her throat and she giggled like a young girl. Glancing at the romance novel in her lap, a broad smile spread across her freshly-painted lips. Who could have imagined that she would be here today?

Jean had done a lot of soul searching after returning from her disastrous job interview in Dallas that hot summer day in 2017. Excited about the thought of expressing herself through her writing, she decided she wanted to write a romance novel set in Italy; a place she had visited and loved several years before. Like most tourists, she had been captivated by the beauty and the culture, and of course the food. As she started outlining her story and researching locations, it seemed crucial that she visit Italy again to renew her sense of wonder and to be better able to describe the architecture, the scenery, the sights and sounds, the tangible feeling of romance in the air.

Over the Christmas holidays, she packed her bags and joined a travel group that was going on a Mediterranean cruise. They flew from Chicago to Barcelona, Spain, where they boarded the ship and then made stops in France, Monte Carlo in Monaco, and then on to Italy with excursions in Florence, Pisa and Rome. The cruise was an absolute dream come true for Jean, and she spent much of her time watching the other passengers and taking in the sights and sounds of the exotic locations. The culmination of the trip for her, though, was Rome. The city held such an attraction to her, and she knew that it was here that she wanted her love story to be written. And what a love story it turned out to be.

On December 29th she was sitting alone at a small outdoor café near the Trevi Fountain, sipping an espresso and watching the tourists as they tossed their coins into the water and made their wishes. She was keenly aware of the busy streets, the melodious Italian language floating on the breeze, and the cool but crisp air that seemed alive with romance. She scribbled impressions into her notebook, trying to capture an array of emotions so she could add them to her book once she got home.

Down the street came a group of high school students who appeared to be part of a choir. They had matching t-shirts and chatted excitedly while posing for pictures by the fountain. They were loud and rowdy, but harmless, and Jean could not help but smile at their youthful enthusiasm. Soon they wandered off, several of them singing "Somewhere Over the Rainbow."

It was only after they left that Jean noticed a smaller group of students who were sitting off to the side, being very quiet and each was busily working on something they held in their laps. Walking among them and speaking softly was a handsome middle-aged man who leaned over each student and offered gentle suggestions. Jean realized that they were a group of art students, and they were sketching the fountain. She watched them for quite a while, each of them so focused on their artwork. But she found her eyes repeatedly drawn toward the instructor. Whether it was his broad shoulders, his sandy hair or his deep brown eyes, Jean found herself instantly attracted to him.

Shaking off these unfamiliar feelings, she went back to her coffee and her notebook, trying to ensure that she had captured all the details she needed. She pulled out her camera and took a few pictures as a way to jog her memory later. One picture just happened to be of the group of students and their teacher.

After writing feverishly for a few minutes, she had the sensation of someone standing near to her. She instinctively pulled her purse a little tighter to her chest, and looked up to see the art teacher with two cups of espresso in his hands.

"Hi, I hope I'm not interrupting," he said softly, "but my students will be busy drawing for quite a while, and I could use a little something to warm me up. Care to join me? My name is Nathan and I'm an art history professor at the University of Cincinnati. I'm guessing you are an American, also?"

"Yes, I'm from St. Louis. I'm a travelling pharmaceutical rep, but here on vacation. I'm writing a book that takes place here in Rome. I'm enjoying the sights while doing some research. My name is Jean by the way. And yes, another cup would be wonderful!" Jean realized that she had spoken very quickly, and felt herself start to blush a bit.

"It's great to meet you, Jean, and to have an American adult to talk to. I love my students, don't get me wrong, but we really are of different worlds it seems. So much technology and music I don't understand........guess I'm dating myself."

"Oh, I know what you mean! I have nieces and nephews about that age, and most of the time I have no idea what they are talking about."

"So, what's your book about, if you don't mind me asking? And how does a pharmaceutical rep become an author?"

"Well, it's a love story, set here in Rome. I haven't worked out all the details yet, but it's about an American girl who falls for an Italian guy she meets here at the fountain. He begs her to stay in Rome with him, but she feels like she must return to the States. Like I said, it's not all settled in my mind just yet how it should end. And as for the other question, that's long story. I haven't been really passionate about my job for a while now, so I'm looking for a more creative way to express myself."

"As an artist, I completely understand the need to express yourself creatively! How long are you going to be in Rome?"

"Just until tomorrow evening. I'm here with a group, and our flight heads back to Chicago and then I return to the real world. Makes me a little sad that my vacation is almost over."

"We are leaving tomorrow evening too......... you don't suppose we are on the same flight?"

After comparing itineraries and realizing that indeed they were to be on the same flight to Chicago, Nathan returned to his students and Jean packed up her notebook and walked to her hotel. Sitting alone in her room, she replayed their conversation, the kindness of his voice, the smile in his eyes. She looked at the pictures she had taken, stopping often to admire the group of students, and Nathan. Then she scolded herself for acting like a silly starry-eyed school girl.

The next morning Jean went with several ladies from her travel group to buy a few last-minute souvenirs and take one more look at the Vatican. Then she finished packing her bags and the group taxied to the airport for the long flight home. She had just settled herself into her airplane seat when she heard a newly-familiar voice behind her.

"Hello, Jean – ready to go back to the real world?"

"Nathan.....hi. No, not really. But it seems I don't have much of a choice. How about you?"

"Oh, no, I'm not either. Good thing the college is on break for another week, so I can recover from the jet lag."

He returned to his seat, and soon the plane took off. Before long the lights were dimmed and everyone was encouraged to sleep their way back to Chicago. Jean found herself unable to relax, though, and got up to stretch her legs a bit. Walking toward the back of the plane, she met Nathan coming toward her with two coffee cups in his hands.

"Just the person I was looking for. Care to join me in a cup? It's decaf, so it won't keep us awake. The seat next to me is vacant and I'd love to visit with you for a while. I always have a hard time sleeping on a plane, especially on international flights."

Jean accepted the cup and the chance to get to know him a bit better. They ended up chatting for several hours, and she found herself growing more comfortable with him as the minutes went by. They had many things in common, from growing up in the Midwest to sharing a love for travel, and the conversation flowed easily. Eventually, they were both getting sleepy so she moved back to her own seat and tried to rest. She must have slept for quite a while, because she was jolted awake by the flight attendants turning on the lights and passing out breakfast. Jean glanced over her shoulder to see that Nathan was still sleeping, his sandy hair a bit messy and he had the beginnings of a scruffy beard. Jean went to the restroom to freshen up a bit, and then ate a cold breakfast of a muffin, fruit and juice. Just as she finished, she felt a tap on her shoulder. She turned to find Nathan standing beside her, looking rested and freshly shaven, and smelling amazing with a hint of a very masculine aftershave. She felt her heart skip and beat and wondered if she was blushing. What was it about this man that affected her so?

"We'll be in Chicago soon, and I wanted one last chance to chat with you. I truly enjoyed our talks, and would love to continue once we get home. Here is my number and my email address," he said as he handed her his business card from the university. All she could do was smile up at him.

"Oh, of course, I'd love that too," she stuttered after a bit. "Let me get my card for you." She fumbled in her purse and felt her hands shaking a little, trying to appear calm but suddenly so nervous. “Here you go.”

“Thanks – and thanks for making this trip so enjoyable for me,” he said with a genuine smile.

The plane landed uneventfully, and Jean shuffled her way off the plane and into the sprawling Chicago O’Hare airport. The line through Customs was long, and Jean quickly lost sight of Nathan and his group. She found her connecting flight to St. Louis and sank into a chair in the waiting area. She held Nathan’s business card in her hands and smiled softly.

Once back in St. Louis, Jean only had two days to rest before going back to work - another flight across the country to Sacramento, more meetings and presentations and reports. But this trip was different in that each evening she enthusiastically worked on her book, which she now titled “Fountain of Love.” She was able to add a richness of descriptive words and a Roman flavor that seemed to make the story come alive. And on her desk at the hotel she kept the picture of Nathan by the fountain with his art students. He was leaned over the shoulder of one of his male students, pointing out an area that could be revised. He was smiling and it was easy to tell that the student was comfortable with him, appreciating the professional guidance. But what Jean noticed the most was the way the evening sun glistened on his tousled hair, the kindness of his eyes, the unimposing strength and confidence he portrayed.

On her third night in California her cell phone rang, and her heart skipped a beat when she realized it was Nathan. They chatted for a while; the conversation still as easy and comfortable as it had been in Rome and on the plane. At first he only called once or twice a week, but within a month or two, the calls came almost every evening, and lasted well into the night. They also exchanged emails regularly, and surprise texts during the day. She was beginning to wonder how she got through her days before meeting him. And she was falling for him, hard.

At the end of March during one of their long phone calls, Nathan asked if she would like to visit him in Cincinnati on one of her weekends off. He wanted to show her around his hometown, and a prestigious gallery was going to be showcasing some of his artwork. He also had a publisher friend he wanted her to meet to talk about publishing her book. She claimed it wasn't ready yet, but he knew she was just nervous and he wanted to encourage her. She gladly accepted his invitation for a visit, and anxiously packed – and repacked – her suitcase numerous times.

April 20th she flew from St. Louis to Cincinnati and he met her at baggage claim. They had grown so close during all those hours on the phone and endless emails and texts, it just seemed natural when he took her in his arms and gave her a lingering kiss on her cheek. He also had a small bouquet of tulips for her. Her big blue eyes smiled at him and she felt more at home than she had in years.

The weekend was a whirlwind of meeting his family, going to the gallery to marvel at his artwork, and then a conference with his publisher friend Greg Mason. Greg was very encouraging of her work, and suggested she send a completed draft to his office as soon as she could. He asked her about any writing classes she had taken, and she had to admit that prior to this book she had not written much since high school, except for a little poetry for the school newspaper while in college. He suggested she find some creative writing classes at a community college to help her brush up on her skills and learn the latest in e-book publishing and marketing.

On their last night together in Ohio, Jean and Nathan sat outside on his porch swing, sharing a bottle of wine and watching the moon rise over the city. Her head was resting on his shoulder, and he had one of her hands clasped tightly in his. Then he asked a question she was NOT expecting.

"I was just wondering........since you work as a consultant and travel all the time, is there any reason why you couldn't have your home base here in Cincinnati instead of St. Louis? I know you have family there, but ....." and his voice trailed off into the darkness.

Jean found herself unable to breathe for a second or two. What exactly was he asking her?

"It's not that I'm trying to rush anything," he added quickly. "It's just that I would love to have you closer, so we could actually SEE each other instead of using face time or text messages. And it will be easier to tell where our relationship is going."

Jean paused for a moment or two, and after catching her breath, answered, "No, there's no reason I can't be here instead of St. Louis. And yes, I think spending more time together would be a good thing. A wonderful thing." She smiled up at him, and he placed a gentle kiss on her forehead. And it was then that she realized that she truly was in love with him, the kind of lovc she had never felt before.

Within three months she had packed up her few belongings and said goodbye to her family. Nathan flew to St. Louis so he could help her drive the U-Haul to Cincinnati. She had rented an apartment sight unseen but on Nathan's suggestions, and was pleased to see that it was more than adequate and fairly close to the airport. Soon she was unpacked, and she and Nathan continued to spend most every evening together that she was in town, either at her place or his, sharing dinner and talking late into the night. She enrolled in a creative writing class at the community college that met only on Saturdays, so she did not miss out when she travelled during the week. The assignments were challenging and really pushed her skills, but she could see the improvement in her writing.

Shortly after her move, Nathan's publisher friend Greg Mason called her with the exciting news that they had decided to publish "Fountain of Love" and were planning an extensive schedule of book signings and television promotion, focusing on her new-writer status and her unusual path to authorship. She was going to be a published author! Nathan took her out to an expensive restaurant to celebrate, and gave her a sapphire necklace that just matched the blue of her eyes. He enclosed a note that said *"I am so very proud of you! I knew the day that we met by the Fountain that you were destined for stardom – I love you, Nathan."*

The rest of the year was a blur of travel for work and travel for book signings. Eventually, she decided that she could cut her job back to part-time and focus more on her writing and schoolwork. And Nathan, of course. In December she accepted the position of mentor to new pharmaceutical consultants, and now most of her time was spent on the phone or answering emails. Her travel schedule was greatly reduced, leaving her even more time for the things (and people) she truly loved. Nathan surprised her with a weekend in the Tennessee mountains for Christmas, and they spent most of the holiday wrapped in each other's arms in front of the fireplace, whispering words of love. She gave him an expensive Italian watch that she ordered from a craftsman she met in Rome, and he got her a soft pink sweater that gently framed her face and accentuated her rosy cheeks. In one of the pockets was a Roman coin he had rescued from the Trevi Fountain all those months ago.

So today, February 13, Jean was in Dallas for the final stop on her book tour which had been a HUGE success, and she was amazed by her growing sales and popularity. Her publisher Greg had recently contacted her about doing a sequel, or perhaps a series of travel love stories. She was exhausted but excited, and ready to go home to spend Valentine's Day with Nathan – her first ever with a boyfriend. He said he had a beautiful night planned for them to celebrate not only their love but also her great book tour. But ice was accumulating on the wings of her plane, and airport maintenance was de-icing as fast as they could. Jean sent a text to Nathan letting him know that she was not sure when – or if - they would get out of Dallas; the weather was deteriorating with each passing minute. She told him she would just take a taxi home from the airport, but of course he insisted on being there to meet her.

Finally after almost two hours, the plane was in the air and heading toward Ohio. Jean leaned back in her seat and tried to rest, but found her mind too excited to let her unwind. She pulled a small mirror from her purse, and checked her makeup and her hair. That was another big change from the past few years – taking more of an interest in her appearance. Her red hair had gotten quite long, and she loved to style it in soft waves. Her blue eyes were now accentuated by a hint of eyeshadow, and she applied her favorite shade of lipstick to her full lips, which always seemed to be smiling these days. Gone was the look of fatigue and depression that haunted her before, replaced instead with the glisten of optimism, of love.

The flight itself was rather uneventful once they got out of the Texas ice storm. Soon they were approaching Cincinnati, and Jean was ready to leap from her seat and into Nathan's arms. As she came down the escalator that led to the baggage claim, she saw him; a dozen red roses in one hand and a cup of coffee in the other. After a lengthy embrace, they found her bag on the carousel and moved toward the exit. But then he stopped in front of a "Visit Italy" travel poster and got down on one knee. Holding a small box out to her and motioning to the poster, said "Jean, I know it's not the real Trevi Fountain, but that is where I fell in love with you. These past several months have only confirmed that love in my heart. Will you do me the honor of becoming my wife?"

Oblivious to everyone around her, Jean held out her hand to him and smiled. "Of course, my dear Nathan! I love you, too."

The crowd around them cheered as he opened the box and placed a beautiful diamond and sapphire ring onto her finger. Then he kissed away a tear that had slid down her cheek, and together they walked out into the cold February night.

STAPLE

BOARDING PASS

BOARDING PASS

Sullivan, Joel

FRA – JFK

Chapter Five

Global Air

PASSENGER RECEIPT 1 OF 1

Sullivan, Joel

SEAT NUMBER

17E

Date and Time

APRIL 16, 2026

05:07 PM

Destination: JFK

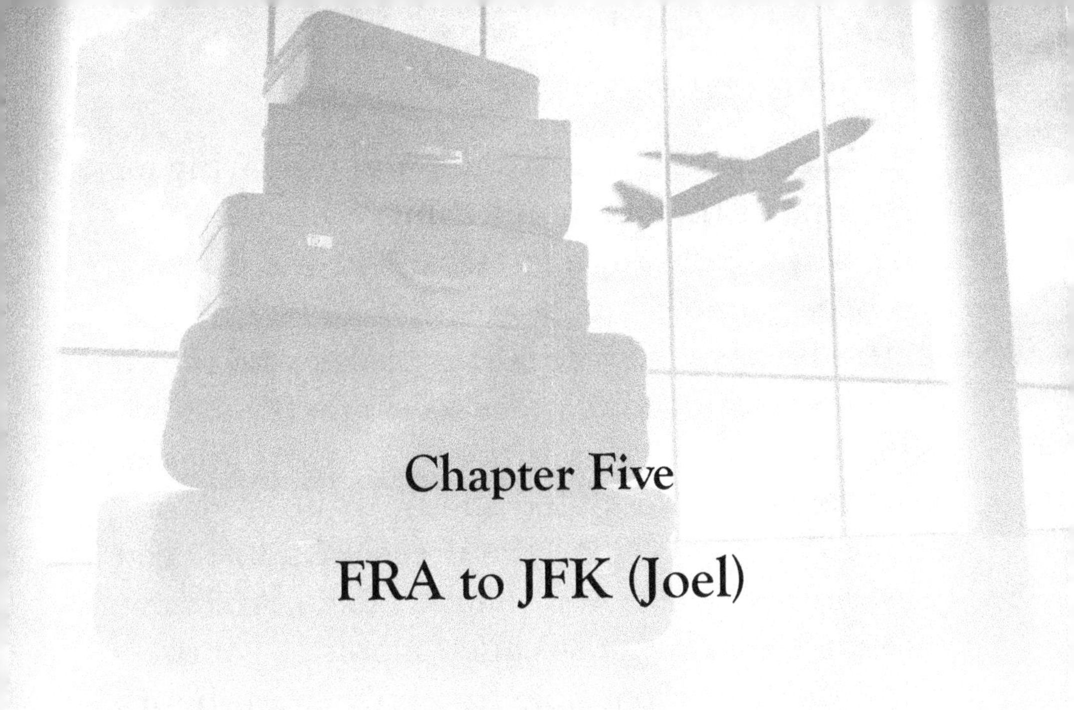

Chapter Five

FRA to JFK (Joel)

Joel Sullivan was numb. That was really the only way to explain it. He had a feeling that people could be yelling at him or throwing things at him and he wouldn't be able to see or hear or feel any of it. It was all static, and had been for the majority of their layover in Frankfurt up to now, as his plane was speeding somewhere over the Atlantic Ocean. In some unfathomable amount of hours they would land in New York City, where they would get on yet another plane that would take them to Dallas. Then there was another hour and a half by car before they would get home.

Home. Joel gave a little grimace as he thought of the state of the place when they'd left it. Kristen's nesting instincts had kicked in, but with all of the rushing around and preparing for their trip to Ethiopia, many things were still half-done. Three out of the four walls in the nursery had been painted a pale green, but one was still white. The bassinet was still in pieces, and they'd somehow managed to order a crib mattress that didn't fit inside the crib they'd bought. Piles of purchased and donated clothing littered one side of the room, since the dresser hadn't been delivered yet. There was so much to do. And now, it seemed, there was so much more.

It didn't seem possible that only seven hours earlier, Joel's beautiful wife Kristen had returned from the airplane lavatory with a pale face and vacant green eyes, telling him that she suspected she might be pregnant. From the way those words weighed on him, he felt as though he'd been carrying them like a burden for years. And indeed, he did remember the first and second times Kristen had come to him with the same message. The first time, he'd been so elated, so overjoyed. The second time, he'd been pleased but wary. Now...he didn't even know how to feel yet.

He'd sent Kristen off to take the pregnancy test in the bathroom at the Frankfurt airport. Though she'd been gone less than ten minutes, it had felt like years. And when she emerged holding the positive test, they'd held one another and sobbed until it was time to board the next flight. They hadn't discussed anything, had tabled all conversation until they could trust themselves to be reasonable and rational.

It was just too much after this roller coaster of a week. Flying halfway across the world and meeting the most beautiful child in the universe, the one that God had chosen for his family--that should have been the height of his excitement. Kristen had succumbed to exhaustion, slouching gracefully against the window, but Joel was wired, brow furrowed against the rising tide of new things to think about and to worry about and to pray about.

First, would this change their adoption plans? It would be so expensive and complicated to back out now. He thought of the little boy, not even three months old, with his delicate skin the color of darkest mahogany. Although he'd agreed to try not to get attached until the court date, he'd begun to narrow down his list of names. He had always teased Kristen that they should name their children Kristoff and Jolene just to mess with people, but he'd had a secret stash of names he liked, family names and such. Ever since meeting the baby boy in the Ethiopian orphanage, he'd toyed with the idea of naming him Seth, after his grandfather. How could he turn his back on him now? It was unthinkable.

Having settled his side of the argument for that point, Joel thought of the next problem. Once little Seth Sullivan came home to them, Kristen would--*could*--be into her second trimester of pregnancy with another baby. If all went well, he would be doubling the size of his family in less than a year. He'd known plenty of men with several children close together in age, and all of them seemed to be slaves to their jobs so that they could be good providers. Would Joel's weekends be full of overtime instead of playtime? Would Kristen be able to drop her part time job and stay home, or would her income be needed to help feed and clothe a second infant?

It was a problem that he would be only too lucky to have, Joel realized. "Third time's a charm" logic was hardly scientific, and he knew there was every possibility that Kristen could miscarry yet again. His whole body shuddered at the thought. He'd seen men die in battle right before his eyes, but nothing had been worse than losing a potential child not once but twice. Seeing the toll it had taken on his wife was unbearable as well. Could they survive another tragcdy like that? Would Seth's presence help or hinder them in that dark time?

Joel pinched the bridge of his nose between his thumb and forefinger and squeezed his eyes shut against this painful train of thought. He knew the only way to survive any of it was to rest in the faith that had brought him this far. He had faith in his God and in his country and in his girl, and that had gotten him through all the hard times leading up to now. He went ahead and let himself daydream that he was blessed enough to be the father of both children. But just as the beautiful picture of their family of four solidified in his mind, a new fear crept up inside of him.

The picture was one of a blended family, something that wasn't so uncommon anymore in most of the world, but it would stand out in rural Texas to those who didn't know their story. Joel was outdoorsy and usually sported a fairly deep tan, but Kristen was as pale as porcelain. Any biological child of theirs would look nothing like the little dark-skinned angel they'd met in that dry Ethiopian village. Even if they gave the boy a family name, he would look different, would be different. Would that mean that he would be treated differently?

Will our friends and family love my biological child more? Joel wondered. *Will the fact that Kristen carried him inside of her make her love him more? Will I love him more because he is my flesh and blood?*

These worries seized his heart and lungs and made it difficult to breathe for a while. He felt guilty for thinking this way, but it couldn't be helped. And while he was beating himself up, he went ahead and let himself worry for the hundredth time about how he would deal with the racial questions that would surely arise. While he was certain there was plenty that he could spiritually and morally pour into his adopted son, at the end of the day, he had no idea how to be the father of a young black boy. He knew with complete certainty that this boy's life experience would be different to his own, and he wasn't at all sure how to prepare him for that. In fact, he didn't even know who to ask for advice. Though he'd had several black soldiers as friends while he'd served in the Army, there wasn't a lot of racial diversity back home. It was one of those things that shouldn't matter, but in his heart he knew that it did.

He glanced to his right at the middle-aged black man in the aisle seat beside him, wondering idly if he should wake him and pick his brain about the subject. The man had put on noise-cancelling headphones and fallen asleep seconds after takeoff and had been unconscious since. But only a second after Joel had turned to look at him now, he began to stir. Not wanting to be caught staring, Joel went back to scowling into space, losing himself to worry while his neighbor stretched and popped his knuckles.

"Sorry, do you speak English?" the man said in a deep voice, thick with sleep.

"Yeah," Joel said, noting the obvious relief that came over the man's face. "What's up?"

"I just wondered what time it was," he replied. "How much longer until we land?"

Joel pulled out his cell phone and checked the clock, but realized that it was still on Frankfurt time. He did the complicated flight math and finally figured out that they would be landing in a little over two hours.

"Ugh, I was hoping my sleeping pill would get me all the way there," the man said. "I'm not a very good flyer."

Joel grinned. He seemed to get seated next to nervous flyers a lot. "You should have been on this flight last week," he said kindly. "Big storms, crazy turbulence. You picked a nice calm day to fly."

The man didn't seem particularly comforted. "I didn't want to do it at all, but sometimes when the mountain doesn't come to Muhammed, Muhammed must go to the mountain." He gave a weak little chuckle. "The mountain in question is my daughter."

"Ah," Joel said, trying to understand.

"I've been begging her to come home for a visit, but decided it would probably be easier for me to go to her. Do you have kids?"

"Uh, we've got one on the way," Joel said awkwardly, glancing over at Kristen to make sure she was still resting comfortably.

"Wow," the man said, removing his neck pillow and setting it in his lap. "Congratulations! You'll be in my boat soon enough. Kids will cling to you and rely on you and then one day *poof!* they will be independent and you'll be useless."

Joel smiled. "I'm sure your daughter appreciated you visiting. Does she live in Germany?"

"For now," the man said. "She married an Air Force Staff Sergeant and he's currently stationed at Ramstein."

"I'm a former PFC in the Army myself," Joel told him. "I know the drill, but I didn't want it as my career."

"Thank you for your service," the man said brightly, and reached out to shake his hand.

"Thank you, sir," Joel replied.

"What's your name, son?"

"Joel Sullivan. That's my wife, Kristen," he added in a lower voice.

"Elias Porter," the man offered, aiming a fatherly smile at Kristen's blanket-covered shoulder. "Is that a Texas accent that I hear?"

"Yes sir," Joel answered with surprise. "How did you guess?"

"My mother's family is from Houston."

"But that's not home for you?" Joel wondered, not detecting any sort of a southern drawl in Elias's voice.

"Oh no, I was born and raised in Jersey. I've barely been out of state, but since my daughter was married, I've visited her at three bases, two of which were overseas. The base in London wasn't so bad. At least everyone spoke English. It sounds stupid, but I really didn't think it would be so hard to get around without knowing the language. I'm a city boy and no stranger to public transit, but German is complicated!"

Joel laughed for the first time in what felt like weeks. "I could say that it's a heck of a lot easier than Arabic or Kurdish, but honestly, anything that's not your native tongue is hard."

"You served in the Middle East then?" Elias asked. "Wow, then I definitely thank you for your service. Are you glad you didn't stay in?"

"Oh yes. It was never meant to be a lifelong commitment. I did what I needed to do so that I could pay for college and provide for my family. Even if I'd had a taste for it, which I didn't, my girl never would have agreed to it." He chuckled and gave a fond glance over at Kristen.

"See, now that's what I would have said about my daughter too," Elias said, scratching his chin, which was slightly prickly with gray stubble. "I turned up in Germany expecting to see her frazzled and ready to get out. Her husband is due to re-up soon, and I thought she'd beg me to try and talk him out of it. I never expected her to make it as a military wife, but she wasn't just surviving. She was thriving. When she was growing up, you could barely walk in her room, she had so much stuff, and she wasn't exactly tidy. But her little apartment on base was neat as a pin and the whole place looked like a page out of a minimalism catalog. She claimed it was just easier, since they would likely have to move over and over, but I could tell it was more than that. She had grown up. She'd found her niche and I was going to have to accept that."

"How's that going?" Joel asked slyly.

Elias let out a rumbling laugh. "To be honest, I had more concerns about her marrying a white boy than the fact that he was a soldier. I'm not prejudiced or anything, I just grew up in a time when that wouldn't have gone over so well. I didn't think she understood what she was getting into. Naturally, as soon as I got to know the kid, I realized that I was the one who'd misunderstood everything. He's a good man, or at least I thought so until he moved my baby girl halfway around the world when they both know I hate to fly."

Joel gave the older man a nudge with his elbow, a gesture of solidarity. "But she's happy there with him. And at the end of the day, that's all that matters, right?"

"It's not anything like the life I would have chosen for her," Elias admitted. "But yes. She's found a way to bloom where she was planted, as they say."

Joel looked over at Kristen. Even dead asleep with her mouth hanging open, looking every bit like a sick person who had been traveling for the last twenty hours, she was the most beautiful thing he'd ever seen. He hadn't always provided the best soil for her, but she had bloomed magnificently anyway. "I think women are just so much stronger than we could possibly give them credit for," he said. "I've done my best to give my girl the world, you know, but life happens. It's never perfect, no matter how hard you try. But she's survived things that would have knocked me flat."

"Sounds like she's got what it takes to be a mother," Elias said with a yawn.

"Oh, definitely," Joel agreed, and this time when his pulse sped up at the thought of not one but two babies coming soon, he didn't flinch away from it. It still terrified him, and his worries were all still there, but it all seemed just a bit more bearable in that moment.

"I wish you all the best of luck," Elias said after a long pause. He put the neck pillow back on but didn't bother with the headphones this time. "I'm going to try and rest a bit more. You'll wake me when we get close?"

"Of course," Joel said, giving the man a grateful smile. "Sleep well."

He turned to look out the window, trying to see where the blue sky ended and the blue ocean began, but he got distracted by the rhythmic rise and fall of Kristen's shoulder as she slept on. She had always been the anchor of peace and strength in his life, and it didn't look like that would be changing anytime soon. He kissed his fingertips and pressed them ever so lightly to her temple as he pushed her hair back. She stirred for a moment, leaning toward his touch in a way that made him feel needed and consoled all at once. And then he crossed his arms over his chest, closed his eyes, and settled in for the final hours of the flight, feeling that even though he was miles above the earth, he was grounded in something unshakeable.

STAPLE

INSERT TEXT HERE

BOARDING PASS

Narong, Patesh

ATL - DEL

Chapter Six

Global Air

PASSENGER RECEIPT 1 OF 1

Narong, Patesh

SEAT NUMBER

14E

Date and Time

November 22, 2018

1:15 PM

Destination: DEL

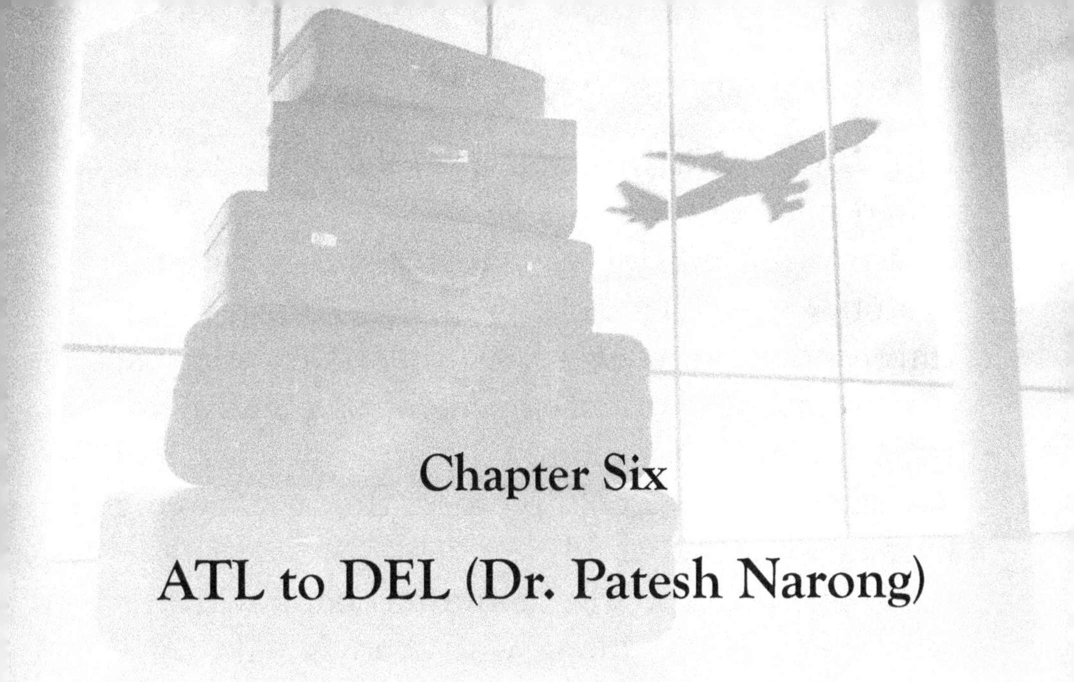

Chapter Six

ATL to DEL (Dr. Patesh Narong)

Patesh was floating in that suspended place between blissful sleep and being awake. He slowly became more aware of the hum of the jet engine, his cramped legs that were jammed into a space much too small, and the soft fragrance of jasmine. He smiled slightly as he inhaled the intoxicating scent again, this time aware of a gentle pressure on his right shoulder. He was almost 50 years old, but was just discovering the joy of the dark-haired beauty resting against him. Patesh glanced to his right and marveled – yet again – that such a gorgeous creature would want to be with him.

Looking around the crowded international plane, he reflected back on the reason for the trip, and how it was one he never dreamed he would need to take.

After his initial press conference in the Atlanta airport 18 months earlier, Patesh found unprecedented success as the CDC's newest researcher. He worked extremely long hours, but within a few short months he and his team had developed a new Ebola protocol that was saving lives around the world.

He spent many weekend afternoons with his new friend Andy, along with Andy's wife Gina and their young twins. He enjoyed the toddlers more than he ever imagined, and realized that he missed having children of his own. They called him "Uncle Pat" which amused him, and he doted on them with toys and books.

He was invited to Andy's house for Christmas, and Gina's sister Gloria was there. They found that they had quite a bit in common, as she was an oncology nurse at the local cancer center. Before long, their friendship blossomed into the beginnings of a romance. Despite their cultural differences and the fact that she was 16 years his junior, they seemed to have a connection that surprised everyone who knew them.

Between his work at the CDC and his new relationship with Gloria, Patesh postponed a return trip to India to see his family. And postponed. And postponed, until now it was too late. About a week ago he got a call from his mother's older brother Ali stating she had passed away in her sleep. Just hours before she passed away, she was calling out for him, begging him to come home. It was as if she knew she was dying, and wanted to see him one last time.

Patesh was awash with grief and guilt. Why had he never gone back, after all that time away and his mother's repeated pleading for him to do so? And what was going to become of his younger brothers and sisters? Even though they were all young adults now, he had a cultural duty as the oldest male, and their futures were ultimately in his hands.

Gloria had been a rock of strength during his initial shock and dismay over his mother's passing. When he mentioned his need to go quickly to India to help with the funeral arrangements and settle her affairs, it was Gloria herself who volunteered to accompany him. She had never flown internationally, and had only left Georgia a few times. Fortunately, she already had a passport for "just in case" and she was able to get some time off from work. Patesh was excited to show his world to her, but recognized that he needed her beside him, more than he ever thought possible.

Sometime during the past week, he realized that everything that had been lacking in his life was fulfilled once Gloria came along. Gone were the lonely days he experienced as a medical student so far from home, and then as a researcher working long hours in the lab. Gone were the sleepless nights when he tossed and turned from worry and guilt. Their romance had progressed slowly but steadily, and just yesterday Patesh had gone to a local jeweler and picked out an engagement ring. The small blue box was tucked safely in the breast pocket of his blazer. Was he really considering such a huge step? Would he know the right time to propose? Would she say yes?

As if reading his mind, Gloria stirred in her seat and opened her hazel eyes to look up at him. She was so tiny – so fragile looking – with her petite frame curled up in her seat and resting securely under his arm. They were such a study in contrasts: he was tall and lean, dark complexioned with eyes so brown they often appeared black. At close to 6 feet 3 inches tall, his always impeccable dress made him a striking figure. Gloria, on the other hand, was barely 5 feet tall with porcelain skin and a pixie cut of raven hair. She was equally as comfortable in a little black dress as she was her nursing scrubs. She was soft and gentle, or could be a force of nature and a bundle of energy – able to be tough when she needed to be but tender when she wanted to be. Her beautiful eyes seemed to dance on her face, and she smiled widely.

"Wow, now that was an interesting way to sleep! Any idea where we are?" she asked sleepily as she stretched and yawned like a tiny kitten.

"Not really," he answered softly, unable to take his eyes off of her. They had flown from Atlanta to LA, and now were somewhere over the Pacific on their way to New Delhi. With the 10 ½ hour time zone difference, his body was confused and wanted to go back to sleep, back to that blissful place with Gloria tucked safely in his arms, her head resting on his chest. But they were both awake now, along with many others on the plane. Seated in the middle section in seats 14E and F, Patesh felt they were crammed in like sardines.

After trips to the lavatory to freshen up a bit, they chatted a while until the flight attendants passed out coffee and a light breakfast. Patesh remembered his first flight to Atlanta when he was too shy to ask for milk to go with his hot tea. He was so much more assertive now, more comfortable in his skin, and he had Gloria to thank for much of that.

The captain announced that they had about three hours to go until they reached the Indira Gandhi Airport in New Delhi. Gloria's eyes widened at the thought of three more hours, after the many hours they had already been in the air. For someone who had rarely been out of Georgia except for a few quick trips to Disney or to Dallas for a nurse's convention, this was quite an adventure.

A young mother paced up and down the aisle near them, holding a sleeping newborn in her arms. Patesh could not help but look at the child's perfect features – button nose, rosy cheeks, head full of dark wavy hair – and wonder what his own children would have looked like. He then noticed that Gloria was watching him, and he shifted in his seat a bit, feeling slightly embarrassed.

"Tell me what you were just thinking," she said gently.

Gloria had been such a good influence on him, and he was more comfortable opening up about his feelings, being honest and vulnerable.

"It was the baby," he said softly. "So beautiful, so perfect, so full of promise. I wonder if I made the wrong decisions years ago and should have had a family when I was much younger. I'll be 50 soon…," he said wistfully and his voice drifted away.

"What about you?" he asked her after a bit. "I'm sure you probably want a houseful. I can imagine you as a great mom."

"Yeah, it's always been part of the dream for me. And of course, we women have that biological clock ticking."

Patesh was totally deflated by her words, and looked way from her beautiful face, saying to her sadly, "Then you should be with someone younger, who can give you that. It's not fair to a child to have a dad who is almost 70 while they are in high school, like I would be."

He felt the weight of the ring box in his pocket, and felt foolish for thinking that young, beautiful Gloria would want an old man like himself.

She reached up to him and gently turned his face towards her.

"Oh Patesh, my dear man. I am here with you because I want to be. I have learned over the years that while life may not always work out the way we planned, the end result is usually so much sweeter than we could have ever imagined. And there are so many other ways to be involved with children – volunteering with groups like Big Brothers and Sisters or scouting, foster parenting, even adopting an older child. I see so many sad situations at the hospital, and I was a CASA volunteer for several years, so I know that there are thousands of children who need a loving home and a consistent, positive environment."

"You would be willing to alter your dream that way, to be with me?" he asked softly, constantly amazed at her capacity for love.

"Of course. The end result is that I want a relationship with a child or children. That can come in many forms, and who is to say which one is right? But more than that, I am happy to be here with you."

Patesh let his eyes wander around the crowed plane, and he observed the numerous families. While most looked pretty traditional, there were many that were not. There were several single parents travelling alone with children. He noticed inter-racial couples with mixed-race children, and also a family with two dads and a rambunctious small boy. Maybe what Gloria said was true, that there was no one right way to be a family.

Patesh spent the rest of the flight deep in thought, evaluating his life and the choices he had made. Gloria attempted – for the 5th or 6th time – to review the maps and travel guides for New Delhi and the surrounding areas, but before long she had fallen asleep again, her long dark lashes caressing the cheek that rested on Patesh's shoulder. He dared not move so as not to disturb her rest – he knew the next several days were going to be very busy, and jet lag would likely catch up with them both.

When the captain announced that they were on initial approach to the airport, Patesh gently touched Gloria's face with his hand. Her hazel eyes slowly fluttered open, and she smiled up at him sleepily.

"All of a sudden I am so nervous," she said once she was fully awake. "The language, the culture, the food – I'm excited to be here with you, but it's so far from home."

"I know," he said gently. "Just stay close to me and you will be fine. The crowds can be overwhelming at times, along with the noise and the poverty. Don't let go of my hand, ok?"

After retrieving their bags and going through customs, they pushed their way through the crowds and out into the street. They hailed an old beat-up taxi and started the long drive through the city towards Patesh's home town of Muthiyani. Childhood memories came rushing back to Patesh – memories of his mother and father, of their daily struggles to feed their large family, of the heat, the squalor, the poverty.

After about two hours, the taxi came to a stop in front of a small, non-descript home on the edge of the town. Patesh's uncle Ali was the first one to greet them. Patesh introduced Gloria as his "special friend from the US" but Ali noticed the tender way he held her hand while helping her from the taxi, and gave her a knowing wink.

Patesh's younger brothers and sisters soon emerged along with various other family members, most of whom were quite surprised to see him with a girl – an American girl – a much younger and beautiful American girl. Patesh had never shown interest in anything or anyone but his studies before, so they were not quite sure what to make of Gloria's presence.

Following his mother's funeral a few days later, Patesh asked Gloria to go with him to a very special place from his childhood. After packing a small lunch and borrowing his cousin Hameed's car, they drove to a remote village several miles away. At first glance, it appeared like any average Indian village, except there was a beautiful spring in the center of town that was surrounded by a small lush green garden. Patesh told her stories about coming here as a young boy and dreaming about far-away places. They sat on a small bench and quietly listened to the babbling water dancing on the surrounding rocks. Gloria closed her eyes to let all of her senses enjoy this experience. Suddenly, Patesh dropped to one knee, and after reaching into his jacket pocket, pulled out the blue box that had been weighing so heavily on his mind this past week. He took Gloria's hands in his, and her eyes opened with surprise.

"My dear, precious Gloria," he said softly. "My life is immensely better because of you, and I would be the most blessed man on Earth if you would agree to be my wife." He opened the box to reveal the modest but lovely ring he had chosen for her.

Gloria's eyes glistened and a smile broke out across her face. "Of course, my dear Patesh. There is nothing I could want more than to be your wife!" He slid the ring onto her finger and kissed her softly. The sparkle of the ring was matched only by the glow of love from her eyes as she gazed at the man she loved.

On their drive back to his family home, they passed by a young girl of about seven or eight who was sitting by herself on the side of the road. Her crudely written sign stated that she was an orphan with no family left to care for her. Gloria insisted that they stop and they rushed to her side. With the help of Patesh as interpreter, Gloria learned that the young girl was named Niree and both of her parents had recently passed away. She had no extended family and was living on the streets.

After asking around a bit to confirm the girl's story, Gloria insisted that she come back with them to the Narong family home. Patesh's Aunt Vedhika got some food together for the girl, and his cousins helped with finding her some clean clothes and giving her a warm bath. The elders of the family held a meeting where they were all in agreement to help her as much as possible.

After dinner, Patesh shared the news with the family that Gloria had agreed to be his wife. Uncle Ali engulfed her in a huge hug, and all of the cousins joined in the celebration. Patesh was just sad that his parents had not lived long enough to meet Gloria and see the happiness she brought to him.

Over the next several days, Gloria became more and more attached to the young orphan Niree, and was dreading leaving her when they returned to the states. What she did not realize was that Patesh had been in contact with the local government to find out the process involved in taking her back to Atlanta with them.

As the day of departure arrived, Gloria was packing her bags while fighting back tears. There was a knock on the front door and Patesh had a hushed conversation with an official-looking gentleman. After the man left, Patesh came to Gloria and put a gentle hand on her shoulder.

"I have one more surprise for you," he said. "Close your eyes and hold out your hands."

Gloria put her hands in front of her, and Patesh slid an envelope between her fingers. "Open it," he urged.

Gloria fumbled with the papers, only to find a legal document she could not read. "Here, I'll help you," he said.

Gloria then noticed that Niree was standing behind him, a big smile on her face. "I won't read all of it," he said, "but the important part is that we have permission to take Niree back to the states with us while her adoption is being finalized, if you want to, that is….."

"If I WANT to?" she exclaimed. "Of course I want to adopt her! But only after I become your wife first!"

Patesh wrapped his arms around his soon-to-be wife and almost-daughter, and knew that his life was complete at last.

STAPLE

INSERT TEXT HERE

BOARDING PASS

MacNamara, G

ORD - LAX

Chapter Seven

Global Air

PASSENGER RECEIPT 1 OF 1

MacNamara, Gerald III

SEAT NUMBER

7A

Date and Time

JUNE 5, 2018

07:14 AM

Destination: LAX

Chapter Seven

ORD to LAX (Mac)

Almost one year after his fateful flight to New York City to try to save his architecture business, Mac found himself again waiting to board a plane, but this time he would be in seat 7A in Business Class, and he was flying west instead of east. This seat was near the front of the plane, with its extra legroom and wider seats, and was in stark contrast to the cramped quarters and humiliation he experienced last year in seat 19F.

The past year had been one of challenges and difficulties, plus a few triumphs along the way. The presentation he made last year for the office building near the World Trade Center site was a huge success, and construction was almost half done. He was able to re-hire of few of the workers he had laid off, and was starting to rebuild the reputation of Mac III. But the satisfaction this brought was tempered by the sense of failure he felt while testifying against his former CFO (and old college friend) who had been caught embezzling over $5 million from the firm.

The trial had been grueling, and it was all Mac could do to avoid hitting the bars after each day of testimony. When it was his turn to testify, Mac noticed that his hands were visibly shaking as he took the stand. The urge for a Scotch and soda was almost overwhelming. He looked at his trusted friend – his college roommate Craig – with tears in his eyes. How could he have been betrayed in this way? How could he have let his drinking get so out of hand that he did not notice the continual discrepancies in the firm's books?

"Do you, Gerald MacNamara the third, swear to tell the truth, the whole truth, and nothing but the truth, so help you God?" the bailiff asked.

"I do," Mac mumbled, as he broke out into a sweat and felt his knees buckle.

Although he was not the one on trial, he was forced to relive the past few years, admitting that he had not paid as much attention to the financial status of the business, and agreeing that his alcoholism had clouded his judgment for months. He recounted how he and Craig had become acquainted at UC Berkley in San

Francisco, eventually becoming roommates. He was the best man at Craig's wedding to a lovely woman named Cindy and godfather of their oldest child Martha.

"So tell me, Mr. MacNamara," the defense attorney probed, "when did your drinking become enough of a problem that, as you testified, you were not paying enough attention to the company finances to notice the missing funds?"

"Object, your Honor!" the prosecutor interrupted. "Irrelevant to the facts of the case!"

"Over-ruled. I will allow this line of questioning but please make it brief," the judge responded.

Mac winced at the insinuation that somehow this was all his fault.

"Once the housing collapse started and we were having to cancel upcoming projects, I started with a drink here or a drink there. As the crisis worsened and we had to start laying off employees, my drinking increased. I began missing board meetings, and usually just glanced at the monthly financials. By the time an outside audit was done and the embezzlement was discovered, I was not functioning well, barely even going into the office anymore."

"Did the defendant ever exhibit any unusual behavior, show any signs of living a more lavish lifestyle, for example? Five million dollars is a lot of money – surely you noticed something!"

"No, I didn't," he said with his eyes downcast to the floor. "But as I said, the last few months I was rarely at the office."

"So, you personally did not witness any misbehavior on the part of the defendant?"

"No. I did not notice much of anything."

The spectators in the courtroom let out a series of whispers and giggles, and Mac stepped down from the witness box, his head hung in shame. They all knew how far he had fallen, how much he had lost. He glanced over at Craig, who was deep in conversation with his attorney. Mac never felt so alone in his life.

Despite Mac's poor performance on the stand, Craig was found guilty of embezzlement and sentenced to 25 years in prison. Mac was visibly shaken by the verdict, and left the courthouse intending to drown his sorrows at the nearest bar. But something stopped him – he had been sober since that fateful meeting with Tess on the flight to New York City last year, when she had tried to convince him that there was hope for his life. He often wondered about her – did she enjoy her trip to Spain and how did the first year of college go? Thinking about her and her optimism for life, he walked past the bar and stopped at a small deli instead. Ordering a pastrami sandwich and a cup of coffee, he relaxed and slowly the alcoholic urges passed. He was getting better at resisting the urges, and he had Tess to thank for that.

As he walked down the aisle of the plane, he was again carrying a tube of architectural drawings and floorplans. He smiled as he remembered Tess's suspicion that he was a spy or a bank robber. He made himself comfortable in the window seat, and as he raised the shade to look outside, he noticed his left hand - still empty of the wedding ring Misty had given him all those years ago. It was odd, though, that his hand did not feel empty anymore. In fact, he hardly remembered how it used to feel.

After returning from last year's trip to New York, Mac had reached out to Misty in an effort to apologize for his behavior in the hopes of winning her back. She remained cold and distant, and within a few weeks their divorce had been finalized. Mac later read in a gossip magazine that she was now involved with an up-and-coming oil company CEO and still travelling in the highest society circles. Maybe she had never really loved him. Maybe he had been totally fooled by her gold-digging expertise. The day he signed the final paperwork to end his marriage (and give her half of his remaining assets) he again ached for a drink or two, or several. But somehow he resisted and instead went for a long walk down by the Navy Pier. He sat on a park bench and felt the sun on his face, the sounds of the water and the birds calming his frazzled nerves. Eventually he made his way back home, and went straight to his drawing board. He found solace in the precision of the lines he drew, and the creativity he felt replaced the pounding in his head, and in his heart.

The plane started filling up, and joining Mac in row 7 was a young man in his late 20's who sat in the middle seat, and eventually an elderly gentleman sat next to the aisle. It was a beautiful summer morning in Chicago, and the plane left right on time. Mac watched out the window as the Chicago skyline faded from sight and before long they were over the expansive farmland of the Midwest. Soon the flight attendants were passing out breakfast and Mac purchased a biscuit sandwich and a cup of coffee. There was not even a passing thought this time about needing something stronger, which was very different from last year when he was craving a drink at 9 AM. He savored the coffee and continued to marvel at how far he had come.

After breakfast was cleared away, the young man in the middle seat introduced himself as Cory Russo. He was on his way to LA to interview for a bank manager position. As a recent graduate from Notre Dame majoring in finance, he was ready to take on the world. Mac remembered feeling that way – it seemed so long ago. Even though Mac was only in his mid-forties, the glow and ambition Cory exuded made Mac smile as he remembered how invincible he once felt, ready to tackle the architecture world with his grand plans for skyscrapers and giant super-structures. Cory had spent a few years paying his dues in small Illinois banks, but now a major financial powerhouse had wanted him for a prestigious regional manager opportunity, and he couldn't wait to make a name for himself in the LA financial community. Mac admired his drive, his determination, his focus for the future. He could not remember exactly when his own focus and drive had faded, but spending time with Tess, and now Cory, had revitalized it a bit. It was easy for him to get caught up in the enthusiasm of youth, and to feel his own heart and spirit restored.

Mac eventually switched his attention to the elderly gentleman seated near the aisle. He introduced himself as Walter Williams, an 87 year—old retired Navy captain who had served in the Korean War. His wife had passed away several years prior, and he was on his way to central California to spend time with his daughter and her family.

"Where in California, exactly?" Mac asked. "I spent my college days in the Bay area, and loved to run up and down the 101 and the PCH whenever I got a chance."

"She lives just north of San Luis Obispo, in Morro Bay," Walter told him. "I love it there – it's about as different from Chicago as you can get. She's been pestering me to move out there permanently, but I'm not sure. My wife Louise is buried in Chicago, and it just doesn't feel right to leave her. But Eve is our only child, the only family I have left. It would be nice to be closer to her and watch her kids grow up. I've missed so much already, and it's hard getting old all alone. I have a few injuries from the war, and it's tough getting around by myself. Maybe I should really consider it."

"Oh, Morro Bay is great! I got caught there one time when the marine layer moved in faster than I anticipated, and the area was socked in with fog. I had to spend the night in a little B&B and then race back up to school the next day. I missed a HUGE test that I should have stayed at school to study for instead of cutting class and driving around, and it almost cost me my grade in the class. Do they still have that great restaurant right on the bay........I forget the name, something about *looking at the water*?"

"Windows on the Water? Yes, it's still there. It's one of our favorite places to go. Wow, such a small world. I've never gotten used to how quickly the marine layer can move in, either. My daughter can read the signs of course, and knows exactly when we need to get home."

"What is a *marine layer*?" Corey asked.

"Oh, you need to learn about it if you are going to live in California!" Mac answered. "It's when there is a contrast between warm air and cold air, and it turns into a really thick fog that sometimes hangs around for days. It was really prevalent up in the San Francisco area, but also all up and down the coast. I can't tell you how many times I drove across the Golden Gate Bridge in fog so thick you could not see the water or the cars in the other lanes. It's crazy! But then the water temperature can raise 1 degree, and POOF! It's gone! Like I said, crazy."

"And it can move onshore really quickly," Walter added. "One minute it looks like it is a hundred miles offshore, just hanging around, then suddenly it has you surrounded with the thickest pea soup that leaves you lost and disoriented. You only need to get caught out in it once to learn your lesson!"

The three men, in three very different and distinct phases of life, continued to share stories. Mac told them about his architectural business, and the new building near the World Trade Center site. He explained that the reason for his trip to LA was a presentation to build a new LA

Convention Center – his biggest project to date. If he got the job, he would be able to rehire the rest of the employees he had to lay off, and it would be a huge step in re-establishing the prestige of his company. But he left out the challenges with his drinking, the embezzlement, or the breakdown of his marriage. The humiliation of his failures was a bit too fresh, too raw, and he was trying to stay focused on the positive.

"Wow, that impressive!" Cory noted. "Big money, big business. Gotta love it!"

"I'm sure it's taken you a very long time to plan such a huge building," Walter said with admiration. "Here I am, sitting with two titans of finance and industry. Impressive indeed."

"Where are my manners?" Mac said with embarrassment. "I never did thank you for your service. And I truly do mean that – what you guys did for our country can never be repaid."

"Yes, I agree," Cory added. "I have many family members and friends who have served, or are currently serving. I admire all of you immensely."

"Thank you," Walter said with misty eyes. "I lost my very best friend about a week before the war was over and we all got to come home. He paid the ultimate price – my aches and pains and discomforts are nothing compared to his sacrifice."

Their conversation lagged a bit, each man returning to his own thoughts, and Mac got out his briefcase to review his notes before they landed in LA. A lot was riding on this presentation, but he didn't feel the sense of panic that he did last year. Tess's words kept ringing in his ears, "Poor is an attitude, and one that you don't have." He had tried so hard over the past year to improve his attitude, to live in a way that would make her proud. Their random crossing of paths had impacted more than just his desire to quit drinking or try to win Misty back.

Mac looked again at the two men who were sharing his row with him. They were such a study in contrasts. Cory – so full of life and the confidence of youth that would allow him to take on the world. Mac, who was in the middle of his career – experiencing some successes but also suffering a few losses and defeats. The stresses of life had caught up with him, and he bore their scars. Lastly was Walter – in the final stages of his life but able to look back with both fondness and tears. Mac could only hope that he was as gracious and kind when he reached that age.

After a while, Mac could see the sprawling city of Los Angeles on the horizon. Cory leaned toward the window and Mac pointed out a few of the most notable landmarks. Cory had never been to LAX before, and both Mac and Walter gave him pointers about finding the baggage claim and where the rental car area was.

The pilot announced that they were on final approach to LAX, and Mac felt optimistic and ready for his presentation. After retrieving his tube of floorplans from the overhead bin, he made his way up the aisle. It was then that he noticed that the main flight attendant had a name tag with "Tess" written in bold letters. He smiled and felt that it was a good omen of sorts. But he knew that however the meeting turned out, he was living in a way that would make her proud, and somehow that mattered more to him than anything.

BOARDING PASS

STAPLE

BOARDING PASS

PASSENGER RECEIPT 1 OF 1

Davis, Lisa

Global Air

Davis, Lisa

SEAT NUMBER

13C

ORD - DSM

Chapter Eight

Date and Time

JUNE 13, 2017

04:00 PM

Destination: DSM

Chapter Eight

ORD to DSM (Lisa)

Lisa was sitting in the boarding area at Chicago O'Hare airport, ready to fly back to Des Moines and home to her family and her quiet life. Just minutes before the ticket agent was to begin the boarding process, the relative calm of the busy terminal was shattered by tornado sirens. Lisa and nearly 100 other women huddled in the ladies' rest room for what seemed hours (but was probably only 30 minutes) while a severe thunderstorm pounded the tarmac with rain and golf ball-sized hail. The crowded restroom was uncomfortable, damp, and just a bit smelly, and Lisa tried to focus on the fact that they were in the safest place possible under the circumstances. Several of the women were obviously not from the Midwest, and were unfamiliar with tornado sirens. A few were crying, and a young girl who was flying alone was being consoled by a flight attendant. Once the storm had passed, they emerged from their shelter and the airport struggled to get back on schedule and to get passengers to their destinations. Several of the planes had been damaged by the hail, and several flights had to be cancelled and re-scheduled. Lisa was thankful that her plane was cleared to fly.

She called her husband Kevin to tell him of the delay, but got his voice mail. She left a message, assuring him that she was fine, and that she would be home as soon as possible.

Settling into her aisle seat 13C, Lisa closed her eyes and reflected back on the past few days with her sisters Rebecca and Susan. She and Susan had done all of the "touristy" things they had planned – shopping, seeing the Broadway play "Wicked" and visiting the Navy Pier. One afternoon was spent at the Shedd Aquarium, and the rest of the time they just wandered wherever they wanted, with snacks at sidewalk cafes and lunches at trendy bistros. Rebecca had joined them for lunch the first day Lisa arrived, but had been pretty absent otherwise as she was tied up with a high-profile criminal case she was prosecuting. She did finally meet them at the observation sky deck of the Sears Tower at 9 PM last night, and they marveled at the spectacular city views at sunset. The conversation was forced and unnatural, though, and she did not stay long, claiming she needed to rush home and prepare for the next day's testimony.

This morning after a leisurely breakfast at Susan's house, the two sisters visited Rosehill Cemetery where their parents were buried. As one of Chicago's oldest and largest cemeteries, Lisa would have gotten lost had Susan not been with her. Brushing leaves away from the grave markers, Lisa placed a small spray of fresh flowers in a bronze urn that was inscribed with her mother's favorite Bible verse. Lisa had not been here since her father's funeral, and it was the first time to see his date of death engraved into the marker.

Susan sensed that Lisa needed some private time, so she silently stepped away to give her the space she needed. Sitting on the ground facing her parents' graves, Lisa poured out her heart to them. She told them about her life in Winterset, how the kids were doing, but mostly how much she missed them. She apologized for not being around more before they died, for sacrificing time with them to be with her own family. She realized now that Kevin and the kids would have gotten along fine without her, and she could have made more of an effort to be with her mom and dad during their final days and years.

After several minutes of weeping tears of regret and asking for forgiveness, Lisa rose to her feet and turned back to where Susan had been standing. To her surprise, Rebecca's BMW was parked down the drive a bit, and she and Susan were in the midst of a heated argument. Impassioned words such as "disrespectful" and "selfish" drifted toward Lisa on the warm summer breeze.

She hurried toward them, and Rebecca flashed an angry sneer her direction. "I suppose you are going to take *her* side again, like you always do!" she growled, pointing at Susan who was visibly shaken by the confrontation.

"Well, if that's the way you are talking to her, of course I will!" Lisa snapped back. "What in the world is going on? What is wrong with you two? Why are you doing this in the middle of a cemetery?"

"Ask the spoiled baby sister – I'm sure she will say it is all my fault, as usual."

Susan looked like she wanted to cry and run away. Lisa put a protective arm around her shoulder, which made Rebecca turn her face away in disgust. "What happened honey?" Lisa asked, peering into Susan's tear-stained face.

"I simply asked why she felt her job and its prestige was more important than us, or our parents. You have no idea what it was like for me, always the one to take care of everything and everyone. She breezes in and out, making a big splash and taking the credit for everything I did for them over the years. I was the one who sacrificed family time to take them to appointments, handle medications, make sure the bills were paid, hold their hands while they were lonely or in pain. She was here in Chicago the whole time, but rarely came to visit or even call. And now that they're gone, she drives around in her big fancy car, bringing expensive flowers and acting all high and mighty."

It was then that Lisa noticed the bouquet of flowers that Rebecca had brought for the urn. To call it *extravagant* was an understatement. Lisa glanced back at the lowly arrangement she had brought, and felt instantly inferior. Again – Rebecca always made her feel inferior.

"You're no better, you know!" Rebecca snapped at Lisa. "You weren't around much, claiming that your husband and kids needed you more than our parents did. But yet, no one was mad at you. How is that possible?"

Lisa looked at Rebecca, and noticed something she had never seen before. For all of the bravado and angry words, Rebecca's eyes were glistening with unshed tears, and her voice quivered a bit.

"And I don't just *breeze in and out*, as you say, Susan," Rebecca continued. "I know I wasn't around as much as you were while dad was sick, but I was at the hospital after mom's accident and rarely left her side. I spent hours working through the probate of their fairly large estate, and while this may not matter much to you, I have been here many, many times, keeping the flowers fresh and working with the landscapers to make sure everything is as beautiful as possible. I am on the Board of Directors of this cemetery, and we meet every month to discuss maintenance and vandalism issues. Did you know that their urn was stolen a few months ago? No? I thought not. I replaced it with the one you see here, with my own funds."

"I had no idea," Susan said sheepishly. "I'm sorry for attacking you." She instinctively reverted back to her role as the baby sister, always deferring to the older and more assertive Rebecca.

Lisa was not quite sure how to react to the emotionally-charged scene she had just witnessed. She knew she carried her own resentments toward Rebecca, and maybe now was the time for all of them to clear the air.

"I have a few questions," Lisa directed toward Rebecca. "Why all the secrecy? Why not just tell us about the stolen urn or the cemetery board? Why do you seem to distance yourself from us so much? You don't return phone calls or emails, and we are lucky to get a Christmas card from you. All we hear about is when you are prosecuting an important case and I see you on the national news. I don't know about Susan, but it makes me feel very inferior and inconsequential."

"Inferior? You? I'm the one who feels inferior! You both have your homes and your families and your pets, and Mom and Dad were so proud of all that the two of you have done. All I have is Lawrence and an empty condo. Oh, it may look like we are happy and successful, but deep inside it is a hollow collection of silent rooms. Lawrence and I barely speak to each other anymore. Early in our careers we were so focused on success that we decided against children. When all is said and done, who is going to miss me when I am gone? Have you ever considered that maybe I keep busy so I don't have to be alone in my empty home, dwelling on the mistakes of the past? I envy you two so much, you have no idea."

Lisa couldn't resist, and rushed to Rebecca's side. Looking deep into her eyes, she put her arms around her big sister. Susan did the same, and the three of them stood there beside the BMW, crying for their parents, and for the miscommunications and hurts of the past many years.

After several minutes, Susan started to giggle, and then Lisa, and finally Rebecca joined them.

Like young girls without a care in the world, they held hands and walked back to their parents' graves. Rebecca took the lead and spoke for all of them. "Mom, Dad, here we are - your daughters who love you and miss you more than you will ever know. We have been stubborn and let our pride come between us, but no more. We have cleared the air, and are here to show you that we love each other, and you. Never again will we let such insignificant things come between us."

They stood their quietly, and then Susan started to softly sing a line from their father's favorite hymn. "Whatever my lot, Thou has taught me to say, it is well, it is well with my soul." The three of them stood there silently, still holding hands, and off in the distance a dove was gently "coo-cooing." After a few more minutes and numerous more hugs, Rebecca climbed into her BMW to drive back to work and Susan took Lisa to the airport for her flight home.

The plane was in the air now – Lisa didn't even remember the safety speech or the plane taking off. She felt like such a weight had been lifted from her shoulders, and she was ready to get home and hug the family she loved so much.

She opened her purse and looked again at a note she had written last night. Kevin had called while they were at the Sears Tower to tell her that their son Shane had decided to go on a college visit to the University of Iowa tomorrow to talk to the baseball coach about a scholarship. After his game-winning home run last week, the school had contacted him about arranging a visit. Coach Hagerman was particularly interested in recruiting him to play 2nd base, a position he loved.

When the flight attendants passed out drinks and pretzels, Lisa savored the snack, realizing she had not eaten since breakfast and was quite hungry. The events at the cemetery and the excitement of the tornado warning had caused her to forget to pick up a sandwich prior to leaving Chicago.

Before long, the plane began to shake and quiver, and Lisa looked out the window to see a scattering of dark clouds and streaks of lightning. The pilot announced that there was a large line of thunderstorms stretching between Chicago and Des Moines, and he was trying to guide the plane around them as best he could. Soon there was a *ping* and the fasten seat-belt sign came on. The flight attendants collected the cups and miscellaneous trash, and everyone was instructed to stay seated and securely buckled in. Without much warning, the plane pitched to the left and dropped a few dozen feet. Several people gasped and a few screams were heard from the back of the plane. Lisa looked out the window again and saw the most violent storm she had ever flown through.

Lightning flashed just outside her window, and the plane continued to shake and reverberate from the thunder and fierce winds. Hail was beating against the plane, and the sound was deafening. The plane was being tossed around like a toy boat in a hurricane. Lisa found herself digging her fingernails into the armrests on either side of her. The middle seat in her row was empty, but the young girl sitting next to the window was terrified, her eyes squeezed shut and tears streaming down her face. Children were whimpering, and she even heard an elderly couple sitting behind her recite the Lord's Prayer. Lisa wished that she could talk to Kevin, but of course she was not allowed to use her phone while on the plane, especially during a storm. She thought of her life in Winterset, her husband whom she adored, her children, even her garden. She hoped that thinking pleasant thoughts would keep her focus away from the raging storm outside.

The sky continued to get darkcr, and the hail seemed like it was about to break the windows. But then, just as quickly as it started, it stopped. Patches of beautiful blue sky could be seen between the towering thunderheads, and the plane was soon sailing smoothly again toward

Des Moines. Everyone onboard seemed to let out a collective sigh of relief. After a few minutes, the seatbelt sign was turned off, and the passengers were free to move about the cabin as usual.

Finally able to breathe normally again, Lisa reached into her bag and retrieved the State Fair article she had saved from *The Des Moines Register* she had read during her flight to Chicago a few days ago. The Fair was only a few weeks away now, and she would be judging pies and cakes and spending her days in Des Moines - something she never imagined she would enjoy so much. When not actually working the Fair, she loved to wander to the other exhibits; the flowers, the livestock, the handcrafts. She would often sit in the shade beside an outdoor band shell and listen to high school bands perform, eating kettle corn and sipping lemonade. She was envious of those kids with such amazing musical ability, since it was a gift she certainly did not have. Her father had loved to sing, and as a small child, Lisa had enjoyed standing next to him in church, his bass voice belting out "Holy, Holy, Holy" or "Victory in Jesus." Such powerful memories, even after all these years. She remembered her daughter Miranda standing on the pew between herself and Kevin. Lisa pointed to the words in the hymnal to help her learn to read, just as her own father had done for her.

The plane was making its approach to the Des Moines airport, and Lisa put the article back into her purse. She was SO GLAD to be this close to home. She wanted to give Shane a big hug, and curl up in Kevin's arms while watching a movie and fall asleep early.

The plane made a fairly smooth landing and taxied toward the gate. Lisa waited impatiently for her turn to make her way up the aisle and into the terminal. Being so close to home made her suddenly very anxious and excited.

As she was about to stand up to leave, she head a *ding* on her phone indicating she had a text message. She glanced at it, and noticed the message was from Kevin. She decided to wait until she was in the terminal to read it and respond to tell him how soon she would be home.

After inching her way off the plane, she stopped at the restroom and then slipped into a chair at Starbucks for a muffin and some juice and to check her messages. Instead of the "Hi honey, welcome home!" she was expecting, her heart sank at the words she saw.

"Hey, love. I know you are probably still on the plane, but needed to tell you this ASAP. Shane was just in a pretty nasty car accident and has been life-flighted to Mercy Hospital in Des Moines. At this point we're not sure how bad it is, other than a broken leg and a punctured lung.

I'm on my way there, but text me as soon as you land, ok? Hopefully I'll have some updated news by then. Love you."

Lisa's hands began to shake, and her throat was dry as she read the words over and over. Shane, her baby.......hurt! She needed to get there right away! She sent a quick text to Kevin letting him know that she had just landed and found his message. She would grab her luggage and drive straight to the hospital. Did he have an update for her now?

Kevin replied quickly, "I just got to the ER a few minutes ago. He's still in x-ray and they are also going to do a CT scan of his abdomen. The doctors are worried about internal bleeding. I'll fill you in on the rest when you get here. Love you."

Lisa's bag was one of the first to come up on the carousel, and she grabbed it and practically ran out the door into the warm summer evening. Fortunately, the hospital was not all that far from the airport, and she was there in just a few minutes. She parked in the ER parking lot and sprinted toward the door. She found Kevin sitting in the waiting room, looking afraid and alone. His eyes lit up a bit and he seemed relieved to see her rush across the room to him.

He filled Lisa in on the details of the accident. Shane and his buddy Tommy had been working on an old Chevy all weekend, and after lunch today decided to take it out for a spin. Tommy was driving up and down the country roads and they were talking and laughing, when suddenly the brakes went out and they flew off the road into a ditch, and then straight into a tree. Tommy was also pretty badly injured, and there was concern for a fractured back and possible paralysis. His parents were back in the exam room with him, while Kevin was waiting in the lobby for Lisa's arrival. Lisa couldn't contain her tears any longer, and she wept in Kevin's arms.

The doctor soon came out and said he wanted to update them on Shane's tests. He had a severe fracture of his left leg and an injury to his lung, but otherwise was in pretty good shape, considering the severity of the accident. He had lots of cuts and bruises, especially a nasty cut above his eyebrow that had been sutured, but there was no internal bleeding seen on the CT scan. They were going to clean him up a bit more and then take him to a private room in a few minutes. They would do surgery on his leg tomorrow to pin the fracture, along with monitoring his lungs for a few days to make sure they heal correctly.

Lisa and Kevin followed the doctor into Shane's exam room, and she was overcome with emotion and love for her youngest child. She gave him a gentle hug, and fussed over him a bit, fluffing his pillow and adjusting his blanket.

Shane was not very talkative, though, and Lisa was a bit worried about him. She knew he must be in a lot of pain. Finally he confessed to her what was really bothering him – he was supposed to go to Iowa City tomorrow for his college visit and talk about a possible baseball scholarship. His dream of playing college (and then professional) baseball was fading before his eyes. Lisa tried to comfort him while Kevin left the room stating he needed to make some phone calls.

After a few minutes, Kevin returned and told Shane there was someone on the phone who wanted to talk to him. Shane listened for a few seconds, then his eyes lit up and he smiled widely. Coach Hagerman from the Iowa baseball team was assuring Shane that they could do the visit at a later date, and nothing minor like a broken leg was going to end his promising baseball career.

Shane was moved to a private room, and his pain medicines were finally starting to kick in. After making sure he was comfortable, Lisa and Kevin told him goodnight and headed toward Winterset in their respective cars. As Lisa drove home, she reflected on the many events of the past few days. As happy as she was that she had resolved things with her sisters, and relieved that Shane was going to be OK, those items paled in comparison to the sight of the old farmhouse looking stately in the glistening moonlight. She rolled her window down and inhaled the cool night air. Lisa was HOME, along with everything that meant to her, and that was the most important thing of all.

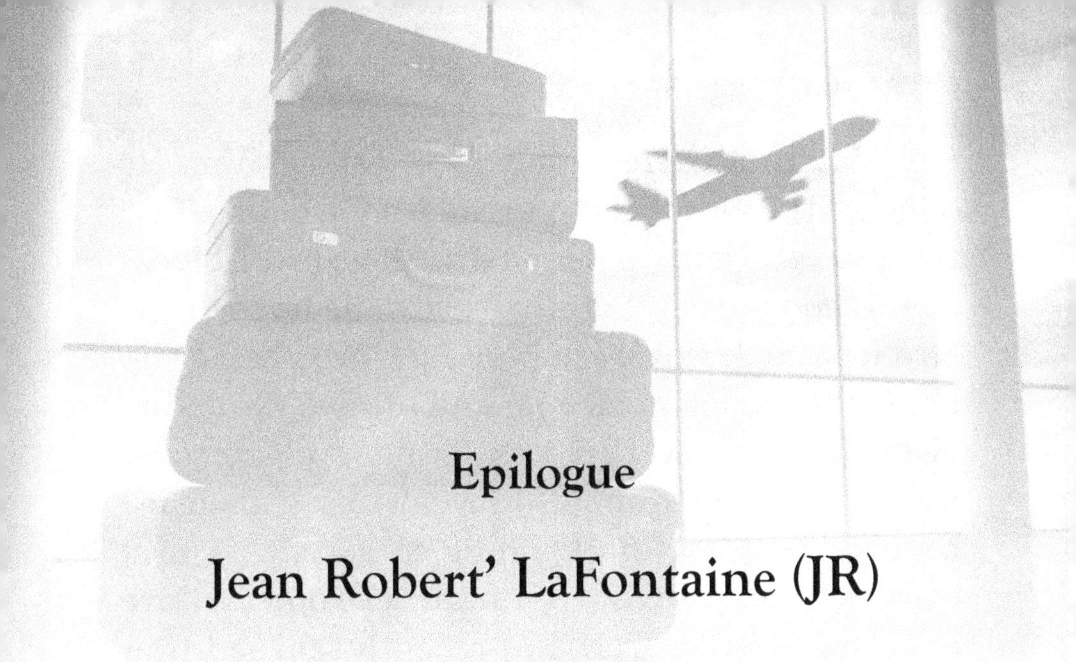

Epilogue

Jean Robert' LaFontaine (JR)

Taking the last of his belongings from his locker, JR glanced around the lounge one last time before walking out into the bright New Orleans sunshine. Turning 65 meant retirement and freedom from the grueling work as a baggage handler, and he was excited to start the next phase of his life. As he headed toward the door, his buddy Manny called out to him, telling him there was some sort of problem with his timecard and he needed to come back.

Walking into the break room, he was amazed to see balloons and a cake, along with many of his friends and his wife. "Surprise!" they all yelled, and JR was overcome with emotion.

After rounds of cheers and congratulations, Manny presented him with a large box and an envelope that represented their gifts to him. He opened the box first and was shocked to find two pieces of very expensive luggage (NOT black, thank goodness!). Fighting tears, he opened the envelope to discover vouchers for two round-trip tickets to Paris; a place he had always wanted to visit but had never had the funds, or the time. Ironically, after almost 40 years as a baggage handler he was finally going to go on his first ever over-seas flight. JR had developed a love of genealogy research and recently learned that his family had emigrated from France over 150 years ago. Finally he had the chance to return to his ancestral homeland, and he couldn't wait to pack his new bags and discover the land of his forefathers.

WHEELS DOWN

3rd Installment in
The Boarding Pass trilogy

BY BETTY GOSSELL AND

KAREN PICKENS

Other Books by Betty Gossell and Karen Pickens

- *The Boarding Pass* - 2017
- *Future Flights* – 2019

Also by Betty Gossell

- *A Home For Molly - 2019*

Excitement for a Third Installment in *The Boarding Pass* Trilogy

"I'm excited for the next book - I loved the first two." Paula M.

"I'm patiently awaiting the final book, and anxiously awaiting the first film! I'm very excited, once again, to take flight with the passengers of seat 19F and see where their life and travels take them! I love the story line! And I really enjoy all the 'Air Miles' I rack up by reading your books!" Mark L.

"I am so excited for the ending. I feel like I was in the seat next to these passengers." Susan H.

"Anxious to hear more of the military couple Joel and Kristen." Wanda G.

"I loved the first two books. Can't wait to see where the adventure takes us next!" Pattie E.

"I am anxious to see where and what these passengers are doing with their lives now." Mary Sue R.

"What's going to happen with my favorite characters? I can't wait to read the next installment of this series. These lives have come to matter to me!" Rosemary F.

"I am very excited to see what paths the passengers I have become invested in from the previous series take - what has been happening in their lives and where have their travels taken them? I can't wait to read and fly with them." Betty D.

"I'm patiently waiting to dive into the next series of this phenomenal story that has no ending. It's like I live the lives of these people, their adventures and their destinations are my destiny." Jennifer D.

Dedication and Thanks

Once again, we find ourselves endlessly grateful for all of the love and support during the writing of this third (and final) installment in *The Boarding Pass* series. It is impossible to list everyone who played a role, but here are just a few special acknowledgments:

To my friends and family who believed from the first day that these eight stories were interesting and worth continuing, even when we had our doubts. Thanks for loving me and supporting me during this amazing process;

To my co-workers, past and present, who lived many similar travel experiences of crowded and delayed flights, crying babies and lost luggage, and yet still love to fly as much as I do;

Immense thanks to Bill H who pushed our original dream toward what it is today, and a special 'thank you' to Jennifer D and Joy K for some additional research help and Janice M for proofreading. And I can't forget Carrie D for her unwavering belief in our stories and talent;

As always, the biggest thanks goes to my amazing daughter Karen who inspired me to take the very first steps of faith into these uncharted waters. I wouldn't be where I am today without you and your encouragement. While we are at the end of this joint venture, I look forward to many more adventures with you in the years to come. Hopefully we can be 'extras' together in the movie someday! I love you more.

Betty Gossell

They say that the third time's a charm, but this whole process has been charmed from the beginning. I am continually shocked by the support and encouragement we have received as we've written these three little books. It's been a true pleasure to create these characters and to nurture them as they go about their various journeys.

I want to say a huge thank you to our faithful readers who have been waiting patiently for this final installment. I hope you find that your curiosity and patience have been rewarded.

To my amazing husband Chris--You let me bounce plot ideas and hypothetical situations off of you, and for that I'm forever grateful. Then you let me ignore you while I tried to make those ideas lay down nicely on paper. You're a truly incredible man and partner, and I'm so blessed to do life with you.

To my beautiful daughter Lilah Joy--I'm blown away by the smart, funny, and creative young lady you're becoming. I'm grateful every single day that God chose to make me your mom.

And of course to my mother and co-author, Betty--I love you so very much. You took a little idea and shaped it into a big dream, one that is still growing; I'm so glad I have the chance to help it come true. Thank you for pushing me and extending deadlines for me and for taking this project higher and higher. It's been so fun!

Karen Pickens

Foreword

The plane has finally landed – the wheels are down and we have taxied to the gate. There was a beginning, a middle, and an end to our flights. But are these really endings, or new beginnings? Does the story ever truly end?

Everyone has a story, but these stories don't always take the course we planned or end how or when we had hoped. Each person we cross paths with is at a different place in their own personal journey. While it is tempting to judge another person by their place in *our* story, we can't immediately know who is just a minor player, and who will become a huge influencer later on. Chance encounters, being in the right place at the right time - whatever you might call it - these seemingly random meetings have the potential to alter our course and take us to places we had never imagined.

Betty Gossell

Contents

Prologue - Jean

The plane landed uneventfully, and as Jean and Nathan were heading through the terminal toward baggage claim, she came to a stop in front of a small bookstore.

"Look!" she whispered to Nathan as she pointed toward the display window. By the door there was a life-size cardboard cutout of her standing beside a table with all of her novels. Inside the store was a large grouping of her books, surrounded by numerous interested shoppers.

"That was my original dream," she said softly, "all those years ago, to be in an airport bookstore. I never dreamed about the rest of this."

Nathan leaned down and gently kissed her cheek. "But you dared to pursue that original dream and you are worth this success, and so much more. I can't tell you how proud I am of you, and how happy I am that I was the one who bought you that cup of espresso in Rome."

STAPLE

BOARDING PASS

BOARDING PASS

PASSENGER RECEIPT 1 OF 1

Narong, Patesh

Global Air

SMF - ATL

Chapter One

Narong, Patesh

SEAT NUMBER

24E

Date and Time

September 4, 2022

10:12 AM

Destination: ATL

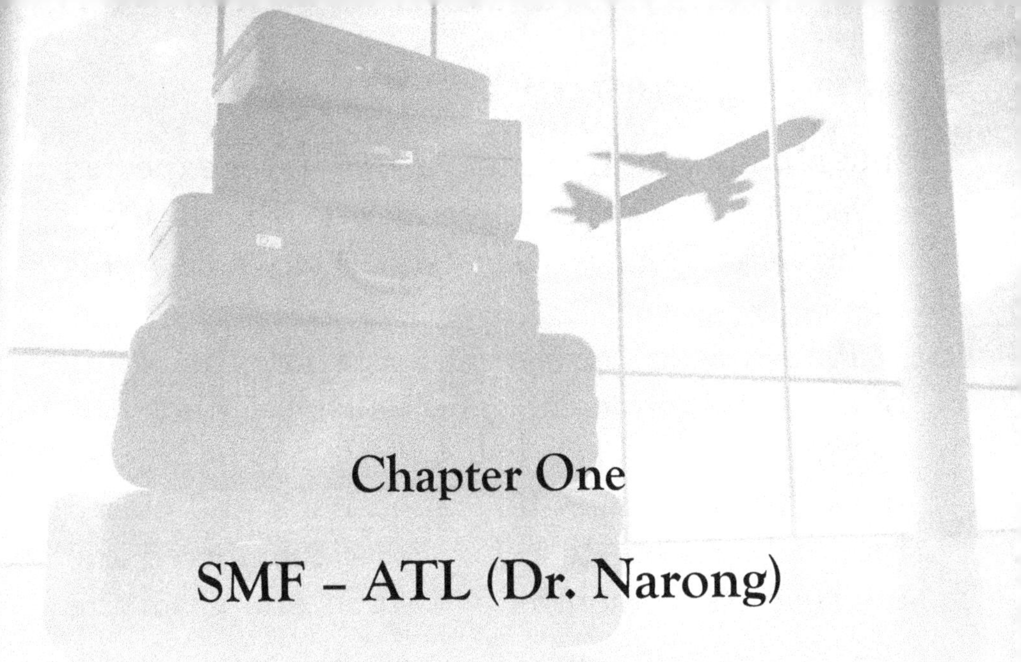

Chapter One

SMF - ATL (Dr. Narong)

Dr. Narong rushed down the jet way and onto a plane headed to Atlanta. He was one of the last to board, and struggled to fit his carryon into the crowded overhead compartment. Since he had requested to fly standby, he had to take whatever seat was available, which in this case was a middle seat near the back of the plane. Squeezing his nearly 6’3” frame into the tiny seat, he felt like his knees were under his chin. But he really didn’t care – he just knew he had to get home to his wife and unborn child – both of whom were in trouble.

Patesh and Gloria had gotten married shortly after returning from India four years ago. Their adoption of the orphan Niree had gone fairly smoothly, and they had quickly and easily settled into a family routine that he had never expected a year before. He loved being a husband and a father, and along with his successful career, his life felt complete.

Patesh was barely seated when the plane pushed back from the gate. He sent a quick text to Gloria's brother-in-law Andy to say he was on his way home, then he leaned back and closed his eyes. Trying to relax, he remembered the afternoon five months ago when she gave him the startling news.

It was a glorious early spring day – not too hot yet in Atlanta – and they had taken Niree to the city park along with a friend from school. Adjusting to American schools had been a challenge for Niree, but her new friend Melissa had been great. She fiercely fended off a few kids who were bullying Niree about her accent, and helped her learn to speak English. The park had an extensive bike path system, and before long the two girls had disappeared around a curve, talking and laughing. They were both mature and responsible girls, and could be trusted to watch the time and meet back in two hours.

Patesh and Gloria sat on a small bench near the duck pond. The sky was crystal blue and there was just a hint of a soft breeze. Patesh was still adjusting to the Georgia weather, but he knew enough to cherish days like this before the summer heat settled in.

He glanced over at Gloria who was intently watching a young mother pushing a toddler on the swing set. She had seemed really distracted the past few days, and he wondered if anything was bothering her.

His arm was around her shoulders, resting on the back of the bench. He gave her a gentle squeeze, and she turned to look at him with those hazel eyes that had melted his heart almost five years before. She was so beautiful and so radiant, even in jeans and a t-shirt and only a hint of makeup. He marveled again that such a glorious creature would love him and agree to spend her life with him.

There was a pretty large age gap between them – he had just turned 54 and she was almost 37. At just over 5 feet tall, the top of her head did not even reach his 6'3" shoulder. He remembered how funny their wedding was – how far he had to bend down to kiss her. But he could not imagine his life without her. "You may now kiss the bride," the minister had said, and Patesh had to almost bend in half to place his lips on hers. The crowd erupted with giggles as they saw her on her tiptoes, reaching up toward him. Such a lovely and fun memory.

"Hey, beautiful," he whispered softly. "Are you ok? You seem a million miles away."

"Not quite a million. I was thinking about our trip to India, when we were talking about babies."

"Babies? What in the world would make you think about that now?"

She dug around in her jeans pocket and pulled out a small white plastic stick.

"This," she said as she handed it to him. He stared at it in confusion for a few seconds, and then his eyes focused on the blue + on one end.

He looked at Gloria in amazement and saw her eyes were rimmed in tears.

"Pregnant? Really?" he asked softly.

"Yes – I was surprised too. You know my cycles have always been a bit erratic, so when I skipped last month I didn't really notice. But when I was late again this month, on a whim I stopped by the pharmacy and then took the test a couple of days ago. I wanted to wait until we were alone to show you."

"The whole story is kinda funny, actually," she continued quickly, suddenly relieved to be able to tell him what she had been keeping a secret. "You know I have been feeling run down lately, but figured it was all the overtime I was working at the Cancer Center, plus getting Niree adjusted to school. Or maybe just that nasty stomach flu that was going around. One day last week I had a strange craving for a peanut butter and pickle sandwich, and one of my co-workers asked if I was pregnant. Everyone laughed at that, but I suddenly realized my cycle was late again. Could I possibly be pregnant? So I stopped at a CVS and wandered around until I found a row of pregnancy tests. Who knew there were so many to choose from? Generic vs name brand. A + sign or a -. One line or two? And then I was oddly nervous at the checkout – what was the clerk thinking? I took the test after I got home and my hands were shaking when I saw the +. I was so excited, and scared, and overwhelmed. How was I going to tell you? How would you react? We never talked about this before, really. Other than that time on the plane."

Patesh reached over and put a protective hand on her belly. She was pregnant and his baby was growing inside her! He was not sure it was possible to love her more than he did right then.

The plane was in the air and the flight attendants passed out drinks and a small bag of pretzels. Patesh ate hungrily, unable to remember the last time he had a real meal – certainly not since last night when he got the call from Andy.

The first few months of Gloria's pregnancy had gone smoothly, but when she had her 20 week ultrasound the doctor noticed an abnormality with the baby's kidneys and the umbilical cord had only two vessels instead of the normal three (which has two arteries and one vein). This was potentially harmful to the baby and increased the potential need for a cesarean section. The kidney issue remained concerning for the next 10 weeks and Gloria was monitored regularly. At 30 weeks they had another ultrasound that confirmed the baby was a boy. Patesh pulled a copy of the ultrasound out of his suit jacket pocket and admired the 3D view of his son. His son – he was still adjusting to the idea of a baby, much less a son!

Seated next to the window was a gentleman about 10 years older than Patesh. His dark hair was graying on his temples, and he was dressed in khakis and a blue polo. He caught Patesh's eye and said, "Ultrasounds are so detailed these days. Your grandchild?"

Ouch! Patesh winced inwardly but politely said "No, it's mine – due in about two months. He came as quite a surprise to his mother and me."

"Oh, sorry. I just assumed........."

"It's ok. I never guessed I would be having my first child at age 57."

"Do you mind if I take a closer look?" the man asked. "I'm Dr. Alan Weston, a retired OB-GYN."

"Sure," Patesh said as he gently passed the picture to his seatmate.

Dr. Weston studied the ultrasound and couldn't help but let his concern show on his face.

"It's ok," Patesh said. "We know about the kidneys and the cord. We've been watching it for a while now."

"How is she doing, if you don't mind me asking?"

"Holding steady, well that is until last night. I didn't want to leave her, but I was slated to be a presenter at a conference here in Sacramento, and was only supposed to be gone for four days. Yesterday she wasn't feeling well, so her sister Gina took her to the doctor – her blood pressure was really elevated, so they admitted her to the hospital. Last night around midnight she went into labor. They have been trying to stop it, but are having trouble. I left the conference and grabbed the first flight I could. I'm so mad at myself – I never should have left her."

"How far along is she now?"

"33 weeks."

"Hmmm…at 33 weeks your son is about a foot and a half long, and probably weighs about four pounds. While it's not ideal to deliver at this size, the NICU would take good care of him. Do you have a name picked out?"

"Yes, his name will be Davin. It means precious. My precious son - I just feel so helpless."

"I know, but trust me – her doctors are doing all that they can to keep your wife and Davin safe. I notice the name on the ultrasound – Narong. I used to work with a fellow with that name…India?"

"Yes, from a small village near New Delhi. I'm a researcher at the CDC. My name is Patesh Narong."

"CDC? Impressive! Is your wife from India also?"

"Oh no, a Georgia girl all the way. Her sister is married to the first friend I made when I moved to Atlanta several years ago. She is a nurse and works at the local cancer center."

Dr. Weston gently handed the ultrasound back to Patesh, who held it for a while longer before putting it back into his pocket.

Patesh closed his eyes and tried to relax, but all that flashed across his mind were images of Gloria – her growing belly, feeling the baby kick, decorating the nursery in a seaside theme with sailboats and seashells. He remembered the excitement of telling their families – the shock and amazement on their faces. And telling Niree was so fun – she was really excited to be a big sister. Eventually he drifted into a restless sleep.

About two hours into the flight, he was jolted awake by a frantic call for help that came from about three rows behind him. A young family was travelling with an infant who had stopped breathing and was turning blue. Patesh and Dr.

Weston quickly jumped from their seats and rushed to the baby. Dr. Weston quickly grabbed the baby and flipped her over to her tummy. He did a few quick pats on her back but nothing happened. The mom was sobbing hysterically and the dad kept crying “save my baby……save my baby!”

Patesh put one of his fingers in the girl’s mouth and felt around. Suddenly she gagged and spit up a large amount of formula. She immediately started crying and her pink color returned. Everyone on the plane applauded, and after checking the baby out further and reassuring the parents, the doctors returned to their seats. The flight attendants brought towels and wash cloths to help them clean themselves up.

“After all of these years, that’s only the second time I’ve had to do that,” Dr. Weston said as he dried his hands. “You were a great help, Patesh – thanks!”

“That was a first for me, actually,” Patesh answered. “I haven’t done hands-on care since medical school. It’s good to know that all of that training came back so quickly.”

After the excitement died down, Patesh again took the ultrasound from his pocket. “Hang on Davin – dad’s on the way.” Dad – he was going to be a dad – maybe today!

The pilot announced that they were on their final approach to Atlanta. Patesh was holding his phone – ready to turn it on once the plane touched down and calls were allowed.

"Welcome to Atlanta's Hartfield-Jackson Airport, where the local time is 5:22 PM," the flight attendant announced. "It is now safe to use your cellular phones. Please stay seated with your seatbelts fastened until we are parked at the gate and the captain has turned off the fasten seatbelt sign."

Immediately Patesh turned on his phone and was flooded with text messages. He soon found one from Andy that just said "Congratulations!" and there was a picture attached. Patesh's hands were shaking as he opened the attachment.

Nothing could have prepared him for what he saw. Almost completely covered in wires and tubes was the smallest baby he had ever seen. At the end of the incubator was a sign that said "Narong, Boy. 4 lb. 2 oz. 16 inches."

Dr. Weston glanced over at Patesh and saw the shock on his face. Patesh smiled weakly and handed him the phone.

"Well, that's about what I would expect at 33 weeks. But look – he had lots of wires but he is NOT on the ventilator – that's a very good sign! I know it looks intimidating in the NICU, but he is getting the best care available. How is your wife?"

"I'm not sure yet – that's the first text I looked at."

Almost as if on cue, his phone *pinged* again. Patesh took the phone from Dr. Weston and read the next text from Andy with a sigh of relief.

"Gloria is great. In recovery after the c/section and her blood pressure is coming down. She did amazing during the surgery. Are you almost home? She is anxious to see you."

Patesh replied quickly. "Just landed. See you soon."

Once the plane came to a stop, Patesh sprinted up the jet way and ran through the concourse to an escalator that would take him downstairs and he could catch a cab. He told the driver to hurry, and then called Andy's cell phone.

"I've landed and I'm in a taxi – how are they?"

"How about I let your wife tell you?" There was a short pause.

"Gloria – are you OK? I've been crazy sick with worry."

"I'm better now that I know you are almost here," she said. "Oh, Patesh – he's so tiny!"

"I'm so proud of you and so very sorry I wasn't there! But I met a retired OB-GYN who explained things to me and helped to keep me somewhat calm. Did they let you hold him?"

"No," she said sadly. "They showed him to me and then whisked him away to the NICU."

"I'll be there soon, I promise. Just a few more minutes. I love you – love you both!"

As the taxi pulled up in front of the hospital, Patesh threw a handful of money at the driver and was out the door before the wheels had even stopped. After running in the front door, he stopped at the Information Desk and asked directions to the NICU. The closer he got to his son, the faster he ran. He introduced himself to a nurse at the desk who escorted him into a room where he could wash up and put on a gown and gloves. He walked into the NICU and gazed at the rows of incubators and machines. The room was noisy and quiet at the same time. Ventilators and infusion pumps were beeping, and EKG's were ticking on monitors. The parents and nurses in the room were all talking in hushed voices. In the far back corner of the room he saw Gloria – so tiny and fragile looking – so exhausted but also with a look of peace. She was gazing lovingly into the isolette, talking softly. Patesh walked up to her slowly and put a hand on her shoulder.

"Isn't he beautiful?" she whispered, not taking her eyes from her child. Her hand was inside the incubator and she was softly stroking the baby's arm. There were tubes and wires everywhere. His eyes were taped shut but he appeared to be resting calmly.

"May I?" Patesh asked as he put his hand next to Gloria's.

"Of course, Patesh. I would like to introduce you to our son. Davin, your daddy is here!"

Daddy. What a beautiful word.

STAPLE

BOARDING PASS

BOARDING PASS

Sullivan, Kristen

DFW to MCO

Chapter Two

Global Air

PASSENGER RECEIPT 1 OF 1

Sullivan, Kristen

SEAT NUMBER

14B

Date and Time

JUNE 2, 2032

09:20 AM

Destination: MCO

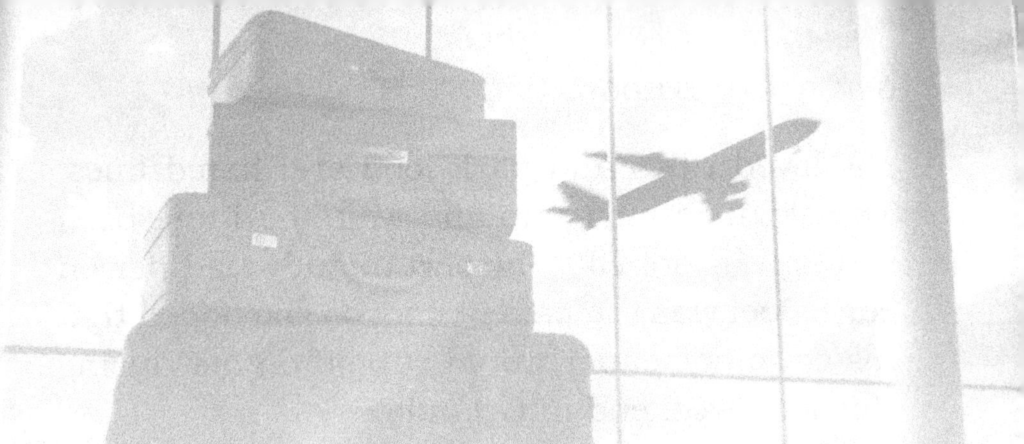

Chapter Two

DFW - MCO (Kristen)

As the boarding passengers began to thin out and get settled, Kristen Sullivan craned her neck, trying to see if she could find where her husband Joel was sitting. She finally spotted the top of his sandy head a few rows up and across the aisle, and could see that he was focused on the little passenger beside him in the window seat. It pained her to be sitting away from the rest of her family, but it would only be a couple of hours before they landed in Florida and began the great Disney vacation, that mandatory rite of passage for kids these days.

Kristen had never actually been to either of the Disney theme parks. They hadn't been able to afford it when she was a kid, but she'd been to Six Flags Over Texas enough times to know that she loved rides and park food and hated lines. The arduous hurry up and wait she'd just been through in the DFW airport already had her on edge. Joel was the patient one, so she hoped that his calm demeanor would rub off on her during this long weekend in Orlando.

She turned her attention to the fidgeting child in the window seat beside her. "Mama, look!" the little boy said, pointing out the window at the ground crew as they loaded bags into the belly of the plane.

"I hope one of those is mine," Kristen said sincerely, trying not to imagine several days in the Florida sunshine and humidity without a change of clothes.

"You can always buy Mickey Mouse shirts at Disney!" he suggested, the corners of his mouth twitching at his little joke.

Kristen giggled fondly, feeling a little sigh of pleasure as she looked at this handsome young boy who called her "Mama." From the moment she'd laid eyes on him in an Ethiopian orphanage six years ago, she'd felt that he belonged to her, and he'd done nothing but enrich her life ever since. He was bright and beautiful, curious and creative. As a son, he was easygoing and eager to please. As a big brother, he was fiercely protective, gentle enough to counteract his sister's wild and dramatic energy. Though he was beginning to be embarrassed by public affection from his mother, she couldn't help but reach over and give his dark hand a squeeze. "Mine," she thought, melting at the feel of him squeezing her fingers in return.

The sound of a large purse dropping into the empty aisle seat made Kristen jump. She turned to see a blonde girl in her late teens or early twenties, hauling a carry-on bag up and failing to get it high enough to stow in the overhead bin. Three different men, already seated and buckled, rushed up to help her and Kristen gave a quiet snort. Even in her days as a perky young cheerleader, she wasn't sure that she could have commanded that kind of attention.

This girl was way more eye-catching than a whole squad of cheerleaders though. At first glance, her t-shirt and yoga pants ensemble was just like many others on this plane, but it was soon clear that these were extremely high-end versions, tailored to perfectly accentuate her Barbie doll curves. She had the sort of face that just didn't exist in the real world, not without surgery or at least pricey spa treatments. Kristen couldn't help but stare at her long lashes and bee-stung lips until she felt her son pulling on the sleeve of her shirt to whisper loudly at her.

"Mama, do you think she's famous or something? She's so shiny!"

"Hush," Kristen said with a little laugh, looking apologetically at the young woman settling in beside her. She was indeed quite shiny with glossy golden hair and dewy, poreless skin. She was wearing a lot of makeup to make it look like she wasn't wearing any at all, and Kristen thought that if she hadn't been sitting practically in her lap, the effect would be pretty flawless.

Kristen knew that she herself was an attractive woman. Yes, she found the occasional grey hair in amongst the dark brown these days, and a few fine lines fanned out around her green eyes when she smiled, but her fair skin was still smooth and bright. She was still told quite often that she was pretty and put together, but she felt sloppy and unfinished next to the girl beside her, who smiled brightly at the young boy's compliment.

"Aw, you're a sweet kid. What's your name?"

"I'm Seth Andrew Sullivan," Kristen's son replied brightly, extending his slim dark hand past his mother to the stranger in the aisle seat.

"Oh, just precious," the girl cooed, taking his hand delicately so as not to spear him with her long, sparkling acrylic nails. "I'm Amber Rae Davies," she said with a gleaming smile.

"Nice to meet you," Seth said somewhat mechanically, dividing his attention between the pretty girl and the world outside his window.

"He's your son?" Amber asked Kristen, clarifying the relationship that wasn't always obvious.

"Yep," Kristen answered, keeping it short and sweet. She hoped that Amber would assume correctly that Seth was her adopted son and leave it at that. Kristen watched her blue-grey eyes tighten ever so slightly as various scenarios and explanations sped through her brain, but miraculously, she didn't probe any deeper on the subject.

"How old is he?"

"I'm six," Seth answered, the words muffled because his face was now squished against the double-paned windows.

Kristen grinned indulgently at Amber. "He's six," she repeated, her tone affirming that it was a tricky age for a little boy to be.

Amber grinned back slightly, but Kristen could see that any subtlety might be lost on this girl. She didn't seem the type to know a lot about kids. How could she possibly interact with children regularly and have such a flawless manicure? Kristen found herself covertly making sure her own unpolished nails were at least clean.

"And you're traveling together, just the two of you?" Amber wondered.

"Oh no, my husband is sitting a couple rows up with our daughter."

"Two kids! Wow, you don't look old enough."

Kristen allowed herself to feel truly flattered by this. Her kids had come along later in life than she'd planned, so hearing that she looked too young to be a mom, especially from this glowing and youthful girl made her smile. "That's nice! They're very close in age."

This was quite true. She'd learned she was pregnant with Charlotte before Seth's adoption was even finalized, making them only seven months apart. This fact was usually just too confusing for people, so she tended to skip over it with strangers.

Just then, the captain came over the intercom, asking the flight attendants to prepare for something called "crosscheck," and Kristen looked up. It seemed that they'd been waiting on one final passenger to board before locking the doors. It was a young woman about Amber's age with vivid red hair and a flushed complexion. She'd clearly had to run to make the flight.

"Oh, crap!" Amber whispered, turning quickly toward Kristen and Seth and putting one hand up to cover the side of her face.

"What's wrong?" Kristen asked, alarmed. Her mom-instincts had her placing a hand on Seth's knee, preparing to protect him from some unseen threat.

Amber didn't answer. She stayed silent and still until the redheaded girl struggled down the aisle past where they were sitting and then gave a relieved sigh, slumping back in her seat again.

"Do you know her?" Kristen asked quietly, glancing over her shoulder as the redhead shoved her bags violently into the overhead bin several rows back. The girl was pretty, but unlike Amber, she had ventured out into the world in a raw state. Perhaps she'd overslept.

"That's Meg. She's...my sister's ex-future-sister-in-law," Amber said, ticking the words off on her fingers to make sure she got all of them right.

Kristen blinked and then frowned trying to translate that. "You lost me," she admitted.

Amber gave one of her glittering smiles. "My sister was supposed to marry Meg's brother but they called it off last minute," she explained.

"Oh! Yeah, I suppose that would make things awkward between you. I'm--um--sorry things didn't work out."

"Yeah, me too. Steve seemed like a nice enough guy. But my sister is a bit high-maintenance."

Kristen pressed her lips together, amused that this primped and polished girl was calling someone else high-maintenance.

"I guess I should have figured I'd run into her. I'm sure I can't avoid her all week so we might as well get the awkwardness out of the way."

"Wait, you lost me again."

"My darling sister planned a destination wedding," Amber said with a roll of her pretty eyes. "The plan was to catch a cruise in Port Canaveral and have the ceremony in the Bahamas. I tried to explain to her that having the whole family along for the honeymoon was bound to be creepy, but she didn't listen."

"So, the wedding was called off, but you're still going on the cruise?"

"You better believe it!" Amber answered with a giggle. "I've been prepping for this vacation for almost a year. Even if I could have gotten most of my money back, I still want to go. Andi, my sister, still wanted to go too, so we're going. She's up in first class right now, probably drinking champagne next to an empty seat, because of course Steve isn't coming."

"Well, that's good, I guess," Kristen said, trying to imagine something worse and failing.

"His parents canceled too," Amber went on. "But most of his groomsmen are probably on this flight somewhere. They're turning it into a dude vacation. Andi's other bridesmaids are flying in later, so we'll meet up with them tonight, and our parents are getting in early tomorrow morning.

I can't imagine why Meg would want to come alone, but I guess it's hard to walk away from a week in the Caribbean no matter the reason."

Kristen nodded absently, still a bit dazed by the story. Her life had been full of amazing adventures, but she'd never heard of anything quite like this one. She felt incredibly sad for the bride-to-be who was no longer to be. If she and Joel had fallen apart right before their wedding, she would have been catatonic for weeks, not sipping champagne in first class, not repurposing a honeymoon into a girl's trip. Perhaps being high-maintenance resulted in resilience.

Of course, Kristen had a merit badge in resilience as well, but it hadn't been quickly earned. It had taken years of sadness and insecurity and worry to find any sort of peace in her situation. Now, however, it felt like she was in the final stages of her evolution. The wild and restless days of her youth had led her to this place of comfort. It was challenging and confusing every single day, but it was the life she'd chosen and she couldn't regret it. Her new friend Amber might have been dazzling, but Kristen was pleased to find that she didn't envy her in the slightest. Raising two kids of different races with only seven months between them seemed so much easier than walking in Amber's designer shoes.

Once the plane was in the air, the two women found themselves speaking to one another often. It wasn't a full conversation, just bits and pieces here and there. They compared itineraries and Kristen tried to keep up with Amber's pop culture gossip. She was pretty sure she could tell the difference when Amber was talking about a celebrity and when she was mentioning one of her beautiful friends.

Meanwhile, Seth had drawn four pictures, played two games on his tablet, and read three comic books, all within the first forty-five minutes of the flight. Kristen had laughed outright when the boy complained of being bored, but did sacrifice her own phone to let him listen to an audiobook about Carmen Sandiego that she'd bought for the kids but was perfectly content to listen to alone.

This finally caught and held his attention because he didn't return her phone and earbuds until after the plane had landed. Seth pressed his face against the window again, trying to absorb all of Orlando at once with his huge dark eyes.

"Let's go meet up with Daddy and Char and get to our hotel room," Kristen urged, tugging the boy away from the sunny window.

"Can we please go to Disney today?" he begged, poking out his lower lip.

"Nope, remember tonight is the big dinner at the hotel."

"I wish it was tomorrow now!" Seth pouted.

Amber gave him a sweet little giggle that sounded a bit like she'd worked on it long and hard to make it sound so playful. "I hear ya, little man," she said. "Tomorrow, I get to go on a big boat and sail away into the ocean. But you can't just think about tomorrow. You have to think about how you can make today even better."

Kristen expected Seth to ignore this near stranger and her advice, but he looked thoughtful for a moment and then gave a solemn nod as though he'd taken her words to heart. Amber beamed down at him and then slipped into the aisle, swimming upstream toward the back of the plane where the ex-future-sister-in-law was sitting.

"That's nice," Kristen thought, almost wishing she was going with them on the cruise before deciding it would be too much work to keep up with those young girls. Her husband and her kids were all the excitement she could handle these days.

Seth was bouncing rather than walking, jostling her as they crossed the jet bridge and moved into the terminal. She found Joel waiting for her with little Charlotte already wearing a pair of homemade mouse ears on her head and tapping her foot impatiently.

Kristen laughed and wondered if they needed to go to the theme park at all. Looking at the family she'd fought so hard for, she was sure she'd already found the Happiest Place on Earth.

STAPLE

BOARDING PASS

BOARDING PASS

Evans, William

STL - MEM

Chapter Three

Global Air

PASSENGER RECEIPT 1 OF 1

Evans, William

SEAT NUMBER

11D

Date and Time

OCTOBER 14, 2020

09:29 AM

Destination: MEM

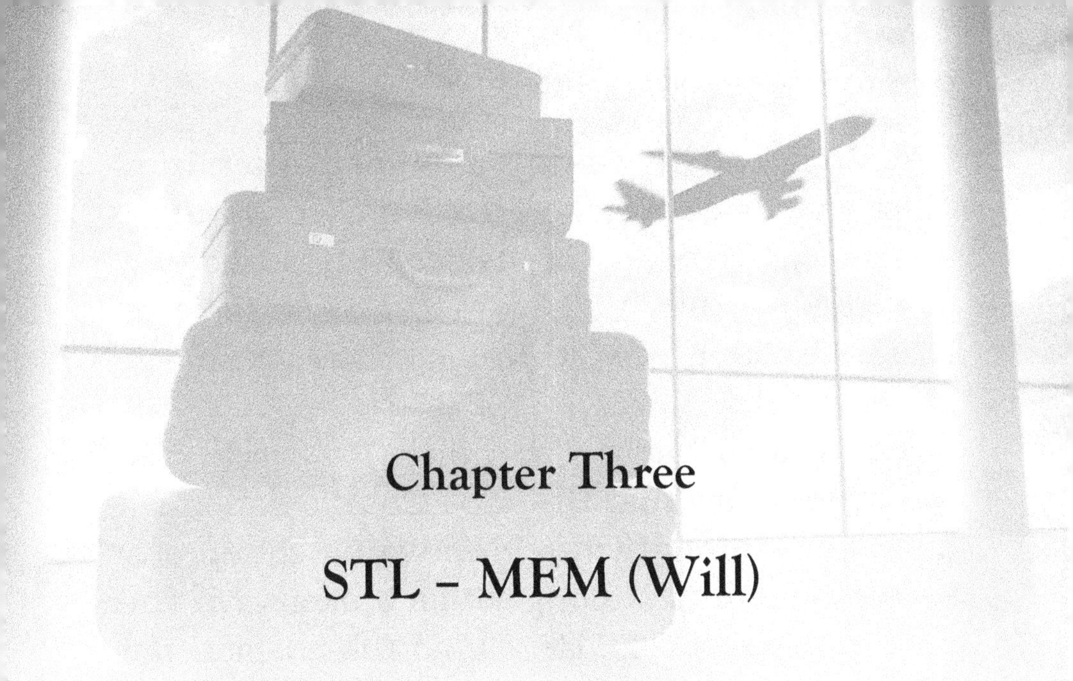

Chapter Three

STL - MEM (Will)

Will choked back tears as he hugged his mother one last time before a flight attendant escorted him down the jet bridge and onto the plane. He found his aisle seat and sat quietly while she explained the process that he already knew by heart. He had flown several times as an unaccompanied minor, but did not have the energy for his usual rudeness or sarcasm for being treated like a child. The funeral had stripped almost every emotion from him.

"I can't believe he's really gone," he thought to himself. "How am I supposed to live without my grandpa – the most influential man in my life – the kindest, most gentle man I ever knew?"

He pulled the memory card from the funeral home out of his backpack. Charles William

Cromwell – Will was even named after him. Master of the corny jokes, teacher of card games, and keeper of secrets. Many people had said they looked alike, but Will wasn't sure he believed them. Probably just trying to make him feel better.

Will's mom had called him a few weeks ago to let him know that Grandpa Charlie had fallen down the stairs at church and suffered a pretty severe head injury, along with a broken arm and several bruised ribs. He was in the hospital but the doctors expected him to be OK. But then the call came last Sunday afternoon that he had suffered a massive stroke and passed away. Just like that, his grandpa – his closest friend – was gone.

Arrangements were made for Will to fly to Memphis the next day. He quickly packed a bag, hugged Etsi and told the girls goodbye, and his dad drove him to the airport. Will was just thankful that it appeared to be a good day for his dad, and that he was sober enough to drive this time.

Things had been really great at first after he moved to Memphis. Sure, there were the usual homesickness and adjustments to a new school, but his dad seemed genuinely happy to have him there.

After about six months, the addition to the back of the house was done and he was able to move back into his own room. His dad owned a software development company and business was going really well. He gave Will $800 to decorate his room however he wanted – paint color, theme, and new furniture -- whatever he wanted! The Memphis Grizzlies had always been his favorite team, so he decorated with the team colors of blue and gold, and put life-sized posters of several players on the walls. He was starting to make friends at school, and had joined the youth group at church. But even with all that, it did not take long for him to realize that moving to his dad's had been a huge mistake.

Will thought back to the funeral service – the singing, the lovely speeches, the tears from everyone in the room, and feeling like he needed to be strong for his mom and grandma. But he felt like a huge part of himself had died that day, too, and was lowered into the dark, cold ground.

The plane began to fill, and soon a young man in his late 20's stopped by Row 11 and motioned to Will that he was supposed to sit in the window seat. Will stood up to let him pass. After tossing his backpack into the overhead bin, the stranger crawled into his seat and slid a small briefcase under the seat in front of him. Then he carefully buckled his seatbelt and gazed casually out the window. Will wasn't quite sure, but there was something about the way this guy moved – so confidently but in a non-threatening manner. He was very tall – maybe 6'2", but thin, with reddish-blond hair and piercing blue eyes. He was wearing jeans, a faded "Keep Austin Weird" t-shirt and cowboy boots.

No one came to sit in the middle seat, and soon the doors were closed and the plane was about to leave the gate. The Flight Attendant stopped by to check on Will, making sure his seat belt was fastened and explaining – again – that he needed to wait in his seat when they landed to be escorted off. Slightly embarrassed, he glanced over at his seat mate.

"They do go out of their way to make you feel small, don't they," the young man said in a thick southern drawl. "I used to fly unaccompanied a lot when I was younger. I've got a whole collection of those wing pins."

"I've got 8 or 10 myself," Will answered. "Not sure what to do with them but hate to throw them away."

"Yeah, me too. I have mine in an old coffee can my mom was going to toss out, plus a bunch of boarding passes and luggage tags. Maybe someday I'll frame them. My parents are divorced and I spent a lot of time shuttling back and forth between them."

"Me, too. I've just been at my Mom's - came up here for my grandpa's funeral."

"Wow, so sorry. I can't imagine losing mine – we are really close."

"We are too. *Were.* I'm gonna miss him so much. He used to tell the worst jokes...what do you call a cow that just had a baby?"

"I have no idea."

"De-caffeinated!"

The young man groaned and rolled his eyes.

"That's the last one he told me," Will said in a soft voice. "I will always remember his chuckle and his cheesy grin..." his voice trailed off as he fought back tears.

"So, you live with your dad?" the young man asked as they taxied down the runway. "My name is Austin, by the way," as he grinned and pointed to his t-shirt. "The shirt is from Austin, Texas, but I just couldn't resist."

"I'm Will, and yes I live with my dad. Have for the past two years."

"So, with your mom before that? How long have your parents been divorced?"

"I was really little – maybe 2 or 3. I have no memory of us as a happy family."

"That's too bad. At least my parents waited until I started school. Although honestly, they probably should have done it sooner. Growing up in an abusive household was no way to live."

Will winced a bit when Austin mentioned abuse. Most of the past year he had been a witness to screaming fights, slamming doors and slamming fists. Broken glass. Broken skin. Broken hearts.

The Flight Attendants were passing out snacks, and Will got his usual Ginger Ale. Austin got a cup of coffee and then pulled a small keyboard-type device from the bag he had slid under his seat.

Aware that Will was watching him, he said, "I just love this new gadget – it's called a Traveler. Kinda like a portable typewriter, but it connects to the Internet so I can transfer files. I'm a sociology major, working on my PhD thesis. I'm writing about victims of abuse, especially the children.

Will shifted uneasily in his seat. "So, where do you get your information?" he asked, trying to sound casual. "Research? Interviews?"

"A bit of both. I prefer interviews though - so much more personal."

"Well, then maybe you should interview me," Will quickly blurted out, not really sure why.

Austin turned to face him and gave him the look of acknowlcdgment that only other abuse victims would understand.

"Oh man – I'm so sorry. Your dad?"

"Yeah. I thought moving in with him and his new family was the answer to my prayers – boy was I wrong."

He told Austin about growing up without his dad, how much he wanted him to be in the stands at his ballgames, to go on the church campouts with him, or to have a reason to celebrate Father's Day. He explained how his dad had remarried and wanted Will to move to Memphis from St. Louis. And while it broke his mom's heart for him to move away, she wanted him to be happy and supported his decision.

"Was he always abusive?" Austin asked gently. "Who was he abusive to – you? Your stepmom? The other kids?"

"No, it didn't start right away. It was after he hurt his knee in a basketball game at the Y and ended up hooked on pain killers. He's been in and out of rehab several times, and gets really nasty when he is relapsing. And no, it was mostly directed at Etsi, at least the physical part."

"*Etsi?*"

"Sorry, my step mom. She's part Cherokee and Etsi is the word for mom. The little girls and I just get the yelling directed at us, and then get to listen to the physical stuff while hiding in a closet or in my bathroom."

"GET? It's still going on? You guys need to get out of there!"

"I know, but Etsi won't leave, even though we've begged her repeatedly. She loves him, and believes him when he says he is sorry and he will get help. Over and over it happens. He cries and apologizes, brings her flowers and she forgives him. And then he's really nice and attentive for a few days. But it keeps happening, a little worse each time. I was tempted to stay in St. Louis with my mom, but felt like I was abandoning them."

"Did you tell your mom about this?"

"No, I just couldn't bring myself to upset her further, since her dad had just died."

Austin pulled his wallet from his back pocket and found a business card. Handing it to Will, he said "Here's the number of a crisis hotline where I volunteer in Memphis. You've got to get your stepmom to call before it's too late!"

"Thanks, I'll try."

The plane was approaching Memphis and Austin handed another card to Will. "This has my cell number and email address. Feel free to contact me anytime, really. Day or night. I can't stand the thought of you going back to that environment. Please promise me!"

"Thanks," Will said quietly, wishing he could turn the plane around and head back to St. Louis.

After everyone else had left the plane, Will was finally escorted off. He fully expected to see his dad waiting to pick him up, but to his surprise, it was Etsi standing there with the three girls. He was shocked to see bruises on her face and neck that were poorly covered with makeup, and she appeared to be trembling. The girls were huddled around her, looking at the ground uncomfortably. But what he didn't notice was that Austin was standing off the side, watching.

"Oh, Etsi," he said sadly. She grimaced when he tried to hug her. "Dad? What happened?"

"He's been arrested, and we have moved out. I don't even know what set him off this time, but it was the worst ever. I tried to pack up most of your favorite things, but probably forgot something. I'm sorry. We'll be staying at a women's shelter for now."

"Please don't be sorry," he said with tears on his cheeks. "Are the girls ok?" he asked softly.

"As good as they can be, under the situation. I know we all really missed having you here. You are so good with them...." she said as tears filled her eyes and she looked away, embarrassed. "I'm sorry, I never even asked you about the funeral. How is your mom?"

"It's ok, we can talk later. Are you alright? Do you need to see a doctor?"

"I was in the ER last night – cracked ribs and lots of bruises. But I'll survive, thankfully. Emma was the brave one, calling 911 and staying on the line until help arrived. I'm not sure what would have happened...."

It was then that he noticed Austin, who was watching the scene and who had instantly recognized their body language and traumatized demeanor.

Will nodded in his direction, and then took his youngest sister's hand. They walked slowly toward the escalator that would take them down to baggage claim, and then outside.

"Hey, Sophie – I have a joke for you. What do you call a cow that just had a baby?"

STAPLE

BOARDNG PASS

BOARDING PASS

Miller, Jean

LAX – CVG

Chapter Four

Global Air

PASSENGER RECEIPT 1 OF 1

Miller, Jean

SEAT NUMBER

2A

Date and Time

NOVEMBER 24, 2023

02:37 PM

Destination: CVG

Chapter Four

LAX - CVG (Jean)

Jean eased herself into her 1st class seat 2A and slid her small carry-on under the seat in front of her. The bright California sunshine was reflecting off the plane next to them, and she pulled the window shade down a bit to shield her eyes. She was operating on almost no sleep, and felt the twinges of a headache about to strike. It was so warm outside, and Jean had to remind herself how much differently late November would feel once they got back to Ohio.

Nathan put his duffle bag in the overhead bin and slipped into the seat beside her. They had been married almost three years now and had taken several trips together, but she still felt excited sitting next to him. He held her hand in his and looked at her tenderly.

"Ready to go home?" he asked gently. "We were so busy this weekend – it was a bit overwhelming. I think we need a vacation to recover from our vacation!"

"I still can't believe everything we did – staying at the Beverly Hilton, walking the red carpet! And seeing *Fountain of Love* on the big screen!"

"Oh, I knew your book had movie potential the first time I read it. I just never imagined that you and I would get to be in it, too! Do we get to add *actor* to our resumes now?"

Jean closed her eyes and thought back over the past few years. She remembered the day her agent called and said a studio executive had read her book and wanted to make a movie out of it.

"You're kidding, right?" she asked in amazement. "My little book?"

Nathan had gone with her to meet with an entertainment lawyer and to help negotiate the best deal for her. One clause he made sure to insert was that they be cast as extras in the movie, an idea which Jean originally felt was pretty silly. But once she got on the set and got to walk hand-in-hand with Nathan near the imaginary Trevi Fountain – well, she understood his motivation. They had both smiled as they remembered their fateful meeting in Rome.

The Flight Attendants offered them a drink before taking off, along with a snack. As she sipped her glass of wine, she watched the coach passengers file past her. Families with children, businessmen and women, college students – such a variety of people were sharing her plane today. Jean had always enjoyed people-watching when she flew, and today was no exception. She noticed that several of the passengers glanced at them as they shuffled past – she wondered what they thought of her? Were they envious of her first class status? Would they have any idea how blessed she felt?

The doors were about to close when one last passenger rushed in and sat in the seat ahead of her. Jean recognized her immediately – Lucy Armando, an up-and-coming country singer who grew up near St. Louis. She was a petite young woman with long jet-black hair pulled into a pony tail and large brown eyes. She was wearing well-worn jeans and a plaid shirt with ruffles down the front. But the Kansas City Royals baseball cap she had pulled down low over her face did little to disguise her identity. Jean had been following her career for several years since she won the national TV talent show "Rising Star." Jean nudged Nathan and nodded in Lucy's direction. His eyes opened wide with recognition. They had watched the show while they were still dating, comparing notes over the phone and cheering when she won. They had even purchased tickets to her upcoming concert in the spring.

The Flight Attendants did their usual safety speeches, and the plane took its place in line for takeoff. As usual, their flight path took them west over the edge of the Pacific, then banked sharply left and made a wide turn before heading east. Jean always loved this part of flying out of LAX – seeing the ocean below and all of the sailboats and cargo ships. She often wished they could keep going west to places unknown. But not today.

The plane had been in the air for only a few minutes when Lucy removed her Royals cap and turned around to look closely at Jean.

"Excuse me for staring, but are you Jean Miller? *Fountain of Love* is one of my favorite books. And the sequel! Wow! I'm so excited to meet you. I'm Lucy Armando, by the way."

"Oh, I know who you are! Probably half on your votes on "Rising Star" came from my husband Nathan and me. Miller was my maiden name – I'm Jean Rhoades now."

"Pleased to meet both of you. What were you doing in LA?"

"Oh, we had the best weekend! This was the premier opening for the *Fountain of Love* movie, and we got to walk the red carpet and everything! We even had a small walk-on part. It was pretty surreal – Nathan and I actually met in Rome near the Fountain, so this book holds a pretty special place in our hearts."

"I was there with a group of art students from my college," Nathan told her. "But the most beautiful thing I saw that trip was this lovely lady here." He placed a gentle kiss on Jean's cheek and she blushed.

"Oh, that's so sweet. I've only been to Rome twice, but it's one of my favorite cities."

Nathan watched with pride as Jean and Lucy continued to share Roman experiences and travel stories in general. How much she had blossomed and grown since he met her that cold December days four years ago!

Lucy reached into her bag and pulled out a well-worn copy of *Love's Reply*, the sequel to *Fountain of Love*. She asked Jean to sign it, and for Nathan to take a picture of the two of them.

"You know I'm gonna Tweet this to all my followers as soon as I can....I have several friends who are huge fans of your books and who will be so jealous!"

Nathan offered to change seats with Lucy so the ladies could chat more comfortably. Settled into the first row, he closed his eyes and listened as Jean recounted their weekend.

"We flew in on Friday morning – a car from the studio took us to the Beverly Hilton – can you imagine? Our room was HUGE and opened onto the pool. The studio had prearranged everything and they treated us like royalty. Even our bellhop Anthony waited on us all weekend, bringing us room service and carrying our bags. Nathan wore a tux to the opening and I had the most gorgeous sapphire gown. The studio provided hair and makeup styling for me – I have never felt so pampered! We had a fancy reception at the hotel and then rode to the theatre in a limousine. All sorts of media outlets were there – it was totally amazing. We saw lots of A-list celebrities, and of course the stars of the movie were there, too. Everyone seemed to love the movie – it was an experience like none I could ever imagine! Afterward, the studio hosted a party and we ate and danced and got back to the hotel really late. Yesterday we lounged around the pool a bit before going sightseeing and then shopping on Rodeo Drive. Let's just say I had to buy an extra suitcase to bring everything home in!"

"So that was this weekend? Wow - I'm sorry I missed it," Lucy said sadly. "I spent the weekend performing in Hawaii….a tough gig, I know. But I really do plan to see the movie as soon as I can. Did it stay fairly true to the book?"

"The essence of the story is there, although they changed several things and deleted some characters. It was a bit unnerving at first – giving my 'baby' over to someone else to re-write and revise. But overall, we were quite pleased."

"What parts did you and Nathan play?"

"We were just tourists in the background, strolling past the Fountain and sitting at one of the cafes. We didn't have any lines or anything. If you blink, I think you will miss us. The filming was really interesting – lots of sitting around and waiting for the lighting to be right, for everyone to remember their lines, you know. I was so nervous, I'm sure I would have messed up if I had to say something. Just walking across the set was scary enough!"

"How exciting, though! To see your dream become a reality like that!"

"Yeah, it really was. And to think without Nathan's encouragement, I might never have tried to get it published!"

"So, where do you get your ideas for your stories?" Lucy asked. "Are they all based on real experiences? Totally fiction? A little of both?"

"Oh, the places I write about are places I have actually been to, but the characters are fictional. Well, mostly, anyway. Why – do you have an idea for me?"

"Well, you could write about an aspiring country singer who meets someone special while on the road but has a hard time establishing a relationship with him because she's always on tour."

"Hmm, sounds a bit like a personal experience there?"

"Perhaps," Lucy said with a smile, but with a hint of sadness in her big brown eyes.

"Actually, it sounds like a promising idea. Want to help me with some of the details? I would need to know a lot more about the music business, and life on the road. I will give you credit, of course."

"I always wanted to write a book but ended up writing songs instead."

"Writing is writing," Jean replied. "No matter the style, it's still opening your heart and risking being vulnerable. You do that every night with your songs. It's the same for me, just different."

The ladies chatted like old friends until the pilot announced they were approaching Cincinnati. Nathan moved back to his seat beside Jean and squeezed her hand with his.

"That was so fun to listen to – you two really seemed to hit it off."

"We did!" Jean exclaimed as she pulled a notebook out of her purse. She handed it to Nathan and asked him to quickly sketch the silhouette of a young girl holding a guitar. When he handed it back to her, she wrote *Country Love Song* across the top and at the bottom wrote "A Novel by Jean Miller-Rhoades with Lucy Armando."

"I know we never really talked about me changing my name, but I think it's time. What do you think?"

"It never bothered me, honestly, but I must admit, this makes me very happy. I love you Mrs. Rhoades."

As the plane was taxiing to the gate, Jean leaned forward and showed the potential book cover to Lucy. She smiled broadly and then gave Jean one of her business cards.

"Call my manager and he will set you up with VIP tickets for the concert next spring – backstage passes and dinner with me before the show. Deal?"

"Wow, thanks! And I forgot to ask – what caused you to fly from Hawaii to Ohio almost non-stop? That's some crazy tour schedule you have. You must be exhausted!"

"Or I'm just trying to sneak in a little romance between concerts," Lucy said with a wink.

"Ah, gotcha!" Jean replied with a wink of her own. "Thanks again for the concert VIPs – that so nice of you."

The plane landed uneventfully, and as Jean and Nathan were heading through the terminal toward baggage claim, she came to a stop in front of a small bookstore.

"Look!" she whispered to Nathan as she pointed toward the display window. There was a life-size cutout of her standing beside a table with all of her novels. Inside the store was a large display of her books, surrounded by numerous interested shoppers.

"That was my original dream all those years ago," she said softly, "to be in an airport bookstore. I never dreamed the rest of this – the movie, the sequels, you."

Nathan leaned down and gently kissed her cheek.

"But you dared to pursue that original dream and you are so worth all of this, and so much more. I can't tell you how proud I am of you, how happy to be the one who bought you a cup of espresso in Rome."

As they rode down the escalator to baggage claim, Jean thought about all the changes in her life since that disastrous job interview in Dallas, and then finding Lisa's boarding pass. Following her writing dream, going to Rome, meeting Nathan and falling in love for the first time in her life, getting her first book published, getting married, and eventually making a movie....her life was so amazing, so much more full than she ever could have imagined! And now, this chance meeting and new friendship with Lucy Armando – who knows what the future will bring? Jean only knew that she loved her life; her husband, her career, and her future. And she could not wait to see what was waiting for her in the next chapter.

STAPLE

BOARDING PASS

BOARDING PASS

Rodriguez, Ana

TPA - EWR

Chapter Five

Global Air

PASSENGER RECEIPT 1 OF 1

Rodriquez, Ana Maria

SEAT NUMBER

12F

Date and Time

May 12, 2023

1:27 PM

Destination: EWR

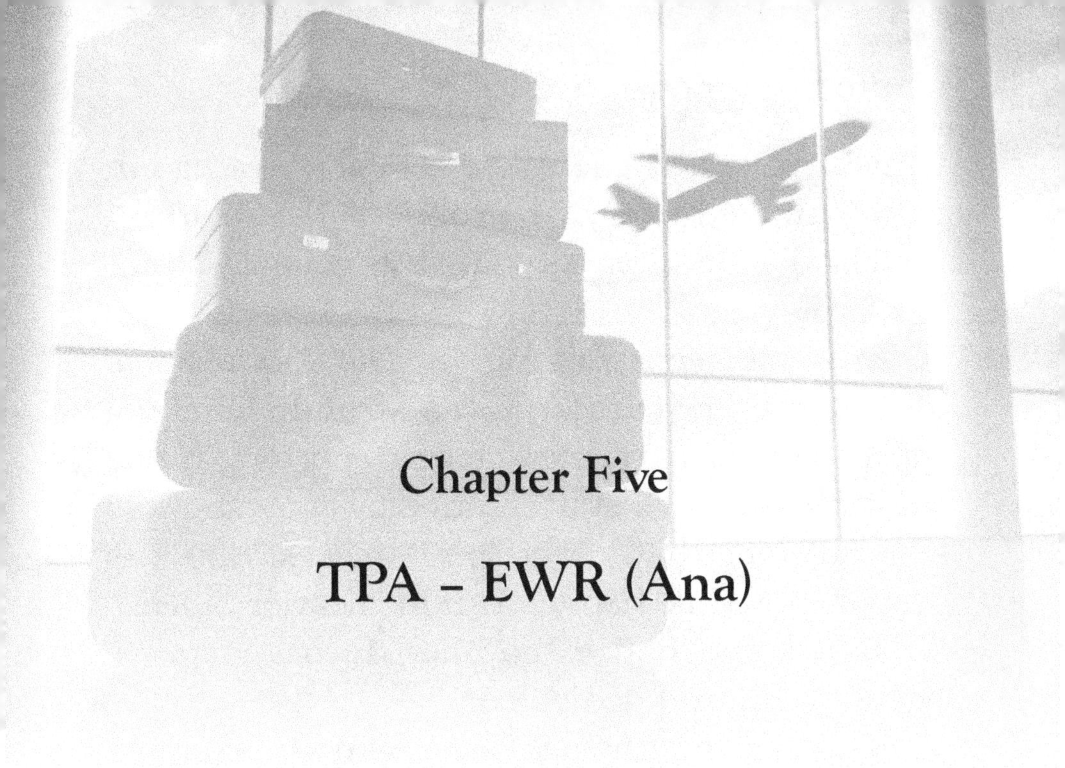

Chapter Five

TPA – EWR (Ana)

Ana sank into window seat 12F after hastily tossing her duffle bag into the overhead bin. She adjusted the A/C to full blast and rested her head on the cool side of the plane. She squeezed her eyes shut, but the noise of the nearby passengers and the hum of the engines was not enough to drown out the screams she could hear in her head, and visions of blood and carnage still flashed before her eyes. Bodies of dead and wounded teenagers were sprawled across the school yard, ambulances were wailing, and parents were lining the sidewalks; sobbing and searching in vain for their children. Ana rubbed her temples in an effort to stop the sights and sounds – but as usual, it didn't work. It had been four days since she had been an accidental witness to one of the worst school shootings in the country's history. The sound of the gunfire – the blood – the screams – was this going to haunt her forever?

Ana had been working for *The Today Show* for about four years and was steadily climbing the ranks as a trusted news reporter. In the beginning, things started out slowly as she was sent out mostly to cover "puff" pieces. She was anxious to sink her teeth into meatier stories, but knew she had to pay her dues and prove herself loyal and dedicated.

About six months ago she began an extended assignment following the campaign of one of the presidential candidates. She had been working long hours with her cameraman Alex Guzman, a stocky but handsome young man with the brownest eyes she had ever seen. When not on the air, the two spent endless hours talking, and learned that they had numerous things in common. Aside from their Hispanic heritage, they shared a love of old Hollywood films, classic cars, and oddly - bbq. They played countless games of Rummy and Cribbage while riding around the country on the press bus with the other reporters. Slowly, their friendship took an unexpected romantic turn, and last week he had proposed – on the bus in front of the rest of the press corps! Still a bit jaded from her failed marriage to Kyle, she did not say yes, but did not say no either. She told him she needed more time, and he was fine with that, or so he said. She worried that she had hurt his feelings by turning him down so publicly.

She honestly didn't think about Kyle much anymore – the fast courtship, the overnight marriage, or how quickly it had all gone sour. Just a month or so ago she had seen his name at the top of the *New York Times* bestseller list again, so obviously his writing was going well. It was rumored that he was practically a recluse; rarely leaving the house except for book signings, which he hated. They both lived and worked in the same city and both were in the media business, but never – ever – crossed paths. She didn't harbor any ill will toward him - that chapter of her life was closed and she had no desire to reopen it.

After the events of the past few days, Ana had asked her news manager for a few days off. Alex elected to stay with the press corps as they continued on the campaign trail across the south. Her boss Bryan approved her time off, of course, and a substitute reporter was assigned to take her place. Ana kissed Alex goodbye as she rushed to the airport for the next flight to Newark. The plane was starting to fill up, and eventually a rather quirky-appearing older gentleman cautiously slipped into the aisle seat. Nervously reaching into his bag to pull out a travel pack of antibacterial wipes, he proceeded to wipe down every available surface of his seat, including the tray table and seatbelt buckle. Folding his hands in his lap, he stared straight ahead and waited for the flight to be over. At least Ana was safe from conversation with him during the long flight from Tampa to Newark. She truly had no desire to talk to anyone. Looking at her own hands, her memory flashed back to when they were covered with the blood of a young student named Emily. Emily Rose Jackman, age 17, who had died in her arms.

There was no stopping the flood of memories now. Presidential candidate Congressman Tom Lewis, a Republican from Arkansas, was scheduled to speak at Eastlake High School in Tampa, Florida. Alex and Ana did their usual pre-event crowd interviews and were setting up in the back of the auditorium to broadcast the rally. Congressman Lewis had not arrived yet, but the students were excitedly finding their seats. Even abovc thc noise of the almost 2000 teenagers, Ana heard a side door burst open as two young men rushed in, firing assault rifles indiscriminately around the room. Things happened so quickly, but yet in slow motion. Ana saw the pain and panic in the faces of the students and teachers as they were gunned down before they had a chance to escape. And she saw the hatred and anger in the eyes of the assailants who were only a few yards away from her. Alex quickly grabbed her arm and pulled her to the ground, shielding her body with his own. She could barely breathe with all of his weight on top of her and felt like she was suffocating. The gunshots seemed to go on forever, but in reality probably only lasted 10-15 seconds. As quickly as it started, the shooting stopped as the gunmen ran out into a hallway. But then what filled the air were the screams and moans of the wounded and the dying.

Alex sat up and held Ana close to his chest. After assuring each other that they were OK, they rushed to the nearest group of students they saw. Most were unharmed, but there were several who were severely wounded. One young Asian male was obviously deceased after suffering several gunshots to his chest. Ana was frozen for a time, staring at his lifeless body. After a few seconds, she shook herself back to action and gathered a small group of frightened students together, leading them out the press exit, while Alex rushed to help some other students. Once outside, Ana hid them behind one of the local TV station vans. She rushed back inside, only to be immediately met by a young girl struggling toward the exit. She had two obvious wounds – one in her left leg and another in her neck – and she was gasping for air. Ana grabbed a male teacher who was nearby, and the two of them carried the girl outside. Once they felt they were safe, Ana fell to the ground and held the girl on her lap. With much difficulty, the girl said her name was Emily and that she was 17 years old. Ana urged her not to speak, but to save her energy. She attempted to speak comforting words to Emily as she pulled off her own cardigan sweater and tried to hold it on the wounds, but it was of little use. She cradled Emily in her arms as she whispered, "Tell my mom I love her....." then she let out a soft moan and died.

The next several minutes were a chaotic blur of police and ambulances, weeping students and anguished parents. After the medics took Emily away, Ana sat on the grass, dazed and in shock, her blood-stained pink sweater in the grass beside her. Alex found her there, and gently held her close to himself.

"Are you sure you're not hurt?" he asked.

"No, I'm fine. It's just..........." Her voice trailed off as she surveyed the chaos around her, and then noticed the blood staining her hands and clothes. She clutched the bloody sweater close to her chest.

After a minute or two, she pulled herself together and slowly stood up. Brushing the blood from her hands onto her jeans, she said "I know it's gonna be tough, but we have a job to do."

"Are you sure? Let me have one of the EMT's check you out, ok?" Alex asked skeptically. "No one back home will be expecting you to file a story today."

"Of course they will! And I'm ok, really, as long as you are beside me. Ready?"

And that is how Ana and Alex spent the next four days – reporting from the school, the hospitals, the police station press briefings, and even the campaign that was being suspended for a few days. Ana could barely remember sleeping or eating, although she is sure she must have done both at some point.

The plane continued to fill, but Ana's eyes were closed, trying to let the routine sounds and voices of the other passengers drown out the pounding in her head. She heard a slight scuffle beside her, and opened her eyes to see the quirky guy reluctantly rising from his seat to let a slender woman in her early 40's slide into the middle seat. Instantly a bit resentful for losing her buffer of personal space, Ana found herself smiling guardedly at the woman who was kicking her purse under the seat in front of her. The flight attendants did their usual safety checks and delivered usual speeches about seatbelts and emergency exits. Finally, the plane taxied down the runway and gently lifted into the crystal blue Florida sky.

Soon the flight attendants were up in the cabin, handing out drinks and snacks. Ana sipped her coke and munched on some pretzels, trying to focus on anything but the memories threatening to overtake her. After the empty cups and trash were collected, the woman seated next to her turned to Ana with a look of recognition in her eyes.

“Excuse me for staring....are you Ana Rodriguez? From the *Today Show*?”

“Yes, I am,” Ana replied politely. She was still having a hard time adjusting to random strangers recognizing her out in public.

“I hate to bother you, I know this has been a rough week for you. My name is Kimberly O’Rourke, and I live in Tampa. I have a 15 year-old daughter Alyssa who goes to JFK High School. I saw your coverage after the shooting at Eastlake, and I just couldn’t take my eyes off the TV. It was so horrible – I hope you don’t mind if I talk to you a bit?”

Ana hated to be rude, so she told her, “Of course, that’s fine. It’s been a rough few days, but I’ll do my best to answer any questions you have.”

“More than anything, I want you to know how comforting it was to see you on my screen each day. Your coverage was compassionate and considerate toward the grieving families. I even watched your report from the funeral today while I finished packing for this trip. That must have been so hard for you."

This morning had been the first of the funerals – 22 students had been killed, along with 14 teachers and other staff. Dozens more were injured with many still hospitalized. The two young gunmen had been captured and were in police custody.

"The funeral *was* quite difficult," Ana said. "I wanted to respect the privacy of the family but still let others know what was going on. I had just signed off from my last live shot outside the funeral home and was ready to head to the airport when I was approached by a family I had seen at various press briefings but did not know their names."

"Ms. Rodriguez?" the woman had said cautiously. "I hope you don't mind, but we wanted to speak with you for a minute. We are the Jackman family – Mark and Lori, and these are our children, Stephanie and Daniel. One of the first responders said you were with our daughter Emily?"

"Emily?" Kimberly whispered. "Isn't that............."

"Yes, Emily was the girl who died while I was holding her. I couldn't believe I was finally meeting her family. It was as if all of the emotions I had pushed down since the shooting were now gushing out – so raw and horrendous."

"Yes, Emily," I whispered back to the family. "I'm so sorry – I tried……"

Emily's mother Lori reached out and grabbed my hand. "We're just so thankful that someone was with her – that she wasn't alone."

"I'm so sorry," I eventually stammered again. "I'm glad that you found me, though. Her last words were '*tell mom I love her.*' If it helps, she didn't suffer long."

"We talked a bit more, then I rushed to the airport and onto this last-minute flight. I knew I had to get away for a few days, to get some perspective on what I had just witnessed and been such an intimate part of."

"I truly don't mean to intrude," Kimberly said gently, "but I really feel compelled to talk to you, to let you know what a difference you made to all of us parents, not just those from Eastlake. Every day wc send our children off to school, wondering if this is the day they don't come home. We try not to dwell on that fear, but it's always in the back of our minds. Our children have grown up in the world of post-Columbine, which actually happened before they were even born. Can you imagine the stress these kids are under? We had tornado and fire drills when I was growing up, they have active-shooter drills and metal detectors at all the doors."

"I remember when Columbine happened." Ana said softly. "I was about eight I think. I didn't understand it much at the time, just remember that my mom cried for days. I grew up in a small town outside of Memphis, but heard about other school shootings over the years. Thankfully, nothing like that ever happened anywhere near me. But to witness it this way.........." her voice trailed away and she and Kimberly sat in silence for a few minutes.

After a short pause, Kimberly said gently, "I can't imagine how difficult it was, especially with Emily, but don't ever doubt the impact you had on the parents, on all of us. You were the right person there at the right time – never forget that."

The quirky guy seated on the aisle was asleep and snoring softly. Ana stared out the window, watching the farmland below her pass slowly by. All she wanted to do was take a long hot shower, crawl into her own bed, and cry. She plugged in her headphones and listened to some soft instrumental music – she may have actually even fallen asleep for a few minutes.

The plane landed smoothly in Newark. Kimberly squeezed Ana's hand gently and they parted company. Ana grabbed her luggage and caught a taxi for the short ride to her condo. Standing in her shower, she leaned against the wall and let the hot water run over her. Before long all the tensions of the past week started to release - she had no idea how long she stood there - the water mixing with her tears, the sound of the shower drowning out her sobs.

Eventually she crawled out of the shower and fell into her bed, sleeping for almost 24 hours straight. It was a very restless sleep, filled with bad dreams and the feeling of helplessness. Sometime the next afternoon she was jolted awake by the sound of her cell phone – it was Alex who was worried about her, and wanted to make sure she made it home ok. Suddenly quite hungry, she made her way into the kitchen to look for something to eat. She kept a supply of frozen dinners and non-perishables on hand, as she did not actually come home very often since the start of the campaign. But she was too afraid to turn on the TV or look at her social media - what if she saw the pictures again? She did check her work email and found several encouraging notes from co-workers, wishing her peace and a chance to heal. Her boss Bryan reminded her to take as much time as she needed, and that her job would be waiting for her when she was ready to come back. The thought of going back to work make her nauseous, and she seriously wondered if she was cut out for this business – maybe she needed to think about changing careers.

For the next three days she did not get dressed or leave her condo, relying on delivery service from her favorite Chinese restaurants, sandwich shops or pizza joints. She slept most of the time, or just sat in a chair looking out the window toward the New York City skyline. On the fourth day she finally pulled herself together enough to walk to the corner deli. Everything outside looked so different – images seemed sharper, the colors more defined. But the world had not changed in the last week, she had.

She took a taxi to the post office to pick up a large stack of mail that was being held for her. Once back home, she rummaged through piles of junk mail to find a wedding dress catalog she had impulsively ordered after Alex proposed, and near the bottom of the bag was a brief note from Kyle that had been forwarded to her from the station.

"Hey, saw you on the news the other day," the note said. *"Kinda reminded me of Jackie Kennedy, you doing your news reports with blood all over your cute pink sweater. Seriously, though, I'm glad you're ok. Kyle"* He was rude and condescending as always, but for once it didn't really bother her. His opinion of her was totally insignificant now.

The wedding magazine, however, was causing her some major anxiety. Not just the usual pre-wedding jitters, but it was the thought of a future with Alex. Or a future with anyone. Why even bother planning a future when there is so much evil in the world? Emily had plans, and look what happened to her.

Her cell phone rang, and it was Bryan from the TV station. He apologized for calling her at home, but wanted to see how she was doing. He also relayed a message from a family in Tampa. They really wanted to talk to her – could she call them back?

After debating an hour or two, Ana returned the call to the family of Jenny Yarbrough. Jenny was a young girl who was injured in the shooting but who Ana had helped lead to safety. Recovering from her wounds at a rehab center, she had a long hard road ahead of her. There had initially been concern about paralysis, but she was showing signs of being able to walk on her own now. Her parents wanted to express how grateful they were, and how different the outcome could have been if Ana had not been there to help. They chatted just a few minutes, and Ana told them to be sure to give Jenny her love.

The next morning she received a text message from Alex telling her that he was going to be coming home in a few days for a long weekend.

He was exhausted, plus he missed her terribly. He was ready to talk to her, to hold her, to cry with her. He wasn't upset about her inability to commit to wedding plans, but he jokingly said maybe they should just go to Vegas this weekend and not wait any longer. Ana smiled at the thought of getting married at a cheesy wedding chapel with an Elvis impersonator doing the ceremony, but part of her was still so uncertain about what direction she wanted to take in her life. If only someone could help her out, give her a sign to help her know what to do.

On a whim, she decided to hop on the subway and go to her office at *The Today Show*. Everyone was thrilled to see her, of course, and marveled at her composure while doing the stories from Florida. Her desk was piled high with mail and gifts from many of her fans. She hadn't realized how much her stories had impacted viewers all across the country. One box in particular caught her eye - the return address just said "Jackman" and was mailed from Tampa. Inside the box was an angel figurine with the inscription "Emily's Angel." For the first time since the shooting, Ana was able to think about Emily without crying – her long red hair, her clear blue eyes, her *Queen* backpack. Funny how she had never really thought about the backpack before. *Queen* had been one of Ana's favorite groups when she was younger, too. She set the angel figurine on a shelf above her computer, where she could see it every day.

Her boss Bryan came into the tiny office, and after some small talk he asked her if she was ready to come back to work. Seeing the panic in Ana's eyes, he explained something he was considering for later in the fall. Watching how composed she was during the shooting coverage, and afterward with how sensitively she dealt with the families, Bryan thought it would be great for her to host her own "making a difference" type of series. The audience had been really receptive to her down-to-earth style and Bryan felt they would respond well to this type of show. Alex could work with her as her photographer, of course. He wanted her to think about it – he saw such potential and talent in her, and wanted to find a way for her to showcase both.

Ana left the studio and stepped out into the invigorating New York City springtime. For the first time since the shooting, she was feeling a bit more optimistic about the future. She reached for her cell phone and sent a quick text to Alex.

"Hey, babe. Just came from the office. Lots to tell you. But instead of flying to EWR, how about I meet you in LAS instead? Think Elvis can fit us into the schedule this weekend? I Love you!"

BOARDING PASS

STAPLE

BOARDING PASS

PASSENGER RECEIPT 1 OF 1

MacNamara, G

BIL - ORD

Chapter Six

Global Air

MacNamara, Gerald III

SEAT NUMBER

3B

Date and Time

MAY 17, 2024

09:14 AM

Destination: ORD

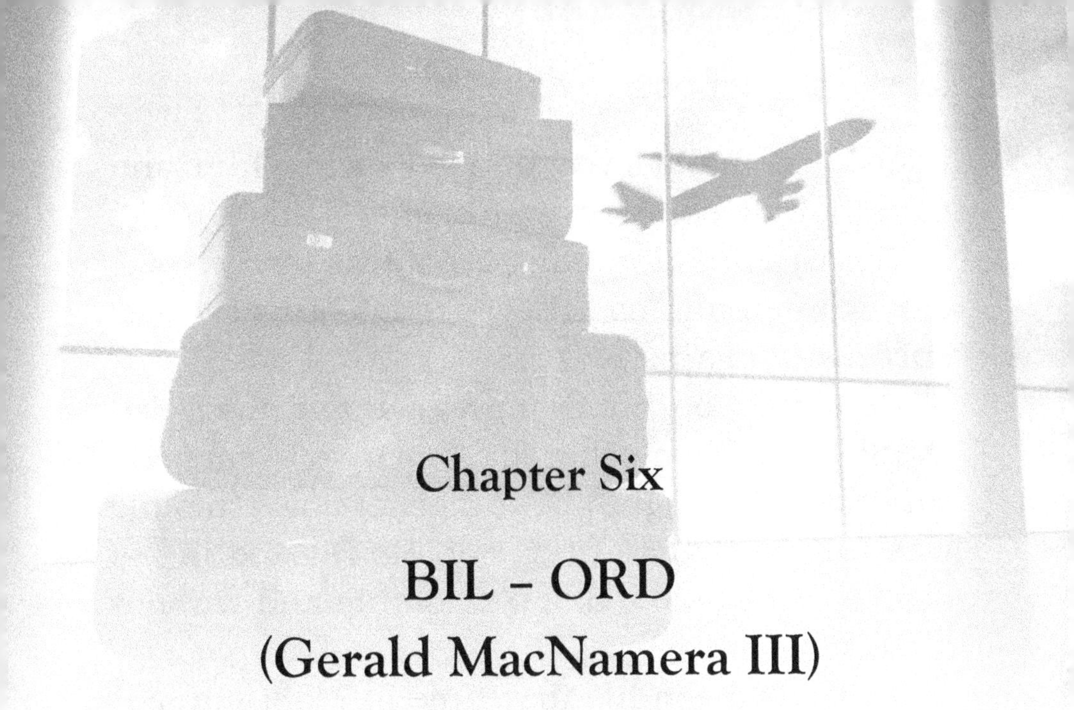

Chapter Six

BIL - ORD
(Gerald MacNamera III)

Once again, Mac placed a tube of architectural drawings in the overhead compartment and took his first class seat 3B. He smiled as he thought of Tess – something he still did fairly often. No, he wasn't a bank robber or a spy, but he did just come from a very successful presentation to build a beautiful new hospital in Billings, Montana.

Life had been going really well these past few years. His business continued to grow and he was back near the top of the architectural world.

Not surprisingly, he had received a call from his ex-wife Misty last fall. Her second marriage had failed and she was hoping to meet with him

– said she had never stopped loving him and missed him so. Mac very firmly said "thanks but no thanks" and hung up. It was obvious she only wanted him back because his business was successful again.

He sipped on his orange juice and marveled that he has been sober for over seven years. He rarely even thought about alcohol now – his life was full and busy without it. He relaxed in his seat as the plane took off smoothly and without incident.

This had been his first time in Montana and he was fascinated by the vast beauty of the state unfolding out the window below him. As someone who spent most of his time in big cities, the BIGNESS of it all amazed him. But more than memories of meetings and mountains, he had the memory of four amazing days with a special lady.

Last summer he had attended the American Institute of Architects annual meeting in San Francisco. It was the usual dull meeting until the second evening when he was sitting on the terrace of the hotel, watching the sun sct over the Pacific, the sky an amazing blaze or orange and red. He heard a soft voice behind him.

"Captivating, isn't it?"

Mac turned around to be mesmerized by one of the most stunning women he had ever seen.

While Misty had been gorgeous in an expensive sort of way, this woman was beautiful in her simplicity, and the intoxicating scent of jasmine floated softly around her.

She was fairly tall, probably 5'8" or so, with flaming red hair that glowed golden in the fading twilight. She was wearing black slacks and a blue and black blouse in a geometric pattern. There was no gaudy jewelry or expensive handbag or shoes. There was just the radiance of someone who was confident about their place in the world and comfortable in their own skin.

After staring at her for several seconds, Mac snapped back to reality and sprang from his chair.

"Where are my manners?" he asked quickly. "Here, take my chair! Yes, the sunset is beautiful. So many things here are. San Francisco is one of my favorite cities."

"Oh, mine too, although I don't get here very often. And we don't have many oceans in Oklahoma."

"No, I guess not. I'm from Chicago, but at least we have the Lake. My name is Mac – Gerald MacNamara actually, but everyone calls me Mac."

"Oh, I know who you are. Mac III is an amazing company, and you really brought it back from the ashes. My name is Lilah Oden, and I'm the owner of OdenSky in Tulsa. We are small and just getting started, but I have big dreams."

"Nothing wrong with starting small and growing gradually. Just make sure you surround yourself with people you can trust." There was a bit of sadness in his voice as he thought about his best friend Craig who had embezzled $5 million right under his previously-alcoholic nose.

"What he did to you was terrible," she said gently. "I'm really sorry."

"Thanks, that was such a dark time in my life. But with the help of a special friend or two, I've been able to recover. In more ways than you know."

Mac found another chair to pull up beside her, and they talked late into the evening – a friendly and easy conversation about life and architecture and world travel. The seminar ended the next afternoon, and Mac worried he might never see her again.

As he was leaving the hotel and waiting for a taxi to take him to the airport, he again heard a voice behind him.

"I suppose you have a direct flight to Chicago? I have to go through Dallas first."

"That's one of the few good things about living in Chicago, to be honest. I was hoping I would run into you, though. Here's my card. If you ever need architectural advice, or just want to talk...."

"I would like that a lot," she smiled at him. "And here's mine. Have a good trip home."

And so it began – a very sweet and comfortable friendship that was slowly blossoming into something more.

After the hurt of loving and losing Misty, he was very cautious about moving too quickly. Lilah was in no hurry, either, since she was so busy starting her new business. But they did share friendly emails and the occasional late-night phone call.

When he had the opportunity to go to Montana for the hospital presentation, he decided to be bold and ask if she wanted to join him for a few days.

At first she was very hesitant. "Oh, I'm not sure that's a good idea....I don't think I'm ready for........."

"Oh, no, I don't mean it that way. I'm going for a presentation in Billings and want to see more of the state since I've never been there before. We will have separate rooms, of course! I was just hoping to share the sights with you."

"I just don't want there to be any misunderstandings, or unclear expectations."

"Of course not! I'm not sure I'm ready for that yet anyway."

So, after his meeting they rented a car and spent the next five days sightseeing – Billings,

Bozeman, Butte, and a day trip to Yellowstone. The scenery was more beautiful than they had ever imagined. They saw waterfalls, Old Faithful, and unbelievable and amazing wildlife. One day they packed a picnic lunch and spent the day watching bison and elk, deer and prairie dogs. They ate their lunch sitting under a tree at the base of a gorgeous mountain with a cold, rushing river nearby. They went shopping in Whitefish and spent a day at the Remedies Day Spa. Neither of them felt any pressure to pursue the relationship physically, and they were they free to enjoy hours of easy conversation and companionship.

This morning they drove to the airport very early, since Lilah had an 8 AM flight to Denver, then home to Tulsa. After they both checked in, they enjoyed a cup of coffee and a sausage biscuit at McDonalds. As she was about to leave, Lilah reached across the table and wrapped her hand around his.

"Thanks again for everything, for including me in this trip. I had a great time, especially getting to know you better. I'm hoping we can do this again sometime?"

"I would like that. I'd love to show you around Chicago. Or is there somewhere else you are interested in?"

"Chicago would be fun – I've never spent much time there. I had better go……" She slowly stood to her feet and he jumped up to stand beside her.

"Bye, Mac," she said with a twinkle in her large green eyes. She gave him a soft kiss on the cheek and disappeared into the security line.

Mac was brought back to the present when the Flight Attendants announced that they were about 20 minutes outside of Chicago. No one was in the seat next to him, and he looked out the window at the Illinois landscape. It was so different from where he had been just a few hours ago.

Once the plane had landed, Mac turned on his phone. Expecting to be met by a flood of work emails, he was pleased to see a text from Lilah.

"The Eagle has landed in Denver. Miss you already."

"I miss you, too," he said softly under his breath.

As painful as his memories with Misty were, he was thankful that he had them and that he now knew the difference between infatuation and real love. What was it that Tess had said to him so long ago?

"That sort of love can fade out. It burns bright and fast and if you don't fan those flames, it can die."

Tess had no idea the impact she had made on him all those years ago. But do any of us really know the influence a chance encounter can have on someone else? What type of impact had he made to others over the years?

Unlocking the door of his condo, his cell phone beeped again. It was the organizer of the convention he attended earlier this year in San Francisco, thanking him for leading one of the education sessions. One young architect in particular had left glowing reviews and was hoping to contact him for career advice. Mac thanked him for the call and promised to be in touch with the student.

He opened his suitcase and took out a photo that was taken in front of one of the waterfalls at Yellowstone. His eyes were initially drawn to Lilah with her flaming hair and wide smile. She was so beautiful, looking so at peace with the world. But then he saw himself – relaxed, smiling, and happy.

Happy. Something he had not been in a very long time. He picked up his phone and sent a text to Lilah.

"Hi! Home. Happy. I miss you."

STAPLE

BOARDING PASS

BOARDING PASS

PASSENGER RECEIPT 1 OF 1

Sullivan, Joel

MCO to DFW

Chapter Seven

Global Air

Sullivan, Joel

SEAT NUMBER

17E

Date and Time

JUNE 6, 2032

03:45 PM

Destination: DFW

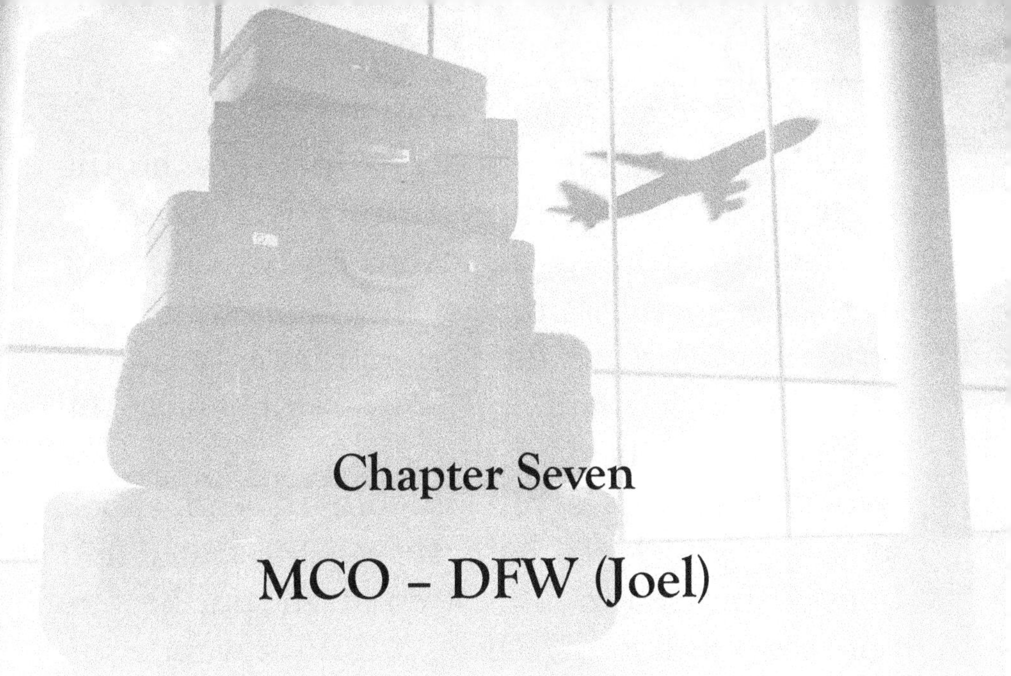

Chapter Seven

MCO - DFW (Joel)

There wasn't a single part of Joel Sullivan's life that was the same as it had been fifteen years ago when he'd flown home from his final tour of duty in Iraq. Even his love for Kristen was different now. It had always been true and strong, but now it had the kind of depth and resilience that only came from adversity. Their life hadn't been simple, but he was grateful for their hardships since it made their rewards seems so sweet and their prior concerns so small.

He used to have nightmares about the fear and violence of wartime. Now, his dreams revolved around the welfare of his little family. While he might have captured Kristen's heart fairly easily, he'd fought long and hard for his two precious children, so it wasn't uncommon for him to worry about them even in his sleep. Just now, on the flight home from Disney World, he'd dozed off into a quick dream about losing his daughter in the theme park crowds. He snapped his eyes open and his heart didn't stop racing until he'd actually put a hand on Charlotte's head as she snored quietly beside him.

Joel blew out a relieved breath and shook away the panicked dream. He was frustrated he'd allowed himself to fall asleep at all, but he was honestly exhausted. Three full days wandering the massive theme park had depleted him, and it seemed that Charlotte felt the same. She'd been snoozing since before takeoff, curled up into a little ball in her seat, and safe from most dangers.

It seemed as though the little girl could sense her daddy needed reassurance, because at that moment, she rolled toward him and snuggled her head into his lap. He grinned and began to lazily stroke her sandy blonde hair, the one feature of hers that resembled his perfectly. She was mostly a carbon copy of his wife, except perhaps even prettier, if that were possible.

He heard a little sigh and turned toward the woman in the aisle seat. She had salt-and-pepper hair, large glasses, and a grandmotherly smile. "She must be a daddy's girl."

Joel gave a little chuckle at that. "It depends," he said quietly, giving Charlotte an affectionate pat on the shoulder. "She might look sweet now, but she's normally quite the manipulative little creature. She's a daddy's girl when daddy has the better toy or the better snack or will let her stay up later. The second I try to enforce a rule, she's clinging to her mother."

"Oh I see," the woman replied. "That's when you have to present a united front."

Joel grinned patiently. He couldn't remember the last day he'd gone without receiving unsolicited parenting advice. It was just part of his life now. He and Kristen might disagree occasionally on treats or punishments for their kids, but he felt more united with her as each year passed. They were an unstoppable team.

When he looked up, he thought perhaps his fond thoughts of his wife had somehow conjured an image of her standing in the aisle, but he quickly realized she was really there. Concern and exhaustion had turned her lovely face into a clouded mask, but her eyes were as green and clear as ever.

"I'm so sorry, ma'am," Kristen said to the woman on the aisle. "I just need to speak to my husband for a moment."

"Oh, yes of course, dear," the woman said, leaning back as though she could flatten herself into the seat.

“What’s up?” Joel asked, his eyes suddenly alert as they swept Kristen’s shadow for his son. He found him there looking sulky and tired, refusing to hold his mother’s hand and resenting her grip on his wrist.

“I know it’s only another hour, but can we switch kids? He’s been whining for you since before we took off. I know he’s tired but he won’t take a nap because it was my idea and not his or yours.”

Joel gave his wife a commiserating smile and glanced down at his lap where Charlotte was still sound asleep. They were both very comfortable, but he knew that Kristen wasn’t really making a suggestion. He couldn’t say no to her even if he wanted to. So he carefully passed Charlotte’s bag and then Charlotte herself into Kristen’s waiting arms. The little girl tucked her face into Kristen’s neck without even noticing she’d been moved. They really were an unstoppable team.

Getting Seth into the window seat was harder. He probably could have squeezed by the woman on the aisle, but he sort of glared down at the ground until both she and his father stood up and cleared the way for him. Joel tried not to roll his eyes, tried not to worry about the boy’s attitude at sixteen if this is what he could be like at six. He met his wife’s gaze once more and smiled as she mouthed the words “thank you” and carried Charlotte up the aisle to her seat. Taking a deep breath, he turned toward his son.

"Hey bud, so whatcha wanna do? There's a magazine in the pocket in front of you. We can do the crossword puzzle or we can practice reading."

As expected, Seth balked like his father had just asked him to jump out of the plane. His incredulous expression made Joel want to burst out laughing. The boy looked just like Kristen, which you would think would be impossible. Somehow, despite the fact that they shared no genetic material, his fair-skinned wife and his black son shared this facial expression and used it when they felt that Joel was being ridiculous.

Seth was actually a great student, smart and sociable, but he was very compartmentalized when it came to his time. Joel had so far been unable to convince him that it was okay to work on reading or spelling words or math problems during the summer break. Those kinds of activities had to be well disguised as a video game or television show or else they were banned from the house until the fall.

"We can play Hangman," Joel suggested, and though his son's eyes were slightly red with exhaustion, they brightened a little and he nodded.

They played several rounds, making each other guess the names of pets and superheroes and rides they'd just experienced at Disney World. Then, as predicted, Seth's exhaustion got the better of him, and he tucked the scribble-covered notebook back into his bag and slumped against the window, succumbing to sleep.

Joel exhaled in relief. He knew they were too close to home for him to bother with napping now, but it would be nice to have calm and quiet for the end of the flight.

"Boys that age are such a challenge, aren't they?" the woman on the aisle said.

So much for calm and quiet. "Nah, he's my easy one. He only gets in a mood when he's extra tired or hungry. My girl can turn on a dime though. She's five years old and we still haven't figured out what flips her switch."

"Is she your real daughter?" the woman asked.

Joel felt the muscles in his back get tight. He hated this question with his entire body and soul. Normally he tried to overlook things, to give the answers that people needed without being rude, but he felt just as tired and cranky as his son had been.

"They're both my real children," he said flatly. "But yes, Charlotte is my biological daughter."

The woman's cheeks went a little pink, but her embarrassment didn't stop her from plowing ahead. "How old was the boy when you adopted him?"

"We brought him home when he was a little over four months old," he told her.

"Oh, where did you get him from?"

This was another question that Joel despised. When Seth had been a baby, he used to tell curious strangers that he got him from Costco. He had long since stopped finding anything funny about it though. "He was born in Ethiopia."

"Oh my!" the woman cooed. "I have some friends at church who adopted a little girl from Honduras a few years ago."

Joel gave a vague nod at this. It was as though the woman beside him were reading from a script written expressly to annoy him. First, the implication that his adopted son wasn't a "real" child to him, then the idea that children were commodities, purchased from third world countries as easily as clothing from a shop. And finally, the need to reference another adoption story.

When Joel and Kristen had first begun the process of bringing Seth home, friends and neighbors and strangers came out of the woodwork to talk about adoption stories they'd heard about. Most of them ended with the birth mother changing her mind at the last minute, or some legal loophole being closed. Joel could never understand why people would share these negative things with him. Kristen had assured him that they all meant well, that they were just trying to relate.

"It really takes a special sort of person to do what you did. That boy is very lucky to have you," the woman added.

It sounded like a compliment, but Joel couldn't help but pick it apart in his mind. Seth had been lucky enough to have been born healthy, lucky enough to be taken in by a well-funded orphanage, that was true. But if Joel and Kristen hadn't adopted him, some other family would have--probably another upper-middle class white, American couple. To imply that the Sullivans had saved him felt wrong.

"To be honest, we're the lucky ones," Joel said. "He's given me more than I could ever give him. He turned me from a man into a father."

The woman looked a bit misty-eyed at this. She put a hand over her heart and absorbed the words. Joel wanted her to end this uncomfortable dialogue now, but it seemed that she was on a roll.

"It's so clear that you're an excellent father to him. He's so blessed to be raised in a...blendcd family. It must be nice to know that you're raising someone that won't even see color."

"Oh, he sees color just fine," Joel replied, unable to let it drop. "He's very aware of his race and his heritage and that it's different than mine."

"I just mean to say that he's lucky to grow up knowing that we're all the same."

"But we're not," Joel pressed. "He's from Africa and I'm from America. We're very different and that's a good thing. If we were all the same, some of us would be redundant. My son knows where he comes from; I wouldn't want to whitewash that. We are teaching him about equality, not sameness."

Joel watched the woman's eyebrows rise up toward her hairline, watched her expression go blank with confusion, and he felt bad about unloading on her. She was hardly the first to make incorrect assumptions about his parenting style. Being in a biracial family was occasionally complicated; it felt like he was always explaining himself to people who would never fully understand. And then of course there was the reality of raising a young black man into a world that was unfortunately biased against him. Joel had always been physically and mentally strong, but he occasionally felt helpless and overwhelmed when he thought about the privilege he'd always had that was and probably always would be denied to his son.

"Sorry about that," he said sheepishly. "I tend to get on a soapbox when it comes to my boy. But I truly didn't mean to be rude."

"You weren't rude at all. I'm sure I overstepped," the woman replied. "I think it's good that you're protective of him and I'm sure he'll grow to be a fine young man like you."

"That's very kind of you," Joel said, pleased that their differences weren't going to result in awkwardness for the next twenty minutes. He saw her smile kindly, then clasp her hands in her lap and close her eyes, letting him off the hook for any further conversation.

He let his mind wander, replaying the expressions of delight on his kids' faces as they saw their favorite Disney characters and gorged on overpriced snacks. He thought about the little pink blotch on the back of Kristen's left arm, the result of hurried sunscreen application one day. As the plane entered its descent, he remembered the much wilder descent of the Splash Mountain ride and how it had drawn an involuntary scream out of him.

Once back on solid ground, he waved goodbyc to the lady on the aisle and roused Seth enough that he could walk on his own and carry his own bag. He wasn't looking forward to guiding a zombie child through the airport, but once the boy saw his mother struggling to balance her own things along with Charlotte's sleeping body, he jumped to action.

"Let me help you, Mama," he said sweetly, shouldering her backpack as well as his own. Then he marched toward the baggage claim area as though he made this trip every week.

Joel looked at Kristen's surprised but pleased face and knew that it didn't matter how tired his muscles were or how ready he was for his own bed. He was sure that his adventures were just beginning, and he couldn't wait to see where his perfect little family would end up next.

STAPLE

BOARDING PASS

BOARDING PASS

Davis, Lisa

JFK - MKE

Chapter Eight

Global Air

PASSENGER RECEIPT 1 OF 1

Davis, Lisa

SEAT NUMBER

17B

Date and Time

August 1, 2024

04:00 PM

Destination: MKE

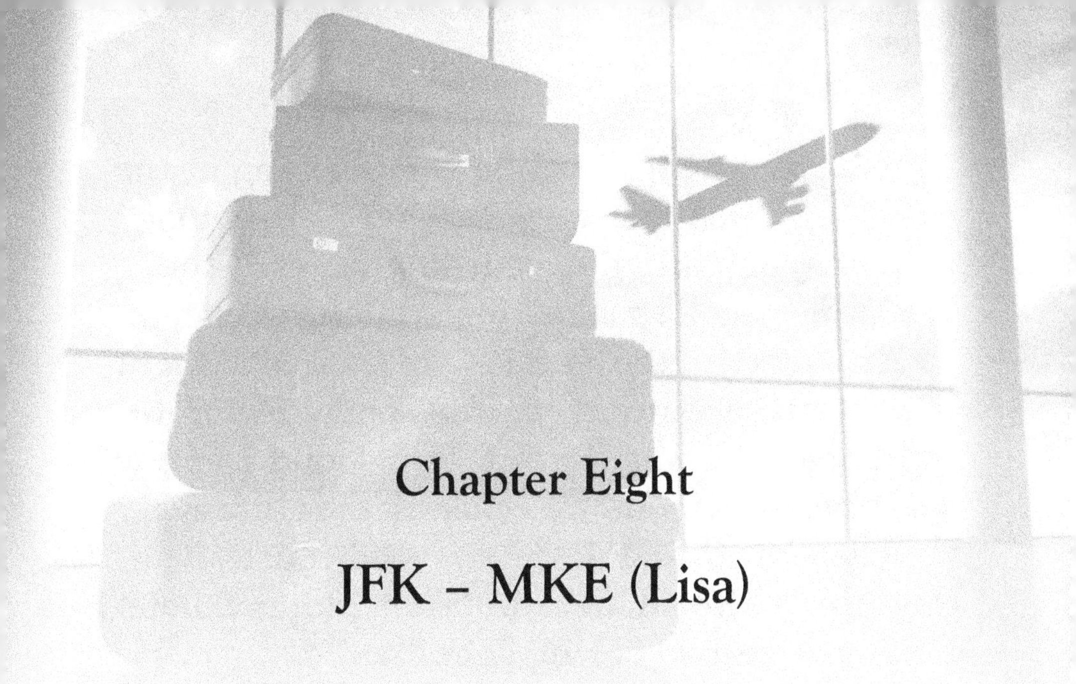

Chapter Eight

JFK - MKE (Lisa)

Lisa stood with her arms outstretched as a female TSA agent ran a wand up and down her body and across her legs. There was a persistent beeping near her right hip, and Lisa reached into her jeans pocket to find a bottle cap. Once that was removed, TSA let her pass and she sat on a small bench to put on her shoes and belt. Kevin was waiting for her with a look of concern – he never was a fan of flying, and found the whole increased security experience unnerving.

"A bottle cap – seriously?" he asked. "Why was it in your pocket?"

"I'm not sure," Lisa answered. "I found it on our hotel room floor this morning when we were about to check out. I meant to drop it into my purse but guess I forgot."

"Ball park root beer," he said, looking at the cap. "Not much is better!" he said as they made their way toward the boarding areas. "And a pretty special keepsake from our long weekend."

They reached the gate 12C for their 3PM flight to Milwaukee. Since there was about 45 minutes until boarding was to start, they found 2 empty seats near a window overlooking the runways.

"There's a Chik-Fil-A in the food court – want anything?" Kevin asked. "That skimpy hotel breakfast we had is long gone."

"Sure – a #1 with a lemonade. Thanks."

After watching Kevin disappear into the crowd of travelers, Lisa opened her purse and pulled out the souvenir program from last night's Yankees game. Across the front cover was the signature "Shane Davis" with a #23 below it. Lisa closed her eyes and replayed the evening again in her mind, watching her youngest son step to the plate for his first Major League at-bat. She knew he was excited and a bit nervous, but he stood there confidently, trying to appear calm before one of the league's top pitchers. 1st pitch – fast ball down the middle of the plate, strike #1. 2nd pitch – high, ball #1. Lisa and Kevin were on their feet cheering wildly. Pitch #3 – foul back into the upper desks – strike #2. Shane stepped out of the batter's box and looked toward his coach. Everyone in the dugout was up and cheering for him. He moved back into the box and adjusted the bat in his hands. Pitch #4 – another fastball to the inside of the plate. Shane's bat made contact and the ball skidded just inside the 3rd base line and rolled into the outfield. Shane got his first Major League hit since being called up from the Minors just last week! Lisa and Kevin had flown to New York City hoping he would get to play this weekend. Tuesday's game was rained out, but Wednesday there was a beautiful blue sky and it was perfect baseball weather. They indulged in peanuts, hot dogs and root beer in a bottle – so cold and fun! They only had a few minutes alone with Shane after the game, but he signed their program and posed for lots of pictures. He went out to celebrate with the team, but Lisa was so thankful to be present to watch his first hit!

The game had gone into extra innings and it was almost midnight before the Yankees won 6-5. By the time they got back to the hotel, Lisa and Kevin were exhausted. Lisa took a quick shower while Kevin called his parents to tell them about the game. Everyone was so excited, and it was hard to fall asleep. After a leisurely morning at the hotel today and a quick call to Shane to wish him luck, they finished packing and grabbed a late breakfast before heading out the door. They allowed a little extra time for the taxi to drive them around Times Square and Central Park a bit before going to the airport.

After a few minutes, Kevin came back with their lunch and they had just finished when the gate agents announced the arrival of their plane from Boston. Lisa made a quick trip to the ladies room and then they boarded the plane to sit in seats 17B and 26E – they didn't get to sit together since they were not able to find two seats in the same row on this last minute-flight.

Lisa squeezed into her middle seat 17B between an older woman who looked to be in her 70's and a young man about her son Tyler's age of 32. She fastened her seatbelt and pulled a notebook from her tote bag before sliding it under the seat in front of her. The first page she opened to said "Baby Davis 2025" and under this the first paragraph began "I am going to be a grandmother!"

Her older son Tyler and his wife Kristal had called just four days ago to share the news that they were expecting a baby early next the spring. They had gotten married almost three years ago in a small wedding chapel outside of Des Moines. Tyler was an EMT and Kristal was the director of a daycare. They met when he came to her daycare to teach infant CPR, and had dated about six months before getting engaged. They had just built a lovely new home in West Des Moines and moved in a few months ago with their tuxedo cat named Molly. They had been actively trying to get pregnant for the past year, and just got the positive test last week. Kristal was a funny and caring girl, and would be a wonderful mother. Tyler was tenderhearted and not jaded by his profession. It was too early to know the gender, of course, and honestly Lisa didn't care – she was so excited to hear a baby's laughter in the big old farmhouse again!

Lisa wrote a few paragraphs about her feelings when she sensed the older woman watching her. Lisa sheepishly started to close the journal but the woman stopped her.

"Don't quit because of me," she said softly. "I have seven grandkids of my own, and each one holds a special place in my heart. But I will tell you – the first time you hold your baby's baby – it's pure magic! It's totally different from the first time you hold your own child – it's as if life has come full circle and you experience a love like you have never known."

"That's what everyone has told me – that I won't truly understand until it happens to me."

"I didn't believe it either, until my daughter placed *her* daughter in my arms!"

They chatted a bit more and then Lisa turned the page to start a list of things she needed to do to fix up a nursery at the farmhouse. Oh, to see a child running in the hallway, or playing on the old swing set again that Kevin had built all those years ago! She remembered decorating that nursery for Miranda, using Pooh and Tigger as the theme. How fun it would be to do that again, since they were still popular characters.

The pilot announced that they were about 30 minutes from Milwaukee, and Lisa put the journal back into her bag. She pulled out the program from the game and smiled as her son's signature.

"You were at the game last night?" the young man to her right asked. "I'm a sport writers for the *Des Moines Register* – do you know Shane?"

"Yes, I know him quite well. He's my youngest son!"

"Wow, this is crazy! My editor sent me to New York City, hoping to see his first Major League appearance, and he got a hit at his first at bat! You must be so proud!"

"Oh, we are! My husband Kevin is sitting a few rows behind us. You know, after the car accident, we weren't sure Shane would ever get to play ball again. But he recovered well, and went on to excel at The University of Iowa. And then he got drafted in the third round!"

"Yeah, I've been following his career for several years, working his way up through the Minor

Leagues. 'Local boy makes it to the Majors.' I remember reading about his accident. So sad about the other boy........."

"Tommy, his best friend. It breaks my heart that he is still paralyzed. But he's an amazing young man and he got married last year. His wife is a physical therapist and they met while he was in rehab."

"How's he doing now? My name is Micah, by the way. Micah Ellis."

"He's doing remarkably well. He graduated with honors from Drake and runs his own graphics design company. Who would have guessed that a car nerd would have such artistic ability?"

The plane landed smoothly in Milwaukee and Lisa waited in the boarding area for Kevin to join her. They only had 39 minutes until their flight to Des Moines, but fortunately their plane was just a few gates away.

Happy that they got to sit together this time, Lisa shared with Kevin her conversation with Micah and the great story he was going to write about Shane.

"You know, it's amazing. All three of our kids are having big events at the same time. Shane, Tyler, and Miranda's Christmas wedding is coming up."

"I'm thrilled she loves her new job in San Francisco," Lisa continued, "and Robert is a great guy, but I feel so disconnected with the wedding planning. I always dreamed we would get to do it together."

"I know," Kevin said softly, taking her hand in his. "But we raised all of our kids to be independent and strong. She was very brave to take that promotion and move to California, even though she didn't know anyone. And I couldn't pick a better guy for her than Robert."

"I know, and she's so happy. The attorney and the court reporter – a perfect match. I just miss spending this special time with her."

The flight from Milwaukee to Des Moines was quite short, and before long they were taxiing to their gate. After collecting their luggage, they walked hand-in-hand toward the parking garage.

"I've been wondering about something," Kevin said after a while. "What would you think about taking early retirement at the end of the fall semester? It would give you the flexibility to be available to babysit, and financially we are in a good place right now. I only have two more years to work – won't retirement be fun? Finally the chance to do what we want, when we want."

"I see more baseball games, more trips to California, and lots of baby-rocking in my future. What about you? What are you wanting to do that we haven't already done?"

"I would love to travel more, but NOT in airplanes! We could get an RV and follow the Yankees around the country!"

"Or, we could visit all the national parks like we used to talk about," Lisa countered. "I love baseball, and enjoy watching Shane play, but there's more that I want to see other than baseball stadiums! Besides, I don't want to be gone for weeks at a time and miss spending time with the grandbaby. The house has been so very quiet these past few years. I'm really looking forward to fixing up the nursery, baking cookies....all the things grandmas do. You probably should check out the old swing set and see if it needs any updates. It's been quite a while since anyone used it."

"Well, we have at least a year until they will be big enough to use it, but yeah, I'll look at it. Maybe it will be a boy.......we'll play catch, I'll take him fishing, or camping. We can get back into 4H! If he wants to raise goats or sheep, we have plenty of room."

"He? Maybe SHE will want to raise goats! It really is exciting, isn't it? To get to do things over again, to pass on what we know and love to another generation. And this time we will have the time to enjoy it."

They didn't say much on the hour's drive home – each was lost in their own thoughts and plans.

But once they got within a mile of home, Lisa reached over and took Kevin's hand. "Mr. Davis, have I told you lately how much I love you? How happy you have made me all these years? How proud I am to have raised three beautiful and talented children with you?"

"Well, Mrs. Davis, you tell me and show me every day in a myriad of ways. And I am the one who is truly blessed by your kindness and gentleness. There is no one I would rather go through life with, and I can't wait to see what the next phase of our life brings."

Kevin turned into the driveway but stopped the car to admire their home and expansive yard together. The sky was clear and there were lightning bugs flickering across the pasture. The farmhouse stood proud and welcoming, silhouetted in fading sunlight. He turned towards Lisa and said "Welcome Home Mrs. Davis. Not many people our age can say they have no regrets, but I honestly don't. Meeting you, marrying you, raising a family with you – the best decisions I ever made. "

After parking in the garage, Kevin carried their luggage while Lisa opened the front door. Home at last, and she knew that there was no place she would rather be.

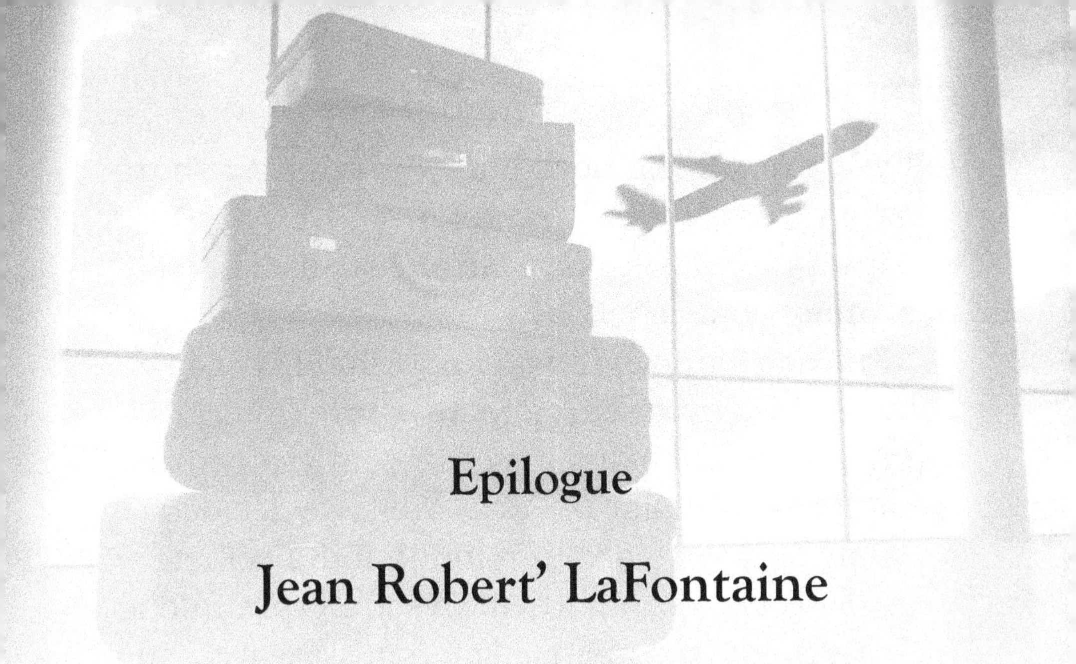

Epilogue

Jean Robert' LaFontaine

Sitting in a reserved area of Antoine's Restaurant in the French Quarter, JR and his wife Paulina were surrounded by friends and family. Photos from their recent trip to France were spread out before them, and the room was filled with laughter and the scents of the restaurant's famous Sunday brunch.

"First off," JR said, standing by his chair, "I want to thank you all again for the amazing retirement gift – France is a place we have always wanted to visit, but it just wasn't possible before now. Of course, adjusting to a life of leisure and not going to the airport everyday has been tough, but I'm trying!" Everyone laughed, and JR continued, "There's way too much for me to tell you everything now, but I did want to share just one story."

"Just one?" his friend Manny asked. "I need to hear more than one!"

"Just one for now. You all know that I have been doing genealogy research in my spare time, and I found that many of my ancestors emigrated from a small town outside of Paris. Well, we decided to do some snooping around and found a cemetery with my great-grandfather Ulysse's grave, along with numerous cousins. I'm not sure why his wife was not buried with him. Anyway, we also drove to the town of Clichy-sous-Bois where I found a cousin Timothée and his wife Camille. They told us stories about my ancestors and dug out this old picture here." He held up a faded tintype from the middle 1800's. It was a picture of Ulysse and his wife Celia. "Who do you think he looks like?"

He passed the picture around the table, and everyone gasped at the incredible resemblance between Ulysse and JR. It was obvious that they were closely related. "But do you want to know the most amazing fact? Ulysse's job was as a luggage maker! All these years later, and I spent my life handling luggage, just like he did. Guess the apple didn't fall far from that tree!"

JR gazed out the window at the city that he loved. Paris and the little towns nearby were wonderful, and he was so thankful that he had the opportunity to see them in person, but his heart was here in the Crescent City with his wife and friends.

He raised his orange juice glass in a toast, and everyone rose to their feet. “Here’s to the past and to the future, but more than anything, here is to the present. My friends and my lovely wife....Santé!”

CPSIA information can be obtained
at www.ICGtesting.com
Printed in the USA
FSHW011605011020
74284FS

9 781952 155918